STEEL PENNIES

Paul R. Lloyd

Paul R. Lloyd

STEEL PENNIES

THANK YOU

Thanks for choosing **Steel Pennies**.

Purchase more of my books by searching Paul R. Lloyd on www.amazon.com.

Dedicated to West Chester, Pennsylvania

CHAPTER 1

1960...

I gawked at the eye holes, gasped, and dropped a chunk of somebody's skull at Bob's feet. We stood in the meadow at the bottom of the hill between the woods on the south side and Strasburg Road to the north. Bob jumped back with wide eyes and mouth open. Old man Utz's dog, Logan, pranced around us stirring up dust.

Utz's Flying A gas station bordered the east end of the meadow. Logan, part German Shepherd and something else, had a habit of wandering away from the station. He followed us into the woods when Utz was too busy with his whiskey to notice. We liked Logan so we invited him to stay with us on our little campout.

A large placard by Utz's business read "Welcome to West Chester, Pennsylvania." Across the road, the blocks of brick row houses began.

To the west, dairy farms and the thoroughbred horse country of Chester County rolled on for what seemed like forever. On either end of the long, narrow pasture, wild bushes like honeysuckle and holly formed a barricade when you pretended the cavalry was chasing you, but the shrubbery made a good hideout after robbing a bank or stagecoach.

Brown grass covered the field on account of the dry weather this spring. No wild flowers bloomed like other years.

Bob wasn't superstitious and neither was I, but as we turned thirteen, wickedness attracted and scared us at the same time. Games we played together for years became childish. Girls transformed into young ladies, breeding fear and awe within us. Will Barnes, who sold newspapers over on High Street, said thirteen was an unlucky number, something Bob and I didn't believe until today.

***

"Where?" Freeman the Cop ran behind me to the skull top with his right hand on the thirty-eight caliber revolver in the holster that dangled from his wide black leather belt.

"Over here," I shouted. A flock of crows lifted in front of us where they cawed and flapped their wings.

Freeman was the most unusual police officer in West Chester because he was as black as the night sky without a single silver star.

We stopped where the skull piece waited for us in the scratched out dirt. Freeman screwed up his face as he picked at the inside of the top of someone's head with the stubby pencil he usually carried behind his ear. The jagged edges of the rest of the skull stuck out where I had scraped away the dirt.

"What were you boys doing here, Tommy?" Freeman stood, hands on his hips, with his pencil stub between two fingers like a cigarette. Except cigarettes never hold skull chunks. You might do it with a good cigar, though.

My stomach twirled around as dots danced in front of everything. "Bob and I were up the hill in the woods when Utz's dog Logan barked and danced that jitterbug mutts do when they want you to follow. When we arrived at the spot, Logan barked louder and faster like he was excited. He jumped around in a circle near what appeared to be a gray rock or old clay pot, honest Freeman. We didn't know the curved lump was somebody's dead head because most of the skull was still buried. I poked around in the dirt with a stick to free enough of the thing to take hold and yank the top off."

I sat down hard on the ground and right away my head began to clear. I closed my eyes to squeeze away the dots, but instead of dots, I saw zombie women from Mars. Flash Gordon's space rocket was in the background. Just as Zelda, the boss of the zombies, was about to grasp my face with a stretched out Hollywood 3-D movie hand, I popped open my peepers. I'd rather spy the dots in the daylight than zombies inside my head, but the dots, like the zombies, were gone.

Freeman hollered for the two other cops in uniform, Higgins and O'Malley, and a guy in a suit who I didn't know. Three squad cars with lights flashing and an ambulance sat along Strasburg Road. The ambulance driver rested behind the wheel with a lit cigarette pasted on his lips. His buddy hung an elbow out the passenger side window. You would think the authorities had better things to do than chase after a yarn spun by a couple of young teenagers.

I walked over to where Bob sat with knees up and head buried on his arms like he was asleep. He had our camping gear down from the woods and stashed in front of him. I flopped next to him.

While shorter than me by a head, broad shoulders marked Bob as an athlete. Meanwhile my muscles waited to pop out.

Bob took after his mom and sister with their blond hair and light freckles. My freckles stuck out like somebody sprayed me with red-brown ink to match my chestnut hair.

We stayed out of the way of the action but close enough to witness it. Freeman faced the other way, and I could see a blackjack and handcuffs on his belt in the blank spot next to the bullets. Like Dad, he was more than six feet tall with broad shoulders and a husky chest. While Dad's gut popped out, Freeman's was flat and appeared firm.

5

Higgins scraped at the ground and lifted a spade of dirt along with some brown lumpy thing with a strap attached like a purse. The uniform cops pointed.

Bob and I glanced at each other. I smiled. Bob's face turned green and then white. He lay back on the grass with his hands over his eyes. I thought barf bucket for him, except we were outside.

I placed a hand on my friend's shoulder. "Maybe it's not hers, Bob. You have to think positive."

"It's hers."

I gazed off to Strasburg Road, but there was no traffic this early in the afternoon. "Cynthia stopped liking us anyway, remember?"

Bob smacked me on the arm and then hid his eyes.

I wasn't anxious to watch the cops dig up people bones anymore so I changed the subject. "How come your hatchet was wet when you came to my house this morning?"

Bob fiddled with the hatchet on the ground in front of him. "Mom told Penny to clean my mess kit, but she got carried away."

"Yeah, right. What really happened?"

"Honest. Sounds stupid, but Penny was doing the breakfast dishes and Mom said to clean my mess kit too. Said she didn't want me to catch ptomaine out in the woods with you like last time."

"We didn't get ptomaine." My stomach churned and for a brief moment behind my eyeballs, Zelda the zombie queen seized my throat. I started to gag in the real world even as I fought to keep my eyes from blinking back to Mars.

"You barfed a gut." Bob pointed a finger down his throat. He showed me no mercy.

"Shut up. We should oil your hatchet at my house if Mom isn't in one of her moods."

"Okay."

"Penny must be crazy." I made an exaggerated long face with my mouth turned way down.

6

Bob punched my shoulder.

"I didn't smile about Penny. She ain't even here." I watched Higgins dump a shovel full of bones and dirt into a canvas bag one of the guys in uniform held. My stomach turned around backwards even though the rest of me still faced forward.

Higgins was tall and skinny with a face shaped like Bob's hatchet. The next shovel full of dirt included a strip of cloth that dangled down. Dark red, like what the girls call maroon, with a green stripe the color of oak leaves in springtime, the material struck me as familiar, but I didn't know why. My stomach swung back around so I felt less afraid.

Bob scanned the cloudless sky. "Think Hitler's in heaven?"

"Hitler? He was like the bad thief on the cross who spit in Jesus' face. He killed, what, ten or twelve million people? Then he topped that off by killing himself. Plus, he had sex outside of marriage. If anybody went to hell, Hitler did."

Bob shrugged. "What if Hitler repented?"

"Are you nuts? Who cares? You can't talk about Hitler when maybe we found Cynthia's bones. Hitler didn't kill her."

"Hitler goes to heaven, there's hope for the rest of us."

O'Malley – a short, fat, hatless uniformed officer with a big bald spot on top of his head – jogged back to one of the squad cars. He pulled a can of paint with that paint-the-world picture on the label and a fat round brush out of the trunk. He returned, puffing hard and spilling paint, to where the other cops dug for clues and bones.

"What are you doing?" Freeman pointed to the little stripe O'Malley was marking on the ground.

O'Malley spilled more paint with the brush. "Outlining the body."

"We don't have a body, O'Malley. We have a grave." Freeman shook his head.

O'Malley stopped to admire his work. "So, looks better with an outline."

Freeman shook his head some more and walked over to where Bob and I waited. "Let's go."

We picked up our camping gear and walked back to the road. I climbed up front in the first of the squad cars parked in a row. Ever notice how the inside of a cop car looks like Flash Gordon's space ship? Okay, it's just a radio and a gear shift knob, but a kid can pretend, right?

Bob collapsed in the backseat with our stuff. Freeman's black and blue police uniform still looked pressed with sharp creases in the shirt sleeves and pants despite the grass stains he had picked up. He started the engine and made a U-turn back towards town.

"Looked like the purse Cynthia Matting used to carry," I said.

Freeman gave me a stern look. He turned back to the road. "Lots of girls have the same kind of purse."

Freeman drove up Gay Street and made the right turn to go south on High. "I want you boys to keep your mouths shut about what you saw today, okay?"

"Yeah." My stomach didn't feel any less queasy as the police car jostled down the street. I contemplated how my hand had been up inside Cynthia's skull where her wet brains used to be.

Bob grunted.

I watched Freeman drive. "Turn on your siren for us."

Freeman gave me a cold stare and turned back to watch the traffic.

Bob refused to say a word while we rode in the squad car. Since his father and brother were put away, he hated playing cops and robbers.

***

Mom told us we could make peanut butter and grape jelly sandwiches. She poured us lemonade. Times are always tough at our house so I wondered about her generosity. Maybe it was because Bob and I spent a lot of time entertaining my five younger brothers and sisters so Mom could work on other stuff.

"We're headed out." I opened the front door as Mom nodded.

"Me first," Bob yelled at the door. He tore down the steps onto Walnut Street.

I didn't see Mr. Bruce's red Cadillac until it was almost on top of Bob. Mr. Bruce's teenaged son Johnny sat behind the wheel. Bob never saw the car until the last second when he fell backwards on the ground to avoid getting run over. The back tires on the red Cadillac rubbed the bottom of Bob's sneakers leaving a black smudge as it sped by.

Johnny Bruce never even slowed down. He spun a right turn up on the corner of Market Street and vanished.

CHAPTER 2

The next day was Sunday. After Mass, Bob and I returned to the meadow where we had discovered the skull. My brother Alan and our friend Jamie Bordeaux joined us. We pulled my little brother's old red wagon with a cardboard box onboard and several shovels. The red wagon used to be mine when I was a little kid.

We dug the hole in the field away from the area the police had roped off. Alan jumped into the hole to check the depth. It was up to his waist.

"Deep enough." He climbed out.

Jamie Bordeaux, a wiry kid about Bob's height despite being a year older than us, stared into the woods.

We followed where he pointed. Will Barnes rose out of a mist near the big oak at the top of the hill. Five years out of St. Agnes High School, Will was more than six feet tall and broad-shouldered. He could have played sports if his eyes worked. He had dark brown skin and curly tight black hair.

Will navigated his way down the hill, waving his red and white cane.

"What are you doing here, Will?" Bob asked.

"A man can sit in his own woods if he wants, Bob Durkin."

"Are these your woods?" I asked.

"Belong to my father, which makes them good as mine. I like to sit among these trees on a warm day. Yes sir, I can see the breeze, too. Sometimes it looks like tear drops are coming. Sometimes I see a sunny day. Sometimes I see love in the wind, Tommy McConnell."

"What else do you see?" I asked.

"I see you boys turning my woods into a burying ground."

"Somebody already turned it into a cemetery," said Jamie Bordeaux.

"Loco, loco, the police came and took those bones away, and now you boys are pretending to bury her bones back down." Will Barnes always called "loco, loco" because he sold the local paper up at the big bank.

Mrs. Lopez, who lived in the upstairs apartment next door to my house, said "loco" meant "crazy" in Spanish. She said Will called everybody crazy when he sold newspapers. But I didn't think so. He loved hawking the paper and the people who bought them.

"How'd you know?" Jamie Bordeaux asked.

Will's hearty laughter said no way was he about to tell his secrets.

We turned in the direction of the bushes where we could still see the area roped off by the police. What we couldn't see from here was a painted white outline in the shape of a body.

"They don't know for certain it was Cynthia," I said.

Bob shoved me. "We both saw the purse."

"May be true," Jamie Bordeaux said, "but Tommy was saying they needed more than an old purse. Maybe they'll find stuff inside, and it will be another girl's handbag."

"Loco, loco, you can read all about what they found when the paper comes out tomorrow, if the police release the information." Will rocked his head around and sniffed the air. "More death and dying before the wind blows the leaves off these woods again."

"How do you know?" Bob asked.

"Like I told you steel pennies before, Will Barnes sees things with his other senses. He sees things borne upon the breeze, he does."

11

"What are you talking about?" Jamie Bordeaux asked.

Will ignored him. "Tell me where your sister is today, Bob Durkin? I know she wants to be here certain."

"Horsepistol. Ran an errand for Mom." Bob emphasized our word for hospital. He twisted the shovel handle into a spin.

I thought about Penny and hoped Bob didn't notice my smile.

"Then all who can gather have gathered," said Will. "Tell me, boys, what do you think of old Cynthia? Was she a good thief or a bad thief?"

I managed to wipe off the grin.

"A thief?" Bob searched Will's blind eyes while a pout formed on his lower lip.

"Don't be upset," Will said. "You are a thief, too. We all are good thieves or bad thieves. In this case, thieving doesn't mean taking what doesn't belong to you. It means sinning. Yes sir. We all are sinners, but some die good and some die bad, Bob Durkin."

"You mean like the good thief on the cross with Jesus?" Alan was my height most of the time. Sometimes I passed him, though he was two years older. But he was husky while I was still way too skinny.

"Yes sir, Alan McConnell. Girls are sinners, too. Sometimes they swipe boyfriends from their girl buddies. Sometimes they bite people they ought not to chew on when they have their little spats. But I'm certain Cynthia confessed of her sins to the Lord."

We watched as Will turned away and drifted up the hill. Before disappearing into the mist at the top, he cried, "Loco, loco," one more time like he did when he hawked his newspapers.

"Where'd that mist come from?" Jamie Bordeaux asked. "And isn't it supposed to be down here with us?"

"Spiritual thing. Happens around Will Barnes sometimes," I said.

Bob lifted a shovel full of dirt, but Jamie Bordeaux stopped him. "We have to pray first and sing a hymn."

I prayed three Our Fathers and two Hail Marys. No one else wanted to pray.

"I'll sing a Protestant hymn. You prayed like a Catholic so it's fair," said Jamie Bordeaux. Without waiting for an answer, he sang, "Amazing Grace, how sweet the fart that's left you and me apart."

Jamie Bordeaux's voice cracked as he struggled for a high note on "apart." He stared at us with a straight face. "Hey, you're not supposed to be happy."

I was on my back on the ground laughing.

Alan held his stomach as he leaned against a tree. "Dumbest Protestant hymn I ever heard."

Bob leaned on his shovel and resisted at first, then cracked up, too.

Alan picked up the other shovel and threw dirt into the hole. Bob joined him in the work while the rest of us supervised. The soil was dry and made a hollow sound off the cardboard box down in the hole. I peered over at the area roped off by the police, where I half expected to see Cynthia Matting come back to attend her mock funeral.

***

Penny Durkin's crossed legs stuck out of her white Bermudas. She sat curled up on the couch with a movie fan magazine in her hands. Penny wore her blonde hair pulled together with a pink ribbon tied in back to hold her ponytail in place. She had a light coating of freckles on her face, like the ones on Bob's mug. Her eyes were large, soft, wet and kind.

I brought Bob back to her so she could comfort him. He was fine when we left the box buried in the meadow, but on the way home, he started to whimper.

The living room and kitchen in the tiny Durkin apartment were combined into one big space. A metal kitchen table with chrome-plated chairs that featured red padded seats and backs separated the two areas. A door in the living room opened to the bedroom and bathroom. The kitchen door opened onto a wrought iron fire escape. Two large windows in the living room faced Market Street. A window over the kitchen sink faced the yard behind the Royal Restaurant, which was on the ground floor below.

I studied the peach fuzz growing on Penny's legs beneath where her shorts stopped and then directed my attention to her blue eyes. She stared back which made me smile and feel warm inside.

Penny shifted her gaze to Bob for a moment and gawked back at me. My smile crumbled under the intensity of her gaze. Why did she stare at me that way? I wasn't crying.

Bob tried but wasn't able to say anything through his tears. If I attempted to speak, I would cry, too. But I wasn't about to cry, not in front of Penny.

"Come here, Bob," she commanded, ever the little mother. "Your pretend funeral didn't go so well, did it?"

Bob walked over to her. She straightened up and planted her bare feet down on the floor. Her left toe nails were shiny red and new-painted. Her right ones had the red paint worn off except for small splotches. I checked around for her nail polish, but didn't see any on the coffee table. She pulled Bob to her and hugged him while he continued to sniffle.

Penny cocked her head around Bob to see me better. "You boys never told me the details, except you found the long lost Cynthia Matting."

I tilted my head, but I couldn't speak. I was not about to cry.

"Well?" Penny asked.

I circled behind Bob to the other side so I didn't have to peer around him anymore.

Her face was so pretty.

I refused to cry.

Penny said, "Crap, I'm bad at this. We need Mom because I'm bad at all kinds of things."

Through his sobs, Bob managed to find bitterness to place in his voice. "I'm not sad because we pretend-buried Cynthia Matting. I'm upset because Johnny Bruce tried to run me over with his father's stupid, brand new, dumb, stinking, red Cadillac."

"Bob, I'm so sorry." Tears welled up in Penny's blue eyes. She turned to me again. "Are you okay, Tommy?"

Cynthia was a couple of years older than Bob and me, but she was about the best girl in the neighborhood for a long time. She was a good friend to me and Bob before she abandoned us to hang around older boys when she turned thirteen. I fought back the tears.

"You need a hug, too, don't you? Come over here." She held out her left arm.

I let out a long breath and didn't have to cry. She knew I was alive!

My eyes dropped to her white blouse. Penny had great boobs for a seventeen-year-old. Bob covered the one on the right. I could plaster myself on the left.

Penny wrapped me in her left arm. Her hug squashed my head against the top of her shoulder. I breathed on her neck below her ear lobe. She felt warm and soft, while smelling rosy like her mom's perfume. Three light-colored freckles decorated her neck below her ear lobe. One was large, the others were tiny. My insides simmered.

Penny Durkin turned her head in my direction so we were eyeball to pretty eyeball and our noses touched, mine slender and straight, hers turned up and perky. I pulled back in time to see her make a big silly grin as she slid her palm down my back and grabbed me in a spot girls don't often grab.

**

Three days later, I saw my first dead person who still had his skin on.

CHAPTER 3

The schoolyard fight was the kind that started when one of us said something stupid, which I was good at, and the other kid thought you were a jerk for saying it. Then you put up your dukes, which my older brothers taught me how to do by picking on me so I had to learn to fight or get beat up. You battled the kid for a while with the punches becoming hand holds and wrestling until the other kid said, "Ah what the heck, you're okay." Salvatore Mercandante put his arm around me and told me to call him Sal.

With the exception of our time at school, I didn't hang out with Sal much because he lived too far out of town.

He caught leukemia last year and was about dead when he bounced down a flight of stairs in his wheelchair at the horsepistol the same day we pretend-buried Cynthia. Penny was at the horsepistol that day so I wanted to ask her if she saw what happened.

Our whole class marched out of school in the middle of the day and headed down Gay Street to attend Sal's afternoon wake. When my turn came to visit his body in the dark wooden coffin, I said, "Sal, why are you wearing a stupid choir boy's outfit? Purgatory is hot. You should have on summer stuff. But you already know that, don't you? Be: you're sweating.

"If you had lived in my neighborhood we could have hung out together. You could have helped us pretend to rebury Cynthia Matting. You didn't know her because she

17

went to public school. But hey, you can look Cynthia up, and you two can become pals. I'll tell Bob about you. He'll like knowing you're an all right guy and up there playing with Cynthia. Hope you feel better now, because you were sick for a while. Gosh, I'll miss you at school."

I didn't cry. Instead, I thought about Penny's hug after Cynthia's pretend funeral. I made the sign of the cross as a new idea popped into my head. "Don't worry about who pushed you down those stairs, Sal. I'll find out for you."

***

Two days after Sal's wake, I visited Will Barnes on my way home from school. He stood in his spot by one of the huge marble columns on the front of the Greek temple bank in the middle of the block on High Street between Gay and Market.

The intersection of High and Gay Streets marked the center of West Chester. If you strolled a couple of blocks west on Gay from High Street, you would arrive at St. Agnes School next to the church.

"Hey, Tommy," Will said before I reached him.

"How'd you know it was me?"

"I saw you approach."

"What are you talking about? You can't see nothing."

"Sure I can. With my ears, I saw you. With my nose, I saw you. Yes sir, I saw you a long ways off." Will laughed.

I parked my olive drab Army schoolbag on the sidewalk by my feet. "You can't see with ears."

"My other senses make up for not having eyes to see. You have any pennies?" Will held out his empty hand.

I yanked a nickel and five pennies out of my pants pocket.

"Give them here," Will said.

"What for?"

"Smart boy. Put them here in my hand. I'll show you something about how my other senses are sharper than yours."

I put the five pennies in Will's right hand, as I marveled at how the palm and fingers were white, but the rest of his hand was a dark brown, almost black. He closed his fist and rubbed the pennies around. I returned the nickel to my pocket.

"These pennies are copper," Will said.

"So."

Will dumped my pennies back into my hand. "Hold your pennies."

He reached into his gray pants pocket with his right hand and pulled out some coins. He picked up several pennies and returned the rest of the coins to his pocket. He held out the palm of his left hand. "You see anything different about any of these pennies?"

"One's steel."

"Correct. They needed the copper for the war effort so they made the nineteen forty-three pennies out of steel. Now watch carefully." Will rubbed one of the pennies between his forefinger and thumb. He put the coin in his pocket. He repeated the process with a second penny. He rubbed the third and stopped. "This is the steel penny. It feels different than the copper ones. You take 'em and feel 'em."

I snatched his steel penny and the two copper ones that remained in his hand. "I can't feel any difference."

"That's because you have eyes. The Lord doesn't give you the blessing of a good feeling hand if you can see."

I removed a newspaper from Will's pile.

Will "watched" me with his ears or something. "Bad day for the steel pennies."

"What are you talking about?"

"I'm saying you be careful around them steel pennies and remember, you are a steel penny, Tommy. A copper penny is

19

in trouble, too. Mark my words; big trouble in West Chester today."

"Some days, you talk crazy. What's the paper say about Cynthia Matting?" I flipped through the front section.

"Loco, loco. That case is full of sad news. Somebody split her head open for her."

"Everybody in town already knows. Does it say who they arrested?"

"Didn't arrest anyone. The police have no idea who did this thing to your friend."

"My friend? She was two years older than Bob and me. She hung out with high school boys when she turned thirteen. Cynthia was more Penny's friend than ours."

"Still, you and Bob played with her when you were little."

"Yeah, you used to do magic tricks for us, remember?"

"Wasn't magic. I truly can feel the numbers. Nobody passes a dollar bill to Will Barnes and asks for change for five dollars. I always know what they hand me."

"And you used to make quarters disappear from Cynthia's hand and squirt them out of Bob's ear."

"You don't know that old trick yet?"

"Sure, but feeling the numbers on dollar bills is magic." I found the article and folded the paper back. "Doesn't say anything we don't already know, but somebody killed her." I gazed up into Will's dull, dead eyes. "Bob and I can find out and tell the police."

"You keep out of police business, Tommy McConnell. Man goes around chopping young girls up the side of the head, you don't want to mess with him."

"He's out there someplace waiting to strike again." I folded the paper smaller.

"Then you be watchful of Bob's sister. She depends on you."

"On me? She depends on Bob. I'll help of course." I stuffed the paper into the Army bag between two of my school books and dug the nickel and five pennies out of my pocket for Will.

People strolled out of the bank.

"Loco, loco," Will cried his name for our local newspaper. It was my signal to move on. Will shouted after me, "There's not but a few steel pennies and the rest are copper. In life it's the other way round." He laughed.

At first I didn't understand, but then it hit me. He meant the way colored people like to call white folks steel pennies because we're light like steel and they're dark like copper.

Paul R. Lloyd

CHAPTER 4

A hint of rotten meat snuggled up my nose as I turned left to go east on Market Street. Down the block, Penny paced back and forth in front of the Royal Restaurant, one of the businesses located between the alley and Rubenstein's toy and sporting goods store on the corner. Penny and Bob lived with their mom above the Royal.

The aroma of dead flesh became worse as I approached Penny. "What's the stink about?"

She raised her hand in greeting which made my right butt cheek feel like twitching as it recalled Penny grabbing it after our mock funeral for Cynthia.

Her voice came from far away, like she had been thinking about something or reading a book and I disturbed her. Her nose scrunched up and her forehead wrinkled. She pressed her bright red lips tight together. When she opened her mouth, a horrible word sprung out.

I asked her what the word meant.

"I ever hear you or Bob use that word, I'll take a bar of soap to your mouths. Brown lye soap, you understand?"

"I didn't say it, you did."

Her face calmed as she lost the scrunched and wrinkled look. She placed her left hand on my right cheek, the one on my face. "I'm sorry, Tommy. We're talking about the baddest, meanest word in the fu… in the dictionary."

"So bad you can't tell me the meaning?"

"I'm not supposed to use it either." She took her hand away and stepped back.

"May I ask you a question?"

"Sure. You might have to kiss me for the answer."

"I'll take my chances. Were you at the horsepistol when my friend Salvatore fell down the steps?"

"Somebody fell down the steps at the hospital?"

"Yeah. We had to go to the wake to say goodbye to his dead body on account of he was in our class."

"Nah, I didn't see nothing. Must have happened after I left. Remember, I was home by the time you guys returned from pretend burying Cynthia."

"Of course I remember." My right butt cheek twitched.

"You're okay, Tommy." She leaned in and kissed me full on the lips.

Something, I think it was a bunny rabbit, squirmed around inside my chest, and my head became a little woozy. "Oh. Uhmm, so can Bob come out?" My voice was high pitched and squeaky.

Penny stepped back but left her hands planted on my shoulders right out on Market Street in front of the whole town. "He's upstairs. Give me another kiss and bang on the door."

Was everybody crazy? Penny traced her hand over my right face cheek, which heated me up. She and I were the same height so it was easy for her to lean in close and kiss me again. She missed my mouth, hit my cheek, and mushed her lips across my skin until she reached my mouth. Then she slid her face down my neck and onto my shoulder. When she pulled me in for a tight embrace, I hugged back.

After what felt like several minutes, she pulled back, smiled, and moved in for another full lip kiss, longer this time. When she released my grinning mug, she had a funny expression on her face like she wanted more kissing or expected me to speak, or I don't know what the look meant. But that rapidly thumping thing in my chest melted into putty. I twirled away so I didn't end up a puddle on the sidewalk but tripped over my Army bag and wondered when it had left my shoulder.

Before clambering through the front door of her building, I worked up the guts to stop and glance back at Penny. She smiled and waved her hand to indicate I should walk up.

Penny Durkin liked me? Why?

Who cared as long as she kissed me?

Through the front door of her building, there was a tiny hall in front of the steps. Bob's bike was parked against the wall. Upstairs, I thumped on the apartment door, but Bob didn't answer, so I pounded again and waited. I lingered a bit more before rapping a third time.

"Breaking my door down?" Bob trudged up the steps behind me.

"Penny said you were in the apartment." My voice was back to normal.

"I was out on the fire escape and came around to the front. You have red stuff around your lips. Is that blood? And what's that big grin about?"

I wiped my mouth with the back of my hand to remove some lipstick and cleaned more off with my shirt front by rubbing it on my shirttail. "Mom will be mad. This is my best school shirt."

"That's lipstick, Tommy. You kissed a girl?"

"No, but one kissed me."

"Chiamaka?"

"No."

"Who?"

"I can't tell you."

"You better."

"Penny knows who kissed me."

"She does?"

"Yeah, she was there."

"I'll ask her." Bob turned as if to go down the steps.

"So when you were out on the fire escape, did you notice what caused the smell?" I knew when to change the subject. I pursed my lips to remove the smile stuck there since Penny's kisses.

Bob turned back to face me. "Too far away to spot anything."

"What direction is the smell coming from?"

"Along Minor Street. We might find out where from your back porch." Bob took off down the stairs.

"Let's check it out."

As we ran past Penny, Bob called, "Going to Tommy's."

She paced back and forth and didn't reply. Bob forgot to ask her about the lipstick.

I liked Penny and now she cared enough to want to make out with me. I never kissed a girl before. Except it was the other way around. Penny kissed me, which doesn't count. It's the first time a girl kissed me like I was her boyfriend, but I didn't want people blabbing stuff all over town.

Perhaps Bob will never get around to asking Penny about the red smears on my face.

***

The odor of rotten meat was stronger on Walnut Street. Bob and I spotted the people gathered down on the corner south of my house at Minor Street.

We crossed Walnut Street in front of old Mrs. Glass' haunted house. The street consisted of red brick row houses on both sides south of the alley. On my side, we had front porches. On the other side, they had front stoops, which made for a two-step walk up to the door. My house was the second south of the alley.

The houses were old and some were run down. Dad was a carpenter and took good care of ours. He enameled the front porch battleship gray last fall and let me help him.

We moseyed into the house where I dumped my schoolbag on the floor. We found Mom and the little ones on the back porch. Mrs. McGillicutty was with them, but she shook her whiskers, curled her tail and took off out of the yard.

"What's happening?" Bob asked.

"They don't even bother to bury their dead." Mom pinched her lips tight. She stared without blinking like when you break one of the good dishes or when she smells rotten meat as she did at that moment.

"The smell is disgusting." I spit over the railing to rid myself of the foul taste of dead things. The "they" mom referred to were the coloreds, but if she was right, how come the colored cemetery over toward Goshen was full of them?

Mom must not have noticed the lipstick smeared on my shirt because she didn't yell at me. She pulled one of Dad's handkerchiefs away from her nose as she dragged the little ones back into the house. Her face scrunched up even more as she meandered inside.

From our backyard, we could see into the yards up and down our street as well as some of the yards of the houses on Minor Street. In one of the Minor Street yards, Freeman the Cop spoke with Juliano, a fireman. They both held handkerchiefs to their noses. Juliano was a short, stubby guy, all muscle and brick.

"Whose house?" Bob asked.

"Johnny Bruce lives there with his father."

"Serve him right to turn up dead."

"Bob."

"What?"

"Somebody might have died. What are you saying?"

Bob turned from the neighbor's yard and stared me in the eye. "He tried to run me over."

"I hate him, too, but you don't kill people for reckless driving."

"I could have turned up dead." Bob twisted away. He lowered his head, and I strained to hear him. "I loved Cynthia."

I placed my hand on Bob's shoulder. "Maybe somebody loves Johnny Bruce. Anyway, it's more likely his father who died." I took my hand away. "His dad sits on the back porch with a whiskey bottle in a brown paper bag. Johnny's still in high school so he ain't dead."

"Don't high school kids die?" Bob peered into the yard again.

"Yeah, of course. Salvatore died. He was thirteen like us and went to my school. Somebody murdered Cynthia Matting, and she was thirteen when she disappeared two years ago." I scanned the neighbor's yard where Freeman the Cop and Juliano leaned over the back fence with their heads down. If they had more to say, we didn't hear it.

"Don't talk about Cynthia," Bob said.

I studied the back of Bob's head. "You still have a crush on her." I gazed back to the neighbor's yard.

"Yeah, like your crush on Penny."

"Except Cynthia told us to beat it. And now she isn't even alive anymore."

Bob pushed with his open hand against my shoulder. "Penny would tell you to beat it if you asked her out."

"I like Penny, but she is too old for me." This was a sore spot for Bob, so I got in a jab. "Maybe I'll ask her out when I'm older unless she asks me first."

"Fat chance."

"You never know what Penny is thinking, Bob. She's kind of like you."

"What do you mean?" Bob pounded my shoulder again

"I mean every time I figure you guys out, you surprise me." I grabbed Bob's wrist as he swung at me again and yanked it down to his side.

"You going out with Penny would be a surprise."

"Yeah, a nice one."

Bob's hand flew up one more time, but I clutched his wrist before he could smash me.

"If you go out with my sister, Tommy, I'll kill you."

"I'll kill you back and then kiss Penny anyway." I let go of Bob's wrist.

Bob turned back to Johnny Bruce's backyard. "Shouldn't date your best friend's sister. Ain't right."

Freeman and Juliano headed back into the house where Johnny Bruce lived with his dad.

"What if your sister and your best friend cared for each other? It'd be okay then, wouldn't it?" I asked.

"You two are not allowed to like each other."

I faced Bob eyeball-to-eyeball. "The odds are it was Johnny's old man, not Johnny."

"Johnny? What are you talking about?"

"The smelly dead meat, remember?"

"Oh yeah."

I rested my butt on the porch railing. "By the way, I prayed to Salvatore in purgatory and told him he could play with Cynthia. Salvatore was okay."

Bob turned around. "Purgletory? What's that?"

"It's where you end up when you die and you weren't bad enough for hell."

"What happens in purlatory?"

"It's a place where they clean you up and make you polish your shoes and stuff so you are ready to meet God. When you are, you can head off to heaven. You really should go to church. You're supposed to know this stuff."

"So you take a bath and wear your Sunday clothes?"

"Yeah, except they bathe you in fire."

Bob's eyes became huge. "Fire? Does it hurt?"

"Hurts like hell."

"Cynthia Matting didn't go to no purpletory."

"In case she did, I told my friend Sal to play with her."

"Thanks."

I turned around to watch the yard. Freeman and Juliano moseyed back out of the house. Freeman took notes with his little pad of paper and stubby little pencil. He stopped to lick the lead every once in a while to keep the point wet.

We strained to hear what they said, but all I made out was "chopped," "week anyway," and "blood everywhere." Those kinds of words make a cop raise his voice loud enough to be heard even when he doesn't want anyone to listen.

"Boring, Tommy." Bob headed for the backdoor.

"Yeah, let's go in."

The windows and doors were closed despite the heat and no sign of rain. We tuned in a rerun of Howdy Doody in the living room. We were too old to watch the little freckle-faced marionette chat with his friend, Buffalo Bob, so I flipped the channel knob to watch the Mouseketeers. It was a rerun, too. We watched it anyway. Bob and I have a crush on one of the Mouseketeers named Annette.

I thought about what Penny would look like with Mouseketeer ears and her name across her chest, like the kids on TV. Would she be a blonde in black and white?

I also considered how "chopped," "week anyway" and "blood everywhere" added up to so much stink in the neighborhood.

CHAPTER 5

On Saturday morning, Penny answered my knock on the Durkin apartment door.

"Hi." She spun around to show off her tiny pajama bottoms and plopped on the couch in the living room area. Penny's pajama bottoms were the same silky material as the top.

"Bob home?" Her outfit made me feel stupid as I stepped through the doorway and stopped.

"Nah, he and Mom took the bus to Sixty-Ninth Street so Bob could spend some of his birthday money." She flipped her pretty legs up on the coffee table.

"Oh." My insides caught fire.

"Ever been to Sixty-Ninth Street? In Upper Darby, the first town coming out of Philly? There are large department stores, lots of little ones, and two big movie theaters. They have restaurants and a huge terminal where the buses, city trolleys and the El come together. They come into the terminal and they come out of the terminal. In and out. Do you understand?"

"Yeah, I get it. In and out. Buses and trolleys. What's the El?" I scratched at my left ear to see if smoke poured out.

"A big, long train."

"Oh." No smoke from the ears, but I swear I felt flames shoot up my back.

Penny's voice sounded weird and she breathed funny, too, like her brain short circuited and set her windpipe on fire.

"You okay, Penny?"

"Yeah, why? Don't you want to go to Sixty-Ninth Street with me?" Penny returned her feet flat to the floor so she could sit up straight. She gazed at me while waiting for my reply. Her facial expression reminded me of the way she scrunched up her face when she kissed me out on Market Street.

"Sounds like a blast. Since you have your license now, you can drive me and Bob to all kinds of cool places our parents never go."

"I wasn't planning to bring Bob."

Why would Penny take me shopping? And why would she leave Bob home?

She strolled over to me. Her arms reached around my neck and held on tight. She had that strained expression on her face like she might cry, but somehow she was happy.

My voice twisted into the squeaky range. "If you're all right, I'll take off now."

"Not yet, Tommy." She didn't cry, but her smile was still strained. She was a big girl.

We stared into each other's eyes. Hers were large and filled with liquid sky. Mine were dark brown. Penny rubbed the skin on the back of my neck with her fingers, which made the fire roaring inside me feel, I don't know, twitchy and good at the same time.

"I know you like me." A smile tried to force itself through the tense muscles on her face. She smelled like a girl, like flowers on a summer breeze.

I shook inside and couldn't make my mouth move.

Penny planted a long, sweet kiss on my lips. She pressed her whole soft self against me and pulled back. She left her hands around my neck. "Guess what, Tommy McConnell. I like you, too." Her voice sounded husky like her insides were on fire.

She seemed happy now but had a tight muscled face like she might cry despite her smile. I grinned back with tense facial muscles.

Was she serious? She liked me, a kid who at the moment was paralyzed with fear? If any more speaking was to happen in this apartment, she would have to do it.

She did.

"Sometimes a girl needs a young man in her life. I know you like me and now I like you, too. Here's a special rule for you. If you like somebody you have to let them know no matter what. Otherwise, you could miss out on somebody special. You don't want to miss out on me, do you?"

I still wore my blue jeans, tee shirt and a gigantic smile, but the words wouldn't come down to my mouth from my brain. Did my face appear strained to her?

"Don't worry. You need time to get used to me, Tommy McConnell. It's called 'Love.' I can wait."

My eyes refused to blink.

"Tommy?"

My mouth was stuck in neutral.

"I'm special. Always remember, okay?" Her voice returned to normal.

I couldn't say anything again.

"Goodbye, Tommy."

She smiled and slid her hands down my chest. I gulped and grinned back while gazing at her gentle eyes which seemed filled with love.

Imagine Penny Durkin, the most beautiful girl ever, liked me. I wasn't sure I was ready for girls, especially an older one. But if I had more guts, Penny and I would still be together yakking about why she liked a thirteen year old. Or she might be teaching me how to make out.

CHAPTER 6

Mrs. McGillicutty, our gray-striped tabby, rested on the top step of my back porch. She waited for the ball to come within claw range so she could swat at it and kill it, maybe even eat it. She didn't understand rubber pimple balls, like the one I was bouncing off the steps.

In my mind, Penny Durkin wore her short nightie outfit with her lengthy pretty legs sticking out. Her hand slid down my back. Her lips pressed against mine. She was about to grab my...

"What are up to, steel penny?" Chiamaka lived in the white stucco house behind our backyard. Her house faced the alley which was not smart. They kept chickens in the backyard and the rooster crowed every morning. She was in the same grade as Bob and me, except she went to public school with Bob while I attended St. Agnes.

You had to listen closely to Chiamaka. She was the brightest girl I ever met and spoke the young Queen's English better than I did, but she loved to talk with an Alabama colored accent. She once told me it was because she was proud to be colored, which made me feel good because kids should be proud of who they were.

"Nothing. How about you?"

"Talking to you."

"Like I knew already."

"You asked." She caught the pimple ball as it bounced off my back porch step and threw it back against the steps.

I caught the pimple ball on the bounce, tossed it and let her catch it.

Chiamaka pointed with it down the row of backyards south towards Minor Street, her arm stretched to full length. "That one, the third house from yours. Cynthia lived there."

"Yeah. She used to play with Bob and me when we were younger."

"She ain't about to get any older." Chiamaka tossed the ball, and we returned to the rhythm of bouncing it off the steps to each other.

I held the ball again. "She's been gone for almost two years. We thought she ran away to New York. Then her Mom and Dad moved away."

"They be running away when they should be staying."

"Why stay? Their daughter moved on without them and she was just thirteen at the time." I tossed the ball against the step one more time.

Chiamaka fumbled the catch but held onto the ball. "She was busy getting murdered. That's not moving away. It's staying put."

"I liked her when she was a kid, then she turned thirteen and was too good for Bob and me."

"She don't be liking us colored folks either, Tommy. And she ain't never played a day with me in her short, tragic life. So you want to walk with me?"

I caught the ball she tossed. "Where we headed?"

"What do you care?"

"Thought I'd ask." I tossed the ball on the porch for the cat to chase.

"Across town. You in?"

"Yeah, not much to do around here. I'll tell Mom."

Turned out Mom wanted me to clean my room because it was Saturday, which led to a squabble. While we were busy yelling, I pulled Mrs. McGillicutty off my little sister, Blair. I'm not sure when or how the cat had gotten back into the house. Mrs. McGillicutty glanced to Mom for protection, but one glare back and she changed her mind. She headed instead for the safety of one of the bedrooms.

Mom said my room could wait for an hour.

Back outside, Chiamaka bounced the pimple ball off the porch steps.

At the gate, I asked "Coming?"

"Hey, I invited you, didn't I?"

"So where we headed, Chiamaka?"

"This way."

We walked side-by-side down the alley into the colored section for two blocks to the train station. We turned north on the tracks until we crossed under the bridge at Market Street. Up the tracks one more block and we arrived under the bridge at Gay Street. The bridges were rusty leftovers from the Depression or older. Bums slept under the Gay Street Bridge and built fires to keep warm. They slept there when they couldn't find an old deserted building to sneak into at night.

"Where are the hobos?" Chiamaka asked.

"I don't know. The cops clean them out once in a while. Most of them don't stay any longer than necessary to hop a freight. The trains have to slow down at the curve up ahead."

"Maybe they went shopping." She flashed a big toothy grin. Her face was like a white girl's except for the chocolate color. She had thin lips and a perky little nose.

"Perhaps they took the bus to Sixty-Ninth Street."

"Fat chance. Colored folks don't shop in Sixty-Ninth Street." Chiamaka made a sad face for a few seconds like her team lost the pennant. She smiled again, took my hand and swung my arm a few times as we walked along. She released my hand.

"Come on," she said and took off up the tracks.

She was too fast to catch so I laughed while stopping to bend over to catch my breath.

A light breeze billowed Chiamaka's dress but not enough to show anything. The dress was pretty with a brown

35

splotchy design on a beige background. She had dark chocolate legs and black canvas sneakers with white socks on her feet.

Chiamaka walked back to me. "Kind of slow, steel penny."

Being a head taller than Chiamaka allowed me to admire her black hair shaped into those corn stalky things colored girls wear. It must have been a lot of work to fix her hair that way.

She took a gander into my eyes with her dark black-brown orbs. They were soft and moist. She made me smile. Don't know why, but she did.

Chiamaka took my hand again and pulled me along. "C'mon, Tommy, we have a ways to travel."

North of Gay Street, we left the tracks and walked past the public high school where Chiamaka watched me pick up a coin.

"Find something?" she asked.

"Steel penny."

"Figures because you are a steel penny."

I fumbled the penny into my pocket. "That's what Will Barnes calls me and Bob."

"My grandmother might call you one, too."

"Who's your grandmother?" I walked beside Chiamaka.

"She be the lady we're visiting for lunch."

"Lunch?" I glanced over at Chiamaka.

"Yeah, white folks eat lunch, don't they?"

"Yeah, of course."

"You're a growing boy. Someday you'll be big and strong like your Dad."

"Guess girls don't get hungry, do they?"

"Yeah, we be mighty hungry, too. Just not hungry like little steel penny boys."

"Uh-huh."

We passed the big nun mother house where they teach the new nuns how to become teachers and beat up on little kids to make them learn. I blessed myself as we continued walking a few more blocks to a street with small, one-story houses.

"This is the neighborhood where Bob's grandfather lives. Bob and I visit him sometimes. He feeds us and gives Bob a dollar."

"It's where my grandma lives, too."

"Your grandmother lives in a white neighborhood?"

"Yeah, the white folks don't like it but nothing they can do according to Grandma. She says the old lady she took care of left the house to her in her will. Gave her the whole house – dishes, furniture, backyard, everything. The old lady didn't care. She loved my Grandma. You'll like her, too. I can tell."

"How?"

"On account of you being hungry." Chiamaka turned onto the path that led to the front door of a small, one-story, brick cottage. She pushed the door open and yelled, "Hello, Grandma."

"We're in the kitchen," a voice returned.

I followed Chiamaka through the living room to the dining room on the right and then left again into the kitchen.

Penny Durkin sat at the kitchen table. Tears streamed down her cheeks. She glared at me and pushed her chair back. She spun around so I couldn't see her face. She wore a white blouse and blue jeans. She mumbled, "Gotta go" and ran out the backdoor. I heard a car start up and rumble away.

Chiamaka's grandma looked at me. "You two know each other?"

"Yeah, Penny is Bob's sister. Bob and I are best friends."

"You don't mind if Penny visits me for advice sometimes because you know how her mama works those long hours and her papa and other brother aren't around any more."

"Not for me to mind," I said.

"Good, because Penny and I are old friends. Now, I have a question for you."

"Yes, ma'am?"

"Who are you?"

Chiamaka jumped in. "Grandma, you didn't give me a chance to introduce Tommy McConnell. He lives near me."

"Oh, you're Tommy McConnell, the boy who's in love with Penny Durkin. Right, young man?"

This was a shock to me so while I fumbled with an answer, Chiamaka came to my aid. "He's my friend, so you have to treat him right."

"You children don't mind a little teasing, do you? Besides, your friends are always welcome at my house."

"Thanks, Grandma."

"Now, I suppose you both want to eat."

"Yes, ma'am." Chiamaka pulled a chair away from the table and plopped down.

I flopped into a chair across from her, the one Penny had sat in. It was still warm from her bottom.

Chiamaka's grandma took away an empty bowl from my place that had chocolate ice cream stains in it. "Tommy, you can call me 'Mrs. Davis.'"

"Sure, Mrs. Davis." I remembered to say "thank you" when she planted a sandwich down for me to eat.

Mrs. Davis smiled back. "You're welcome." She pointed out the half empty jar of pickles on the table in front of me when I asked for some.

"Mrs. Davis, you make great sandwiches." I chomped on mine while flashing a puffed cheek smile at Chiamaka.

"She learned from her Aunt Flora, right, Grandma?"

I swallowed and peered over at Mrs. Davis. "Did your mother teach you, too?"

"She did when I was a small child, then she sent me up north to live with Aunt Flora."

"How old were you?" I asked.

"Younger than you and Chiamaka. I was only ten years old."

"Why'd your mama send you north so young?" Chiamaka asked.

"She said so I could attend school but there was another reason, too." Mrs. Davis folded her arms across her chest.

"Tell us!" Chiamaka's eyes gazed up at her grandma like she expected a story.

Mrs. Davis wiped the table. "Grandma doesn't like to talk about those long ago memories."

"Sounds like there was a boy in the story somewhere." Chiamaka's mouth crept into a big grin.

"Not like you think." Mrs. Davis shook a finger at Chiamaka.

Chiamaka sat back in her chair. "Then you better tell us so we won't be thinking the wrong way."

"The best thing is for you to eat and then run along to play," Mrs. Davis said.

Chiamaka looked down at her plate for a moment, but then raised her face with another oversized grin. "Yes, Grandma, but I want to hear the story someday."

"Maybe I'll tell you and maybe I won't."

"We be needing to run now anyway, Grandma." Chiamaka stood and carried her plate to the sink. I didn't know why she carried her plate away, but kept silent.

Mrs. Davis placed her right hand on her hip. "Chiamaka, I told you about using correct English. You're not an ignorant country girl so don't speak like one."

"I know lots of country girls be smart," Chiamaka said.

Mrs. Davis's eyes narrowed. "Then I bet they don't be 'being this' and 'being that' every time they speak."

Chiamaka must have noticed the glare in her grandma's eyes because she backpedalled. "I say a thing 'be's' a certain way because that's the way we talk on the colored side of town."

Maybe Mrs. Davis had a rule that said you had to take your plate to the sink. At my house, Mom made us kids take turns clearing the table and scrubbing the dishes.

Mrs. Davis pointed a finger at Chiamaka and moved it up and down. "I don't want to hear no more about this. And you be minding your school teachers. No more getting your face slapped by them white teachers, you understand?"

Chiamaka opened her mouth for a second before words came out. Her eyes grew big, too. "How'd you know?"

I was ready for a story. "I didn't hear this one."

"Grandma knows many things, Chiamaka," Mrs. Davis said.

Yeah, like how to put her hands on her hips when she's not happy with her granddaughter.

"Do you know why my teacher slapped my face?" Chiamaka gawked up in one of those sweet, innocent looks girls are so good at.

"I suspect I don't need to know except you must have sassed her proper." Mrs. Davis crossed her arms and leaned against the sink.

"I want to know," I said.

Chiamaka placed her hands on her hips and spun in my direction. I expected her to scold me, but instead she must have realized one of her stares was enough to shut me up. And it was. She focused her attention back to her grandma. "I did sass her proper. Do you know what I said?"

"You're about to tell me whether I want to hear it or not." Mrs. Davis grinned.

I stayed busy keeping my mouth shut.

"Mrs. Peabody at school told me it wasn't fitting for an American not to have a good Christian name, but I told her I was a good Christian girl so my name is a good Christian's name, and my people have been Americans since our country started in seventeen-seventy-six and they've been living in the New World since long before the Revolution, so what was she talking about? I suspect our ancestors about got off the first slave boat to land on these shores. I said, 'What you are implying, Mrs. Peabody, is I should have a white girl's name, but as you can plainly see, I ain't no white girl and I ain't about to change into one or pretend I might. What you see is what you get with Chiamaka, Mrs. Peabody, with all due respect to you.' She didn't like what I said, but not much she could say back except not to use the word 'ain't' because it ain't no word and then she punished me good for sassing her and said, 'About what I'd expect from a dumb colored kid who doesn't know a good name from a bad one.' So I told her, 'But I know my name and it's a good one. It means 'God is beautiful' and comes straight from Africa, like my people, and I'm proud of my people, and I'm proud of my African heritage, and I'm proud of the color of my skin, and I'm proud to be an American, and I'm proud to be a Christian, and I'm proud to be a girl, and I'm proud to be poor. It's the way God made me, and God don't make nothing the wrong way. You can get along with me or move along without me.' Then Mrs. Peabody slapped my face something fierce."

Wow, who knew colored people thought about such stuff? I was proud of Chiamaka at that moment because she stood up to her teacher, but she was pretty stupid if you think about it. Why get your face slapped because some white teacher hated coloreds?

I didn't hate Negroes. In fact, I felt like I should fall in love with Chiamaka, I was so proud of her, but that would be stupid, too. But I couldn't help the way I felt. I was so proud of her, but I had a crush on Penny. You can't love a colored girl, if you're a white boy. You have to fall in love with the right kind of girl. Chiamaka was pretty, don't get me wrong, but I had this crush on Penny since first grade practically, and she had this wonderful blonde hair and those deep blue eyes.

Mrs. Davis wiped tears from her eyes. When she finished, she gathered Chiamaka into a hug. When she pushed her back from the embrace, she smiled, but you could still see tears leaking. "Outside and play you two. And don't let me hear you say that 'be' word unless you speak proper."

I carried my plate to the sink, so Chiamaka wouldn't yell at me for not hauling it. A guy had to think about these things.

41

"Yes, Grandma. Thanks for lunch." Chiamaka kissed her grandma on the cheek and hugged her. "You know I speak proper English when I want to."

"I know you do. Thanks for visiting with me, children."

Outside I said, "Your grandma is nice, Chiamaka."

"She sure is."

"What you said about your teacher inside was cool."

Chiamaka popped out one of those girly smiles for when they like you. She ran down the street for all she was worth.

CHAPTER 7

A chunk of broken bottle glass spun by us so close it almost pierced Chiamaka's ankle. We were up on the street level above the railroad tracks on our return from her grandmother's house. As we crossed the Gay Street Bridge, some colored kids had seen us from down below on the tracks and attacked. We tore off west on Gay Street as glass fragments zinged past. The projectiles stopped as soon as we were out of sight of the tracks. I glanced back after a block, but the colored kids hadn't followed us.

At Matlack Street, we turned south past Market Street to the head of the alley in the middle of the block. We turned west up the alley towards our homes.

"Those kids might have thought we were boyfriend and girlfriend," Chiamaka said.

"What a dumb nigger thing to say," I replied. Who said you have to think before you talk? Guess I should have listened when they mentioned it.

Chiamaka was in front of me when she twirled around and planted her nose right up in front of mine, which was a trick since she was a head shorter than me. "Don't you ever call me that, you white stale cracker!"

"Didn't mean nothing." I didn't either. I had opened my mouth without thinking. You could find yourself in a lot of trouble in my neighborhood if you didn't use your brain once in a while.

"I'll show you what you meant." Chiamaka bolted me in the stomach with her right fist as hard as she could.

Who expected her to let loose? I doubled over and held my throbbing stomach. I croaked in a hoarse whisper, "What'd you belt me for?" I'm not sure which was worse, the pain in my gut or the ache of receiving a royal butt kicking from a colored girl.

"I'll show you why." Chiamaka crushed me as hard as she could with an uppercut.

A flash of bright light blinded my eye. The force of Chiamaka's thump spun me sideways. I toppled over with a thud as my shoulder hit the pavement. As the rest of me landed, I squeezed out a loud "oomph" while the air emptied from my lungs. Gravel and bits of broken asphalt pressed into my right cheek. The air didn't seem to want to come back into my chest. No tears welled up in my eyes, so that's one thing at least.

Gut pain and eye soreness outweigh the insult of a girl tearing me apart. Chiamaka was way too nice for me to call that horrible word. Of course, this raised the question of who it was okay to use it with. Somebody a lot weaker than Chiamaka for sure. I decided that I wouldn't say such a horrible word anymore so I could spend less time on the ground chewing gravel.

With my good eye, I spied Chiamaka as she stormed up the alley. In the distance, she whirled around, smiled at me, and threw a couple of punches in the air like a boxer. I figured she had cooled off enough to realize I didn't mean nothing personal when I called her a nasty name, which I didn't. She ran home.

I pulled myself up to a sitting position and scooted over against somebody's garage door.

A two-tone white and powder blue Chevrolet two-door hardtop roared up the alley from Matlack and squealed to a halt next to me. It was a top-of-the-line nineteen-fifty-seven

Bel-Air model with the cool tail fins. The passenger door opened.

Penny stared me in the eye through the open car door as I stood up. A smile crossed my lips. I covered my sore left eye.

"Get in," she ordered. I was no sooner on the seat when she floored the engine. The car roared up the alley across Walnut and squealed to a halt by the backyard of old Mrs. Glass' haunted house. Good thing Johnny Bruce wasn't driving up Walnut in his father's Caddy like the day he almost ran over Bob or that Chevy would have been smashed.

Penny glared at me. She didn't have the tense, strained love appearance from this morning. This was the fuming Penny. Didn't she love me anymore?

I glanced her way. "What?"

"Don't you ever tell anyone you saw me in that nigger's house," she shouted.

I waited for her anger to pass. How could she not love me so soon? What did I do?

I whispered, "They don't like when you call them that, Penny."

"Shut up and listen. Don't you ever tell anyone you saw me in that house. Do you understand?" Her voice was still too loud.

"Yes, but why?" Did she hear the fear I felt?

"There ain't no why. You shut up and listen. Don't never tell nobody you saw me."

"Okay, I understand." Good. It came out like a complaint.

"What do you understand?"

"I'll never tell anybody I saw you in Mrs. Davis' house."

"Perfect. I like you, Tommy. I don't like to see you get hurt. Let me give you another rule. Don't ever let a colored girl cold cock you. Do you understand me?"

"That I understand."

45

"Fine. Go home and wash up." Her voice was soft so she liked me again.

"All right."

"Scram."

Angry. Wished she would make up her mind.

"Penny?"

"What?" Less perturbed.

"Where's the car from?" I gazed down at a white rabbit's foot that dangled from the key in the ignition. It swung back and forth above Penny's knee.

She still had on her blue jeans. She also wore white bobby socks with brown penny loafers, which always made me smile because her name was Penny.

"Don't ask me stuff like that, Tommy. I don't want you in any trouble."

"Sure."

"Anybody asks…"

"I know; I never saw you drive a car."

"You're a fine boy, Tommy. I'll see you later."

I climbed out of the Chevy. Guess I was just a boy again.

Penny called after me, "Don't forget what I told you."

"Don't use the awful word you like to say, the one you promised you would wash my mouth out with lye soap if I said it?"

"No, silly. Always remember that we love each other."

CHAPTER 8

Mom looked up from Blair's bottom. "About time, Tommy. Clean your room. You promised to be back hours ago." She returned her attention to the safety pins she fastened in my baby sister's freshly washed diaper.

"Let me grab some ice because the knife stuck in my ear hurts." Sarcasm was the last refuge of a teenager called to be a writer.

"Refill the ice tray and tell Alan to dust under his bureau. You too. Now get out of my sight."

I wrapped the ice in a clean dishtowel and smacked it against my eye. Soon my skin cooled. By the time I arrived upstairs, the towel had a wet spot and a speck of blood.

I found Alan on his bed with a book. He raised his eyebrows. "What happened to you?"

"Don't want to talk about it."

"Did you have a fight with Bob?"

"Naw."

"Somebody beat you up?"

Mrs. McGillicutty sauntered into the room and jumped onto my bed. She curled against me, to provide cat comfort for my beleaguered eye. I petted her with my left hand and with my right adjusted the towel so it remained in place on my face.

"You know the cinderblock wall along the backyard of the Royal?" No sense embarrassing myself with the truth.

"Let me guess. You fell off?"

"Yeah."

"Into the Royal backyard?"

"What do you think, I'm stupid? I made sure I went the other way."

"Let me see." Alan pushed Mrs. McGillicutty onto the floor and sat on the bed beside me. He jerked the towel and ice off my eye. He squinted, stared, and puffed his cheeks out, pretending he was fat old Dr. Blue, our family physician.

"Yep, you'll have a shiner," he said.

"Crap."

We were quiet for a while. Alan lay on his bed again so he was in no hurry to touch his messy bureau. I sagged on my back with the ice over my eye. Mrs. McGillicutty parked on my chest. She purred to the rhythm of my heart beat.

Penny was so pretty and she liked me. Why would an older girl like me?

I asked Alan what the awful word Penny used meant.

"You don't know?"

"Would I ask if I knew?"

"It's having sex."

"Oh, okay. Now I know."

Alan continued to avoid his bureau. I pictured Penny wearing those incredible Bermuda shorts, and she kissed me.

"Alan?"

"Yeah."

"How old do you have to be to fu…, I mean have sex with someone?"

"Old enough so she wants to do it with you."

After more not cleaning our room, the ice was about melted on my face. Mrs. McGillicutty scampered out the open door, having spotted her favorite tom through the window. I thought about snagging more ice from downstairs.

Alan asked, "Why are you asking these questions? Does Chiamaka want you to bang her?"

"No, I was just curious."

"Somebody made you interested. Bet Chiamaka wants to lose her virginity with you."

"I heard Penny use that word, and I didn't know what it meant."

Alan's bureau gathered more dust in the summer heat. I coaxed the last of the coldness out of the wet towel on my face.

Alan rolled on his side to face me from his bed. "I'll be. You love Penny Durkin."

"She's Bob's big sister. I'm a kid. She used fu… I mean that stupid word, and I had never heard it before."

"At least you're learning how to use it. Now, say the whole word, not just the first two letters."

I sucked the water out of the towel while Alan lay motionless with a thoughtful expression on his face like he wanted to figure out what to say to Mom about not cleaning his bureau.

Alan sat up. "You better think of a better story before Dad comes home."

"Story? About what?"

"You fall off a wall, you break your arm. You don't get a black eye."

"Is it black?"

"Not yet. Will be by morning."

"I'll keep ice on it."

"Might work. Your story won't. Tell me what really happened."

I sat up and leaned over to Alan, "You won't blab it all over town?"

"Nah, I won't tell nobody."

In a soft voice I said, "I called Chiamaka a nigger."

Alan fell off the bed laughing. "That'll work. Tell that one to Dad."

CHAPTER 9

Penny had a bald head as she danced in her shorty pajamas across my daydreaming mind. Alan, Bob, Jamie Bordeaux, Dickey Nelson and I strolled back to our little neighborhood from a matinee at the Warner Theater on High Street north of Gay a few blocks. Dickey was a skinny kid who lived with his mom next door to Bob and Penny. He was only ten, but we let him hang out with us anyway. He was a good ballplayer, and sometimes I had to take my little brother Danny with me, and he was ten, too.

The Warner was the fancy big theater in town. The Harrison over on Gay Street was the dumpy little one with the cheap seats and cheaper horror flicks.

We saw a movie called "Five Branded Women" about these ladies who got their heads shaved during the War. Pretty impressive when Vera Miles galumphed down the street bald.

"Loco, loco!" cried Will Barnes as we passed the First Bank of Chester County on High Street in the middle of the block between Gay and Market.

Alan asked, "Selling any papers today, Will?"

Will's eyes spun around with no place to settle because he'd been blind forever. He closed his eyes for a minute and took on a look of extreme concentration with his black skin wrinkled up and his lips pursed so he was either about to say something profound or else fart. He held this position for two or three minutes like we weren't with him. I stopped the daydream about Penny's bald head and thought about how Chiamaka should have a bald head.

"What's he up to?" Dickey whispered.

"Crapping his pants," Jamie Bordeaux said.

"Nah, he's consulting with the spirits and dark powers," said Bob.

"Don't think so." I smiled because I knew the answer.

"Why not?" Jamie Bordeaux asked.

The guys scowled in my direction. "Will's a devout Catholic. Goes to church and communion every Sunday."

Alan, Jamie Bordeaux, and Dickey turned to Bob and whispered, "Oh."

Meanwhile, in my daydream, Penny appeared more attractive with a blonde head, but Chiamaka was awesome with a sweet chocolate bald head. I tried to picture Penny as a colored girl with a blonde head, but it didn't work.

Will Barnes' eyes popped open, and he stared at my brother with his eyes not fluttering. "Woe be unto Alan."

Everyone peered at Alan who lost the color from his face. He also backed up. "Why me?" Alan swallowed a big gulp of air. "What kind of woe am I in for? Fall-down-and-skin-your-knee woe or somebody-beats-the-crap-out-of-you woe?"

Dickey said, "I'm scared, too. Can we leave?"

Alan shoved Dickey. "Didn't say I was scared!" He moved off towards Market Street, and we followed him. Behind us Will sang, "Loco, loco," which was about all you ever got out of Will after one of his pronouncements from the spirit world. I felt like a giant spider crawled up and down my spine. I don't think Will would say "woe" to somebody unless he meant the worst kind.

We made our way to Market Street and turned east. Between the apartment building where Dickey Nelson lived and the Royal Restaurant, with Bob's apartment above, was a walkway of red brick. The ground was paved in brick as were the two walls and the arched ceiling.

Alan, Bob, Jamie Bordeaux, Dickey, and I walked through the narrow alleyway single file because that was the only way we could fit. We didn't want Menoitios to see us so we tried to be quiet.

Menoitios Demeter was the craziest Greek I had ever met. Of course, I only knew four Greeks including Menoitios, his father Iapetos, his mother, Mrs. Demeter, and Philomena Pokonapolis, a girl in my class at St. Agnes. Philomena was nice for a girl. Mrs. Demeter was kind. She waited on the tables in the Royal. Iapetos was the cook and owner. Menoitios did whatever needed doing. He was in his twenties and didn't like kids.

At the end of the walkway, Bob charged up the black iron fire escape that led to his apartment. An exhaust fan blew the greasy air out of the Royal kitchen and onto the fire escape. Bob spat into it as he ran past. We laughed, and I spat into the fan, too. Then Jamie Bordeaux spat. Dickey spat and Alan screamed.

From above we saw the long, white-coated arm of Menoitios snatch my brother and drag him through the backdoor of the Royal into the kitchen.

I was paralyzed with fear because who knew what Menoitios would do to my brother? Whatever it was, wasn't going to be good.

Jamie Bordeaux yelled, "Go!"

We scrambled up the rest of the fire escape and through Bob's backdoor. Penny was reading a fan magazine as we huddled in the living room. She practiced looking sexy in shorts while sitting cross-legged on the couch.

Bob asked, "Feel any better, Penny?"

"Yeah. Thanks for blabbing to your friends." Penny glared at Bob.

"Sorry, but you've been waking up sick lately." Bob dropped his head like a kid in trouble.

"Girl stuff, Bob. You wouldn't understand." Penny buried her face in the fan magazine.

"Monthly girl stuff?" Jamie Bordeaux did a crappy job of imitating an innocent expression on his face. I guess because he was older, Jamie wasn't embarrassed by girl junk, but I felt my face become hot. A rock lodged inside my stomach.

"What's "girl stuff?" I whispered to Bob.

Bob whispered back, "You have to have a big sister to understand. Ask Alan after he gets away from Menoitios."

"Yeah, I have girl stuff. Now, you creeps skedaddle and leave me alone." Penny closed her eyes. She rested her head against the arm of the couch and placed her magazine across her chest.

Alan was a good brother sometimes. Like at this moment because I could use him to get sympathy from Penny. "Poor Alan, I'll never see him again."

Penny tilted her head in my direction and blinked like she had a question. At least she wasn't angry this time. "What happened to Alan? Was he bad like me?"

"You're not bad," said Bob.

"You look great to me." Whoa, what'd I say? Bob will make me pay for blurting my big mouth. Penny might not like it either, especially in front of the guys.

Penny stared at me as her face melted into a smile. She sat up to gaze at Bob. "Of course, I'm bad. Daddy always said I was bad." To me, she asked, "But what about Alan?"

"Not as pretty as you." There I went again, but at least nobody seemed mad, except Bob.

"Tommy, that's the nicest thing you ever said to me." Penny's smile softened, but I could see what was coming next.

Not in front of the guys.

She did.

Penny climbed off the couch and grasped me by the head. She parked her sweet lips on mine. Stayed parked for a good long time before she let loose. I glanced around, and the guys stared at me with big eyes.

"Can I be next?" Jamie Bordeaux asked.

Penny wrapped an arm around my elbow and smiled at everybody. To me she said, "Now, tell me about your brother."

"Yeah, does he kiss as bad as you?" Dickey asked.

Bob's face reddened. "Shut up. Kissing my sister ain't funny."

Jamie Bordeaux gave Bob a shoulder tap. "I laughed."

Bob yanked away from Jamie Bordeaux and flopped down on the couch.

Penny's eyes narrowed. "Okay wise guys, out with you."

"Don't you want to know about Alan?" asked Jamie Bordeaux.

"Only if you tell me something worth hearing," Penny said.

Jamie Bordeaux turned his palms upward the way he did when he explained stuff to you that he made up. "Put it this way, Penny, you don't want to eat lamb stew anytime soon at the Royal."

Penny turned white and clutched her belly with both hands. "Eww, disgusting. Why would you say such a thing?"

I lowered my head. "Menoitios."

The rest of the guys glanced my way with heads bobbing up and down at each other.

"What's with Menoitios and Alan?" Penny asked.

"Menoitios caught him spitting into the kitchen fan," said Dickey.

"Why was Alan spitting into the kitchen fan?" Penny's face returned to its normal beautiful self. She seized my arm again and leaned in close.

Bob rose off the couch. "He wasn't."

"Yes, he was," Jamie Bordeaux said.

"No," Bob said. "We spit. He got caught. He was last in line and didn't get to spit."

"What are you boys doing about it?" Penny asked.

"Hiding up here," said Bob.

"Brave bunch you are." Penny held fast to my arm.

"You won't find anyone meaner than Menoitios Demeter." Bob glared at me. "Your brother is in a pot of boiling water right now. Too late for him."

"We're lucky we're still alive. Poor Alan," said Dickey.

"If he's so mean," said Jamie Bordeaux, "maybe he killed old man Bruce."

"Don't scare Penny," I said.

Jamie Bordeaux flashed me his quizzical look. "Why not? He's guilty. Johnny Bruce was framed."

"They have to catch Johnny Bruce before they can frame him," I said.

Jamie Bordeaux ignored me. "What do you think, Penny?"

"I hope he… well, I mean I hate the thought of that young man killing his own father, but on the other hand, I hate thinking the killer might be right here in the building where Bob and I and Mom live. You're a creep, Jamie Bordeaux. I won't be able to sleep at night." Penny snuggled closer to me, almost knocking me over. I side stepped to keep my balance.

"Menoitios isn't here at night," said Bob. His eyes still boiled in my direction but I couldn't help it if his big sister liked me.

"Why would Menoitios kill old man Bruce?" Dickey asked.

"Doesn't need no reason," Bob said. "Kills for the pleasure of killing."

"He's too mean for pleasure," said Jamie Bordeaux. "He kills out of meanness. Pure and simple meanness. He kills because he can get away with it. Maybe he killed Cynthia Matting."

"Who cares? Let's play ball," said Dickey.

"Can't," Bob said.

"Why not?" Jamie Bordeaux asked.

"His turn to clean the kitchen," Penny said.

"I'll join you guys later." Bob headed for the kitchen sink.

"No more talk about killing people!" Dickey said.

I pulled away from Penny and took off with the guys out the front door. Before closing the apartment door behind me, I gawked at Penny. She yawned but giggled in my direction. I smiled back and saluted like a sea captain.

As I started down the stairs that led to the street, I wondered if Penny was safe in her own home.

***

Four cops ran through the backdoor of the police garage from the station. They piled into two cars and zinged out of the garage. Their sirens blared and red jelly bean lights flashed as they zoomed up the alley towards Market Street. We ran over in time to watch them swing right on Market.

We were playing ball on the parking lot across the alley from the police garage. It was a two-level lot with a three-foot drop separating the front half from the back. We used the upper part for the infield and the lower for the outfield. The drop resulted from the lot being on a hill and the builders wanting the parking areas to be flat.

Freeman the Cop came out through the police garage. "Tommy, go home. Your mother needs you."

"Alan!" I tore off for the cinderblock wall that ran down one side of the backyard of the Royal Restaurant. I was on top of the wall when I heard Jamie Bordeaux slap the top of the wall next to me on his way over. He landed a split second after me. Bob was right behind. I heard Dickey scuffling over, too.

Up towards the kitchen door and the black iron fire escape, two police officers stood around a crumpled, lumpy olive drab Army surplus wool blanket. These were not the same cops who sped out of the police garage, so something had been going on for a while. One end of the blanket was wet and murky with spilled blood darkening the concrete. A guy in a suit held the wool cover up near the other end. He drew with a piece of chalk. I ran over and lifted the end with the blood.

A thing, an evil spirit, grips your throat at moments like this with one hand and pounds you on the chest with the other so you can't breathe. Then the monster pounds you again right in the stomach, and you double over.

I wanted to scream, opening my mouth so far my jaw was about to kiss my knees. The demon was on my back now. I moved away but couldn't straighten up.

One of the cops yelled, "Hey, get away from there, you."

But it was too late forever.

Backing away I bumped into somebody who grabbed me. It was a kid. Jamie Bordeaux? Yes, because Bob had my arm and tried to spin me around away from the blood-red death. Bob was my best friend and like a brother to me.

My breaths came in short, deep gasps. Acid burned my throat. I was about to barf. A big pressure, not the evil fiend, but Bob pushed me down on the grass which was a better landing spot than the concrete walkway that ran down the middle of the yard towards the garage in back. I didn't need a black and blue bottom for the funeral.

Jamie Bordeaux pushed my head between my knees. Bob held my legs so my knees stayed up. I rocked back and forth, back and forth.

"Oh, my God, oh, my God, oh, my God…" I rocked like a baby and tried not to see Alan under the blanket, tried to wish him alive, tried to pray him back to life, but all I could say was "Oh, my God, oh my God, oh, my God…"

"It's all right to cry, son." Freeman the Cop's voice was big, mellow and soothing, but I wouldn't let the tears sneak out. I was a big boy and big boys don't cry.

Somehow, I was on my feet and someone hugged me. Bob no longer held my legs to keep my knees up. Instead, he squeezed me so tight I had trouble with my deep breaths. I let my knees drop and made a gagging sound. Bob backed off, and I gaped at him as my butt hit the grass again.

Bob knelt on my right side. I felt Jamie Bordeaux's hand on my back. Big tears streamed down Bob's cheeks.

I started to get up. Jamie Bordeaux took hold of me under the arm. Bob seized my right arm. With their help, I rose to my feet. I was dizzy and could hardly breathe.

"Tommy, listen to me," Freeman said.

I opened my eyes. How come they were closed? Freeman the Cop stood in front of me with Dickey next to him. "Go home to your mother, Tommy. She needs you. You're a big boy. Your little brothers and sisters need you, too."

I nodded a tiny bit so Freeman knew I had heard him.

Bob took my arm and pulled me towards the garage at the back of the Royal Restaurant yard. He opened the door at the right side of the garage and pushed me towards the opening. I stopped and turned around.

Menoitios Demeter, with his hands behind his back, was led out of the kitchen door. A police officer on either side had him by the elbows. His black hair hung down his olive forehead. Menoitios must have been in handcuffs, but I couldn't see for sure. He glared at me with what must be defiance. I had never seen that ugly, harsh stare from anyone before.

I refused to move my eyes off his. No way would I let Menoitios Demeter know he intimidated me. That he was big, husky and mean didn't matter. A cop tugged at his arm, and Menoitios turned away first. At least they caught him.

Bob led me through the garage past a row of trash and garbage cans and out another door into the alley.

Jamie Bordeaux patted me on the back a few times when we reached Walnut Street. He headed towards Market dragging Dickey with him. What tales would they tell around the dinner table tonight? They better remember to say I didn't cry. I was a big boy.

Then I heard the wailing.

Two men, one a police officer and the other a man with a suit and tie, came out the front door of my house and down to a parked police car where they climbed in and drove away. To the tune of my mother's screams, a dirge as ancient as death, my friend Bob led me home.

CHAPTER 10

I heard the clump-clump of feet lumbering down the linoleum floor. Dad poked me on the shoulder so I stood up and trudged over to the coffin where Bob, his mom and Penny waited. They didn't appear to know you were supposed to kneel, though I told Bob about Salvatore's funeral. They were Catholics, even if they never went to church.

Bob patted me on the arm a couple of times and I smiled at him. It was my first smile in a week. His mom patted my head. She leaned forward and kissed my forehead. She smelled the way Penny does when she kisses me. Mrs. Durkin took Bob by the hand and walked over to Mom and Dad.

Penny stayed behind. She smiled at me through her tears. She hugged me so my face was plastered against her neck. Her boobs pressed against my chest. She smelled like her Mom's perfume again. She kissed me on the lips and licked them. Yech.

She took my hand. I wiped a tear from her cheek with my free hand and led her to my chair. She glanced at me as if to ask if it was okay. I nodded and pulled down on her hand so she knew to sit. Dad made the little ones scoot over to make room so I could have the seat next to Penny. My big brothers were on the other side of Mom and Dad. Bob and Mrs. Durkin sat behind us.

My brothers and sisters will never let me live this down. The neighborhood was already whispering "Tommy

McConnell loves Penny Durkin." Now, they'll shout it around town. It was all I needed. Bob will kill me.

A few minutes passed before the unmistakable sound of school kids marching down the aisle of O'Leary's Funeral Home snagged my attention. The whole tenth grade class of Archbishop Shanahan High School marched in with Sister Agnes Marie at the head of the line. The girls wore their school uniforms which were way too short on them because it was summer. They bought these uniforms last year, and nobody would be school shopping for at least another month. The guys wore their school uniforms, too. They had shirts, ties, blazers, and long pants. The pants came way up on their legs and the jacket sleeves ended about halfway up their forearms.

Alan's friends gawked over at me while they waited their turn at the casket. Great. So when school starts, the whole tenth grade class from Shanahan will be waiting outside the eighth grade at St. Agnes to beat up Tommy McConnell. They'll tell me the beating is in memory of their dear departed friend Alan who died in the summer and made them come to a funeral home in their school clothes.

Gaping at the girls in their short skirts was fun when their turn came to gawk at Alan in the casket.

Later, a bunch of parishioners arrived after their workday to "pay their respects" as Dad said. Father Murdoch came in to lead us in prayers and to give a blessing. He started us in saying the rosary so we wouldn't notice old man O'Leary close Alan's coffin. I watched it though. So did Mom who slumped down into Dad's arms. She was bawling again. My brothers gawked at her like she was crazy. We were not crying. Even my three little sisters didn't blubber. We weren't much of a family for weeping.

We drove home, and the relatives came for a visit. Mom wandered upstairs to put my little sisters to bed. Nobody expected to see her again before breakfast.

Somebody showed up with a giant platter of sandwiches.

"A gift from the Knights of Columbus," one of the deliverymen said. Uncle Jack poured him a whiskey and one for the other Knight. Uncle Jack used the little tiny glasses he brought along with the booze. He gave them a bottle of beer for a chaser, he called it. Mom and Dad didn't keep liquor in the house so Uncle Jack always brought plenty with him. Meanwhile, Mrs. McGillicutty took a special interest in that platter of sandwiches.

After the Knights left, Uncle Jack spied me on the couch minding my own business. One peek and I knew I was in trouble. I tried to think of something clever to say about kissing older girls at my brother's wake but didn't come up with an answer.

"Come over here." Uncle Jack wiggled his upturned index finger at me.

"Whatcha want, Uncle Jack?" He was about to interrogate me about kissing girls in public.

"How old are you, Tommy?" Uncle Jack tilted his whiskey bottle at me.

Not old enough for kissing girls at my brother's wake. "Thirteen."

"When will you be fourteen?" Uncle Jack lifted one his little glasses off the table.

"Next year."

"Close enough." Uncle Jack filled his tiny glass from his bottle of Bushmills and handed it to me.

I was off one hook and onto another.

The Irish whiskey didn't look like much as I waved it around in front of my face. The Knights had swallowed their shots in one gulp. I lifted the shot glass to my lips, opened wide and let'er rip.

I clutched my throat to keep from choking, but gagged anyway.

"That's why you use such tiny glasses." My voice was a hoarse whisper.

"Here, you'll want a chaser." Uncle Jack handed me a jelly glass filled with beer. It had an inch of bubbles at the top of the bronze nectar. I glanced around while sipping. Everybody laughed. I didn't care. I just had my first shot of whiskey with a beer chaser.

"Want another?" Uncle Jack asked.

"Not right now." My voice was still hoarse. The room exploded in laughter.

"Way to go, Tommy. Pace yourself for a long evening." Uncle Jack poured a shot and handed it to Uncle Pud. He poured another to cure his own dry throat.

I finished my beer and wandered out to the back porch where I found my little brothers, Danny and Banning.

"What are you guys doing out here?" I asked.

"Hiding," Danny said.

"Don't you want to go to bed?" I asked.

"Scared," said Banning.

"Too much family?" I placed my hands on my hips.

"Too many people," said Danny.

"You're related to most of them, so you have nothing to be scared of." I pointed them to the door.

"Suppose they step on us?" Banning asked.

"Don't worry." I gave Danny a little shove on the back.

Banning, the younger one, took my hand. Danny followed us through the crowd. We turned up the stairs to their bedroom. They both relaxed once they were in their own beds.

"Goodnight." I headed for the hall.

"Don't leave," Banning begged.

"Now, what's wrong?" I asked.

"What if Alan turns into a ghost?" Banning asked.

I sat on Banning's bed. "Alan won't come around here. He's already in purgatory burning off his sins."

"Alan gots sins?" Banning asked.

"Sure, we all have sins," I said.

"Purpatory burns them off?" Banning asked.

63

"Say it right, Banning," Danny said. "It's pronounced 'purpletory.'"

"Don't worry about it, Banning," I said. "The nuns will explain it when the time comes."

I turned out the light and pushed Banning over in the bed to lie down next to him. My head spun. I closed my eyes. When I opened them, the morning sun brightened the room. Danny and Banning were still asleep so I traipsed downstairs to see about breakfast.

Aunt Katherine was making eggs and bacon in the kitchen. I grabbed a chair and sat at the table. She was talking to my other aunts and didn't say a word to me. In a few minutes she placed a plate with two eggs, two slices of bacon, some fried potatoes and a piece of toast in front of me. She poured a glass of orange juice for me also.

I was wiping up the last of the egg yoke with my toast when Uncle Jack came in. He made his way over to me, put an arm around my shoulder and shouted, "That's my boy, a true Irishman if ever I saw one. Why Tommy here took his first shot last night like a man, nary a flinch. Took a beer chaser, too. Then he's up first light and downs a full breakfast, not a hangover in sight. A true Irishman, I say."

"Jack, shut up and make the coffee," said Uncle Pud, sounding much like he had a hangover. Somewhere in this muddle, Mom and Dad wandered into the kitchen. Mom sat but didn't eat. Dad drank a cup of coffee with sugar and milk like usual.

Mom noticed me. "Go up and get ready, Tommy. And don't dawdle." She sounded almost like her usual angry self.

I headed upstairs. This was no time to open my mouth and have Dad whack me and tell me to respect my mother.

By ten o'clock, parishioners filed into the old oak pews of St. Agnes Church. Alan was up front in the aisle in a big pine casket. Dad said it was a nice one. He knows quality woodwork because he's a carpenter.

The nuns made the kids from school come to the funeral Mass. The guys looked ticked off in their jackets and ties. The girls looked happy in their short skirts, but the nuns were livid. Every once in a while during Father Murdoch's funeral Mass, the sound of a ruler cracking on flesh punctuated the sorrow.

After Mass, the relatives piled into cars. We drove to St. Agnes Cemetery. We buried Alan next to little infant brother Bobby McConnell whose stone said he was born and died the same day.

The kids from school didn't have to visit the cemetery. That's one thing they can't be mad at me about.

As we walked hand-in-hand back to the line of parked cars after the burial, Penny kissed me on the lips with the little lick thing she does. Yech. But I let her. I wanted to make her happy.

Uncle Pud walked by. "She your girlfriend, Tommy? A mite old for you." He laughed and shoved off.

Penny called after him, "I'm his best friend's sister."

"Yeah, I heard that one before," Uncle Pud called back.

"I'm riding home with you." I took Penny's hand.

"Of course you are." Penny dropped my hand and pulled the rabbit foot with the key out of her purse. We made our way to a brand new black Chevrolet sedan. We climbed in and she drove off. I didn't care who saw me with Penny Durkin or who saw her kiss me. Wasn't my funeral.

CHAPTER 11

"What's the hatchet for, Bob?" I peered up from my bowl of cereal.

"Johnny Bruce's head." Bob raised his hand like he was ready to scalp me.

"Don't think that's a good idea."

"Why not?" Bob leaned back against the sink in my kitchen. He fiddled with the hatchet holster on his belt.

"Head bashing might land you in trouble."

"Mom won't mind." Bob flashed one of his silly grins.

"I'm thinking Freeman the Cop here. And your mom will not be pleased if you scalp Johnny Bruce."

"Freeman not like it?"

"No, Bob. He supports this thing where you have to arrest the criminal, have a jury trial, and then you clobber bust them."

"Hatchet stays home?"

"Yeah. If we see Johnny Bruce, we high tail it for Freeman."

"Good. Freeman has a gun."

We traipsed over to Bob's apartment where I let Penny kiss, lick and hug me while Bob put his hatchet away in the bedroom. Bob said the best place for Johnny Bruce to hide was under the Gay Street Bridge so we headed around the corner to the alley by my house and then east toward the railroad tracks. We passed Chiamaka's house, but we didn't see her around.

"You know there will be bums," I said.

"Hobos," Bob said.

"Bums, hobos, what's the difference?"

"Bums treat you mean. They're thugs on the lam. Or ex-cons on the lookout for trouble. Hobos are poor. They want food and work. Some have wives and children back home starving to death."

We crossed Matlack Street where I dodged a high speed junker of a pickup truck with a colored driver. He waved his big finger at me.

"Hobos aren't bums?" I scratched my head.

"Nope."

"How do you know?"

"Penny." Bob kicked a rock down the alley.

"Oh."

Bob bounced a rock off somebody's garage. "Johnny Bruce is a bum by now."

"He has his father's red Cadillac." I threw a stone against the same garage.

"Maybe he sold it for cash."

A colored person's voice yelled, "Hey, scram."

"If he's a bum, he's living under the Gay Street Bridge." Bob called back to me as he ran down the alley.

We sprinted the rest of the way to the train station. Bob picked up half a pack of Chesterfield cigarettes off the ground. "Maybe Johnny Bruce killed Cynthia."

"What makes you think so?" I turned north up the tracks with Bob at my side.

"No reason except she's dead and he's a bum."

"Could he have dated her, and they had a fight?"

Bob didn't reply.

Under the Market Street Bridge, he said, "Let's put some here."

He opened the Chesterfields and dumped out two cigarettes in my hand to take across the tracks to the east embankment under the bridge.

I dropped them on the dry, brown dirt and crossed the tracks to Bob.

"Bait for Johnny Bruce," Bob said. "He'll need a smoke bad by now."

"If he's around."

"Where else would he hide?"

I pointed west. "Coatesville or Downingtown."

We stopped under the Gay Street Bridge. Bob gave me three cigarettes and took the rest of the pack over to the east embankment. He tossed it in the dirt.

"We should smoke one." I spread my three like a fan on the ground.

"Penny would kill us."

"We should bring some to Penny to smoke and then keep one for us to share." I held each one to my nose. They smelled sweet and weedy.

"Naw. Bait."

We continued north along the tracks.

"We need evidence to prove Johnny Bruce killed Cynthia." I said.

"Maybe Menoitios did it."

"They didn't both kill her." I picked up a lump of coal that had fallen onto the tracks.

"Johnny Bruce."

"Why?" I tossed the coal until it shattered against a railroad sign.

"Don't know. Hitting on her?"

"Do you mean did he slap her around?" I picked up a stone.

"Sex, stupid."

"He's colored." I tossed the stone straight up a few feet above my head to play catch with it.

Bob caught the stone in midair. "That's why he had to kill her."

We spotted three white men dressed in greasy, black clothes lumbering towards us on the tracks.

When they came up to us, I said, "We left some cigarettes under the bridge for you."

They gaped at us weird like we were cops.

After they passed by, one turned around. "Thanks. You don't want to play down here no more. No place for kids. You could get hurt. But thanks."

"Sure," I said.

"Explain?" Bob tossed the stone up the tracks. It bounced on a rail and then skipped up the embankment.

"Don't know. Saying this is not a place for kids didn't make sense. Where else can you meet hobos and bums?"

"Yeah, and hang out under a real railroad bridge? Two real bridges."

"And dodge freight trains when they come by."

"We've never seen a train, Tommy."

"It could happen."

"Yeah. Why'd you tell them bums about the cigarettes?"

"They were hobos. Their pants were greasy so they must have been working somewhere. Figured they were bound to find the little suckers anyway so we might as well get the credit."

Bob kicked at a stone. "Blows our bait."

"Didn't tell them about the cigarettes under the Market Street Bridge, did I?"

Bob grunted.

I hurled a rock up the tracks away from the hoboes. "Let's climb up on Gay Street where we can have a great view of the action under the Market Street Bridge."

"Now?"

"Sure. Why not?"

We already passed the Gay Street Bridge so we turned around and climbed a path that led to street level. The hobos were lighting their cigarettes when we started up the path.

We picked the southwest side of the bridge. I poked my head around the corner of a red-brick building so I could see under the Market Street Bridge south of us by a block. Bob peeked around me and watched, too.

After a while, I tired of staring. "What do you think? Is Johnny Bruce coming today?"

"He'll be here. His home's down there 'cause he's a bum."

"My neck is sore from craning around this corner."

Bob grunted, "Have to wait longer."

"So you think Johnny Bruce wanted to have sex with Cynthia? He's too old for her, isn't he?"

"She'd be fifteen if she didn't croak. Johnny is eighteen. She was thirteen when she disappeared, so Johnny would have been sixteen."

I'm trying to keep up with the math. "They were far apart in age."

"Penny has four years on you." Bob can add?

"What's that have to do with anything?" I asked.

"You two like each other."

"What makes you think so?"

"You two stare at each other. And you kiss each other. Penny kisses you right in front of me. Don't think I forgot about the day you showed up wearing lipstick smears."

A creepy smile popped on my face. "You mean the day they found old man Bruce's body?"

"Yeah, clever you said Penny was hanging around when some girl kissed you. Bet it was Penny all along, huh?"

"She kissed me, honest, Bob. Wasn't my fault. She took hold and laid a hot one on me."

"So, she knows you've had a crush on her since diapers."

"I didn't know you guys when I was in diapers. I moved here when we were six, remember?"

The three hobos came out from under the Gay Street Bridge. One of them still had a cigarette in his mouth. He took a long drag before pinching it between his fingers to extinguish the burning. He carefully placed the butt into his shirt pocket. They headed south towards the Market Street Bridge.

"Does it bother you when Penny kisses me?" My neck stiffened.

"Yeah. You're my friend, Tommy, not hers."

"I've always been your friend. Nothing will change that." I heard cars behind us on Gay Street, but I continued staring down at the tracks.

Bob said, "Maybe Johnny wanted to be friends with Cynthia."

"She didn't like coloreds. Chiamaka said she never played with her. Besides, Cynthia was too young to have a boyfriend." My neck felt like pins and needles.

"Yeah, but she hung out with older white boys."

"But not us."

"Cynthia wanted the older guys so she could make out."

"Yeah, I know."

"She could have made out with me, Tommy." Bob punched my shoulder from behind.

"If Johnny Bruce didn't show up by now, he's not coming."

"Just wait. He'll pop up."

"My neck ain't any less crinked, Bob."

"I have a crink, too. Let's keep staring. Maybe our necks will crink up so bad we'll have to walk around with our heads sideways all summer."

"Cool."

Bob slapped the back of his neck. "My crink's starting to hurt."

"Yeah. Let's come back later to check our bait. Once Johnny discovers the cigarettes, he'll have to wait around and smoke them."

We headed up Gay Street towards Walnut, leaving Johnny Bruce for another day.

CHAPTER 12

Freeman was not loud, but I could hear him blabbing through the wall. "We're barking up the wrong tree with that kid, Chief. I don't care how many red Caddies he's driving or where he's driving 'em. He didn't do it."

I was last in line at the water fountain in the police station and didn't want to get kicked out before my drink. The other kids were talking so we sounded loud. The good news was when one of them finished drinking, off they went back outside to wait for the rest of us.

Chief Hanson must not have heard Freeman even though I could. He said, "Three red Caddies in Downingtown. Six in Coatesville. Fourteen in Philly. Fourteen? Has to be more."

"The kid's scared. Any kid would run off if he came home and found his father butchered. Leastwise, any smart colored kid would." Freeman sounded miffed.

"I received a call from the Virginia State Police for cripes sake. They had a white kid driving a red Caddy with Pennsylvania tags. The officer sounded disappointed when I told him our kid was colored," said the Chief.

"I'm guessing some teenagers from the neighborhood broke in while the old man slept, but why'd they kill him?" Freeman's voice went way up when he spoke.

"Call came in a while ago from South Carolina where they hauled in a boy, I mean young man, driving a blue Caddy. Wanted to know if our man painted the car. They said they didn't want to turn him loose because they had beat him up pretty bad and he wasn't much good for anything at the moment so if he were guilty of something that'd be better. Haven't heard anything from paint shops, have you, Freeman?"

"Maybe they were looking for money and booze when the old man woke up from a nap. The kids panicked. One of them had a big knife or a machete and started hacking. We should ask the store owners about anyone buying knives and machetes, anything big and sharp. Shame we didn't find any prints except for the family." Freeman's voice was deep and resonant.

"Then there's the idiot out in Ohio. State trooper I think. Pulled over a red Ford pickup for crying out loud. Colored kid from Cleveland had his skull fractured in that one. The pickup had Ohio plates for Pete's sake," Chief Hanson said.

"I have to run, Chief. I want to check out Rubensteins and some other stores to see if anybody bought any kind of knives or axes lately," said Freeman.

"You walking patrol, Freeman?" Chief Hanson asked.

"I was promoted four years ago, Chief." Freeman sounded miffed again.

"Keep your eyes peeled for a red Cadillac. Has to be around here someplace. The boy can't be bright enough to wander too far," said Chief Hanson.

"Right, Chief. Thanks for listening." Freeman's footsteps echoed on the linoleum floor in Chief Hanson's office loud enough for me to hear.

My turn came at the water fountain. The water splashed in and out of my mouth for a while. The cold water felt special. You can't drink a big gulp with a water cooler, so you have to sip what you can.

With my thirst satisfied, I started to leave but bumped into Freeman. "Hi, Freeman."

"Hi, Tommy. Whatcha doing?"

"We're playing ball. Came in for a drink of water."

"Good. Play ball." Freeman's face turned weird. "Wish I could play ball, too."

"You can. Come on out back and join us."

"It's not that easy, Tommy, but thanks for the invitation."

The kids were waiting for me when I ran outside.

CHAPTER 13

"Steel pennies stirring up a storm," said Will Barnes in front of the Greek temple bank on High Street.

Bob and I watched as Will closed his blind eyes and contorted his face for a minute. He opened them wide. "Big trouble for Tommy McConnell and Penny Durkin. Your brother is in this edition."

"My brother?"

Will flopped a paper in front of us. "He's big news in this town. He was a star basketball player at Shanahan High School. He was murdered, and the police are investigating. There's blood on the fire escape down by the kitchen of that restaurant."

"What about me and Penny?" I pulled a dime out of my pocket and snatched the paper.

The story was on page one, but Will interrupted as I was about to read aloud. "Be careful what you read, boys."

"Why?" Bob asked.

Will leaned his head way back like he was reaching for an answer from the stars, which would have been tough since it was still daytime. He returned to normal. "There's only one truth, but that doesn't mean the person telling the story got it right. The reporter doesn't always see the whole truth and some things the storyteller chooses to believe are lies."

"We'll be careful," Bob said.

To Will Barnes' cry of "Loco, loco," I took off south on High Street.

"See you later, Will," Bob called as he ran to catch up. "What was he talking about, Tommy?"

We walked around the corner to Market Street headed for Bob's apartment. "More of Will's spiritual stuff, I guess."

"Let's read the paper at your house."

"Naw, Mom'll grab it and start to cry. The kids'll become upset and we don't need that right now. Let's hang out at your place."

"Penny might throw us out. She's big on kicking me out these days."

"Why? Aren't you the one she likes?"

"She loves me, Tommy, even though she knows she's pissing me off. Now, she loves you and you love her."

"Who told you?"

"Everybody sees how you two gawk at each other."

"I'm thirteen, Bob. Do you love any girls?"

"You nuts?"

"See."

"You two have been kissing, Tommy. You shouldn't go around kissing your best friend's sister."

My big, stupid grin slithered onto my face again. "Ain't my fault your sister likes me. She told my uncle it was because you and I are best friends and so she was like a big sister to me. Except she ain't my sister. But I'll still give you one of my older brothers for her. Want to trade?"

"Last time you offered your baseball cards. I don't need another big brother. One's enough. He's why Penny kicks me out. She wants me to get used to staying away from home. Doesn't want me sucked into a life of crime with Dad and Mickey."

"They getting out soon?" We crossed the alley being careful around the pot holes.

"Yep."

"When?"

Bob rubbed his chin. "Dad has a hearing coming up. Mickey will be released when Dad gets out. That's what the judge said when he sentenced Dad. Figured Dad would behave in prison this time if he knew his kid wouldn't get out of reform school until he was released from jail."

"That's too bad." I patted Bob on the shoulder.

"Yeah. I like them where they are."

"You guys ever visit them?"

Bob opened the door that leads to the stairway up to his apartment. "You kidding? Mom won't let me near no jail. Bad influence. So's reform school. Besides, Dad's in Sing-Sing. Way off in New York someplace."

"What's he doing so far away?"

"Busted out of jail in Pennsylvania last time he was in. Kicked him up to Sing-Sing. Send you to Sing-Sing, you stay there until your time is up. If you're bad in jail, your time ain't never up." Bob led the way through the front door of his family's apartment.

Bob flopped on the couch and motioned for me to sit next to him. We read the story on the front page.

According to the paper, Menoitios was in the Chester County jail. His lawyer said he was innocent. He had alibis, customers and his parents, who saw him chase Alan out the backdoor of the restaurant, alive and screaming.

Bob slid down the couch. "They're saying stuff to make him sound innocent. Mom would lie her teeth off to keep me out of jail, so you have to expect the same thing from Mrs. Demeter."

"Did your mom lie for your brother and dad?" I asked.

"You kidding? I said she'd lie for me."

"Paper says the police found my brother's blood on the fire escape."

"That's what Will Barnes told us. Menoitios banged Alan's head against the steps."

From the bedroom, we heard Penny yell, "What did the paper say about blood on the steps?"

Bob called back, "Paper says police found blood. Menoitios must have swung ol' Alan by the feet and banged him on the steps. Probably what killed him."

I put my head down on my knees. I missed Alan, but I wouldn't cry.

"Okay?" Bob put a hand on my shoulder.

"Yeah."

"Miss Alan?"

I shook my head yes. Not going to cry.

We're quiet for a while. When I was able to speak, I said, "Alan was too big for Menoitios to toss around."

Bob swung his fist like a boxer. "Maybe he knocked him out first. Maybe poisoned him in the restaurant. Got food, don't they?"

"Tommy's right, Bob," Penny shouted from the bedroom.

Bob turned to me. "So what do you think really happened?"

I leaned over and shook off the wrenching feeling in my gut. "Depends on what step the blood's on."

***

"Total?" Bob asked.

My index finger pointed at the next to the top step, then the top. "Thirteen."

"Figures."

Bob located a wide smear of blood on the sixth step of the black iron fire escape outside his apartment. I checked out a black stain on the concrete at the bottom of the steps where chalk marks faded away in the sun and wind.

"Bam. Alan was nailed here," Bob said.

I bent over like the time Chiamaka punched me in the stomach. I struggled to catch my breath and straighten back up. "No, he hit on that step."

"What'd I say? Bam."

I was okay again. "You said he was nailed there, but he wasn't. His head hit the step after he fell or was thrown. His head was smashed before he fell."

"Looks like a big bam to me, Tommy."

I shake my head a few times and do a lot hand waving. "Say you take a bam on the back of the head at the bottom of the steps. You try to run away. Which way do you head? Alan's running up the steps 'cause he thinks we're in your apartment. We were heading there when he last saw us. Of course, we're out playing ball, but Alan has no idea. Besides, Penny is up in the apartment, and she would let him in. So Alan charges up the steps, but he's had his noggin knocked, and he's dizzy. He stumbles. He starts to faint. He does faint. He falls backward, and the back of his head, where Menoitios smashed him, hits the edge of the sixth step. He must have been about on the top step, too. He almost made it. Once he thumps his head from falling backwards, he tumbles to the bottom of the steps where somebody finds him and calls the police."

Bob stared at me like he had gears spinning around inside his head and he was too busy to make his face muscles do anything but sit there like a doll's empty stare. How I could even talk like this about my dead brother?

A switch kicked in to light up Bob's face. "Maybe Menoitios threw something at him and conked him on the back of the head. Then he fell backwards like you said."

I rubbed my chin. "Nah, a conk on the back of the head would have knocked him forward. He would have stumbled onto the platform at the top of the steps. Menoitios clobber busted him at the bottom. There's no other way."

Bob did a little fist pump. "Yeah, I know. Alan runs out of the kitchen. Thinks he's escaping. Menoitios chases him He has something in his hand like a meat cleaver, a big, giant pot or a frying pan…"

"Couldn't have been a frying pan."

"Yeah, it could." Bob swung his hand over his head to imitate throwing a frying pan.

"Nah, a frying pan would make a big smash like a rock. Something zonked Alan a clean one according to what Freeman told my Dad. The back of a meat cleaver could do it."

"Nah."

"Sure could."

"Too sharp."

I stared off into space. "Didn't say the front of the meat cleaver. Had to be the back. It's like a flat, thick surface running the length of the blade, about five or six inches. Menoitios could bam you and you'd be out."

"Okay. Back of the meat cleaver..."

I slammed a fist into my hand. "No, wait, couldn't have been."

"Why not, Tommy?"

"Now I think about it, the back is still too sharp."

"That's what I said." Bob stuck his head forward tight lipped and frowning.

"You were right. We need something long like a meat cleaver, but with a blunter surface."

"A what?"

"A wider, flatter surface. You know, blunter. Blunter means it ain't sharper."

"Opposite of sharp?"

"Correct." I judo chopped my hand to demonstrate.

"Then why didn't you say so?" Bob sounded angry.

"I did."

"Did not. You said 'blunter.'" He spoke louder now.

"It was blunter. Flatter. That's why it killed Alan the way it did." My voice sounded loud, too.

"What was?" Bob calmed down again.

"What we're trying to figure out." I was still too loud.

Bob made some motions with his hands like he was holding a stick. "So it was this long, flat, wide but not too wide thing?"

"Yep." My voice returned to normal. My face cooled off.

"So what was it?"

"If we can figure that out, we can show how Menoitios was the only person who had one of them whatever it wases."

"Maybe the handle of the meat cleaver?"

"Right shape, but you wouldn't have enough pop to do any serious damage. At best, you'd raise a bump."

Bob's face lit up. "Hey, what about a long metal rod? You know, the kind your dad is always shoving into the back of his pickup?"

"Yeah, could have been. Causes a problem."

"Why?"

"If it was a solid metal rod or a lead pipe, anybody could have had one that day."

Bob pointed to the kitchen door of the Royal. "They keep all kinds of tools and junk around to fix the ovens or the sink or the stove when they have problems."

"It could have been a table leg."

"How can we prove he did it, Tommy?"

"God, I miss Alan."

CHAPTER 14

"Say, you hear the latest about Johnny Bruce?" Mrs. Brownell asked Mom.

My eyes met Bob's. I placed my fingers to my lips so he wouldn't say anything.

Mrs. Brownell added, "Down at the Rig, people say he's living high as a hog in Alabama someplace up in the hills. A regular colored hillbilly he is. And him a murderer, too. Guess if you're colored, you can get away with murder. At least in the north you can."

June slopped over into July in our neighborhood of West Chester and it was hot. We hadn't seen rain since April. Most everybody on Walnut Street sat out on the front porch or stoop after supper yakking with their neighbors.

Mrs. Brownell, next door to us towards Minor Street, liked to talk about cooking and recipes, which Mom enjoyed, but she picked this moment to bring up Johnny Bruce. Bob and I tried to stay cool by playing checkers.

Bob mouthed the words, "What's the Rig?"

Our talking wouldn't bother the adults, so I leaned over close to his ear. "The parachute factory down in Rig Town. On the south side someplace where Mrs. Brownell works."

"Ain't the college on the south side?"

"It is. The college is west of High Street. Rig Town is east. A lot of the Irish kids at St. Agnes live there. They tell me about it."

"Nice neighborhood?"

"You kidding? Won't catch me down in Rig Town during the daytime, let alone at night."

Mom laughed at something Mrs. Brownell said which perked me and Bob up. Mrs. McGillicutty picked this moment to wander up from the sidewalk, swish her tail in my face, and park on the checker board.

Mrs. Brownell was talking, "... and the paper was saying today some farmers have reported seeing a red Cadillac on the back roads late at night. Can't be Johnny if he's in Alabama like people say."

"Maybe he ain't in Alabama," Mom suggested.

"I'll be. Why it wouldn't surprise me if he's the one who murdered your boy, Mrs. McConnell. Wouldn't surprise me one bit." Mrs. Brownell waved a finger at my mom.

Mrs. Brownell ticked me off because she had caused Mom to start sniffling. Mrs. McGillicutty hopped up onto Mom's lap.

"I better see to the children, now, Mrs. Brownell." Mom rose up off her rocking chair, the one Dad made for her, and started for the door. Mrs. McGillicutty screeched and scrabbled to the corner of the porch out of Mom's way.

Mrs. Brownell flapped the newspaper in her hand. "Paper says the judge let Menoity off Scot free. Says he has too strong an alibi. Paper also says your boy just took a bad spill. Don't look at me like that, Mrs. McConnell. It's what the paper says, not me. Never knew the paper to be wrong so I guess that's the way of it."

"Goodnight, Mrs. Brownell." Mom opened the door and headed in without waiting for an answer. The closing door smacked Mrs. McGillicutty's tail as she tried to sneak in. After letting out a screech, Mrs. McGillicutty managed to scoot into the house.

Mrs. Brownell glanced down at me. "Tommy, doesn't your mom feel well? She don't look so good."

"She's sad on account of Alan, Mrs. Brownell. You have to cut her some slack about him. Upsets her if you know what I mean." I smile like I know something and ain't telling.

Mrs. Brownell lifted her huge self up from her metal rocking chair and shooed some flies with her newspaper. "It'll be a bad day in this town when an old lady can't speak her mind without her neighbor crumbling to pieces."

"Give her more time, Mrs. Brownell. She'll be fine." I spoke like I knew what I was talking about, but Mom ain't never been fine the thirteen years I've known her. She's always either blue or angry. You don't stick around when she's on a tear. She'll take hold of a stick or belt and commence to beating on you. Best thing is to be someplace else them times.

Bob removed three of my black pieces off the checkerboard.

***

Whoever thought you could miss your ornery old brother?

On July fourth we sometimes drove to the shore and other times to French Creek State Park for a dip in the water and playtime on the beach. Either way, it was a same-day trip. Can you imagine trooping into one of those hotels or motels and saying we needed a room for two adults and eleven kids? Not about to happen. Who would pay for all those rooms? Not Dad. He was happy just to buy the groceries.

This year we stayed home because of Alan. Hitting the road without him wouldn't be right, but Alan would never want to spoil one of our picnics. Or one of our summers either. But my summer was spoiled without him.

Bob and I staked out Old Glory, the statue on the corner of the courthouse property at Market and High Streets. Old Glory was a bronze World War I soldier holding a flag in his hand. We took turns climbing the base of the statue so we could sit at Old Glory's feet. You had a great view of the Fourth of July parade from up there. The highlight was watching the vets march along from the American Legion. The ones up front were from the War, the big one. Then some younger guys followed who fought in Korea or, like Elvis, got drafted to drink beer in Germany. Bringing up the rear were the old guys left over from the First World War.

After the parade, I was invited home with Bob for a picnic dinner in his apartment. His Mom was off for the first time this summer. She made us fried chicken, potato salad, Jell-O and other cool stuff. And I didn't have to fight off a bunch of brothers and sisters and... this is the best part... you were allowed to have seconds on everything. When you have eleven kids at home, there's no such thing as seconds.

"How are you holding up, Tommy?" Mrs. Durkin parked fried chicken on everybody's plate.

"Doing fine. Miss him is all."

"I bet you do, you poor boy." Sympathy would have killed me last summer at age twelve. Not this year. I picked up my chicken and chomped. I peered over at Penny to see what she was up to. Figured if she made a face, I'd crack up and be safe.

She slurped iced tea. When she put the glass down, she scrutinized me. "I went to Alan's wake and funeral."

"We all went to the wake, dear," said Mrs. Durkin. "Did you go to the funeral, too? That was thoughtful, wasn't it Bob?"

"She gave Tommy a big kiss at the wake." Bob pointed at his sister with his fork.

"She was just being nice, I'm sure. Penny knew Tommy felt sad." Mrs. Durkin nodded.

Bob folded his arms and smiled before opening his big, fat, stupid mouth. "She licked his lips."

"No, I didn't," Penny's face turned red.

"Bob, if you can't say anything nice..." Mrs. Durkin pointed a finger at her son.

Bob exhaled and then lowered his head and his voice. "I know, I can go to my room, except it's not my room, it's everybody's."

"We'll be moving to a new house after your dad and brother are released." Mrs. Durkin sliced off a chunk of fried chicken breast meat and placed it on her plate.

"You're moving?" First I heard. Judging from the looks Bob and Penny gave their mom, it was the first they heard, too.

"Are we moving?" Penny asked.

Mrs. Durkin waved her fork around in the air. "We can't stay here forever. Once your dad comes home and finds a job, we'll have two people working, and we'll want a bigger place. With two incomes, we may be able to afford a house. Penny will have her own room, and Bob, you can share with Mickey."

Bob shook his head. "I ain't sharing nothing with that creep."

Mrs. Durkin slammed down her fork. "That's no way to speak about your brother. He and Dad made mistakes, and they are paying for them. Once they're out, we will welcome them home and start over again as a complete family."

"Mom, are you thinking about the same Dad and Mickey I know?" Bob asked. "Anyway, she did lick his lips."

"I did not." Penny stumped her foot under the table.

"Bob, I warned you..." Mrs. Durkin flashed Bob her sternest watch-out-buster look.

Bob leaned way back in his seat. "Tommy, you tell her."

Great, now I had to stick up for my best friend, which meant that Penny would want to clobber me later. Bob was not thinking about the consequences of his actions like the nuns always taught us. Of course, Bob was a public so he didn't hear the wisdom of nunnery.

"She was sad, Bob. Her tongue slipped out of her mouth by accident." I didn't even believe this one. "She didn't mean nothing."

Mrs. Durkin nodded. "There you are, sweetheart. Now, we'll have no more such talk. And Penny, we'll have no lip licking around here. Do you understand?"

"I didn't do it, but if you say I'm bad, then I'm bad."

Mrs. Durkin slapped the table hard with her fork hand. "Penny Durkin, stop. You're not bad and I didn't say you did anything wrong. I said no lip licking, but you already know not to so we'll have no more talk about you being bad. Now, who wants cherry pie?"

Bango, she hit my smile button. "Me, Mrs. Durkin."

Penny grabbed the dirty plates and took them away. Bob tried to hold onto the piece of chicken leg Penny pulled out of his mouth.

Mrs. Durkin asked, "Have you children heard anymore about who may have been responsible for Alan's uhmm … you know?"

Penny said, "They released Menoitios, Mom. He's right downstairs where he can sneak up here anytime and bash our heads in."

"He's not downstairs, dear. Mr. Demeter sent him off to live with relatives in Philadelphia. Wouldn't surprise me if they sent him back to Greece," said Mrs. Durkin.

"Is he from Greece?" I asked.

"You didn't know?" Bob asked.

I shrugged. "I knew he was a Greek but thought he was born in this country."

"I do believe he came to America as a little boy, Tommy," Mrs. Durkin said.

I smiled. Bob nodded his head as if agreeing with his mom. Penny stuck her spoon on the end of her nose.

Two things guys don't do. One is cry. The other is split a gut at the wrong time. I was good at one of them. The laughter climbed up my gullet and danced on my tonsils. It exploded out of my mouth with bits and pieces of chewed cherry pie.

Bob laughed which made me roar louder. Penny appeared innocent except for the spoon on the end of her nose. This was the nose which she now wiggled.

Mrs. Durkin poured herself a cup of hot coffee while Penny and Bob did the dishes. Mrs. Durkin told me to take a break because I was in mourning. I sat across the table from her and watched as she drank hot coffee on July fourth. I broke into a sweat as she sipped the hot liquid on an evening when it was still about ninety-nine degrees outside and hotter in here from the cooking.

Over by the sink, Bob said, "Menoitios didn't do it."

Penny said, "Of course he did. Who else could have?"

"Johnny Bruce," Bob said.

"Johnny Bruce?" I asked. "Didn't you hear he was way off in the hills down in Alabama someplace, a regular colored hillbilly he was. That's what Mrs. Brownell next door told my Mom. You were with me, right, Bob?"

"Yeah, she said it, but I heard the farmers around here have spotted a red Cadillac late at night on the back roads. Mrs. Brownell might have said that one, too."

Penny continued washing the dishes while Bob dried.

"Why would Johnny Bruce kill Alan?" I asked.

Bob faced me with a dish in his hand and a towel in the other. "Once you get to murderizing people, you don't stop. You let the bodies pile up. By the time the police catch up with you, it would be Judgment Day in West Chester. Wouldn't surprise me if he was the one who killed Cynthia Matting."

Penny let out a loud fart and took off towards the bathroom. Bob and I looked at each other. Before we both cracked up, Bob turned around to the sink. He took over washing.

Once my laughing was under control, I said, "He could have been sneaking around out of sight, up on the roof. He could have stood on the fire escape railing and reached up. I'm tall enough to do it, so Johnny Bruce could, too."

Mrs. Durkin chuckled, blew on her coffee to be sure she had our attention, and slurped. She parked her cup back on its saucer. "Why would Johnny Bruce hide on top of our building in the middle of a hot summer? During the daytime? He'd burn to death. Die of dehydration. Doesn't make any sense at all. You boys have to come up with better."

"He could hide out in old Mrs. Glass' house," I suggested.

"There's a thought," Bob said. "We have to check it out."

"I ain't checking nothing out." I said.

"Why not?" Bob whacked at me with a dish towel but missed. He went back to work on the dishes.

I was not afraid of much. Girls and ghosts. And my older brothers whenever they rampaged. Nuns who asked me to turn in my homework which I never did. My Mom on a tear. Dad ran amok sometimes to chase my older brothers off me, so his rampages weren't so bad. Unless I was the one picking on my little brothers and sisters. Dad became angry if he caught you slugging a girl.

"Haunted," I said.

Bob placed a wet plate on the drying rack. "We ain't out to bother no ghosts. They'd be happy if we got rid of Johnny Bruce for them."

"Great, so we creep into an old haunted house and scare up Johnny Bruce and some ghosts. What do you think can happen?" I asked.

"We'll catch Johnny Bruce. Maybe we can collect some reward dough. Cops should be offering a bundle, you know." Bob scrubbed chicken yuck from a large frying pan.

I pointed a finger at Bob's back. "I'll tell you what will happen. You'll be chased by a bunch of ghosts and a mad killer who chops people up. Not a good thing."

Bob turned around from the dishes and glared at me. "If you are afraid…"

I threw my hands up with the palms out. "Didn't say I was afraid. Said it was haunted."

"Then you're in?" Bob asked.

"No." I shook my head.

"Why not?" Bob dunked the frying pan in the rinse water.

"Haunted. Told you already," I said.

Somewhere in the middle of this conversation, Penny returned. She sat at the table with her mom and me with her hands wrapped around a magazine. She raised her head. "What's haunted?"

"Mrs. Glass' house," Bob turned back to the dishes.

"Everybody knows that." Penny planted her pretty nose back in the magazine.

"We're sneaking in," said Bob.

"What on earth for?" Penny gazed at Bob.

Bob spun to face her. "Find Johnny Bruce."

"Then let's bust in." Penny smacked a fist into the palm of her other hand.

The conversation died while Bob wiped the last of the dishes. Penny announced she would stroll out with me.

Bob checked if his mom had paid attention. "He lives around the corner."

Mrs. Durkin had her head in a newspaper and didn't seem to hear us.

Penny stood up. "I just want some fresh air, Bob. You can stay here."

"Nah, I'll come, too. I don't trust you guys alone."

"Stay here, Bob," Mrs. Durkin did not raise her head from the paper.

"Why?" Bob's face reddened and his lower lip formed a pout.

Mrs. Durkin turned a page in her paper. "Maybe Tommy and Penny want to be alone, dear. You're always with them."

"Do I have to?" Bob whined.

"Yes, Bob." Mrs. Durkin still didn't look up.

"Aw, Mom." Bob shook his head.

I put my hand on his shoulder. "It's no big deal, Bob."

Bob yanked his arm away. "It better not be. Don't you dare mess around with Penny."

"Sounds like fun," Penny teased. "Come on, Tommy, we have some messing around to catch up on."

"Penny." Mrs. Durkin's head remained in her newspaper. Guess she can read and listen at the same time.

"Yes, Mom?" Penny tapped a foot.

"Don't tease your brother," Mrs. Durkin said.

"Okay." Penny took my arm and pointed us to the door. She stuck her tongue out at Bob as we passed him. I hid my face so Bob couldn't see the giant grin that ran from my left ear to my right ear.

Penny and I walked down the steps to the street and then east on Market. The street was well-lit as we passed Rubenstein's toy and sporting goods store on the corner. At Walnut we turned south towards my house.

Penny said, "Tommy, come up the alley with me for a minute."

We strolled up the alley across the street from my house. Penny snatched my hand and led me to Mrs. Glass' backyard under the big cherry tree where the night was black dark.

Penny stopped. She faced me while holding my hand. She placed her free hand on the back of my neck and kissed me a long, syrupy one. I liked it.

Why was Penny Durkin kissing me? She was seventeen, way too old for me.

When she disconnected, Penny said, "Good, now kiss me."

I leaned in and kissed her full on the lips with her body pressed against mine. At least I wasn't frozen this time. Where the guts to kiss her came from, I didn't know, but kissing her was fun, even if it made me breathe funny.

While we kissed, I thought about Cynthia Matting. Had she joined the other ghosts in Mrs. Glass' haunted house? Cynthia's eyes peeked out the window. She watched me kiss Penny Durkin, the first girl I ever made out with. Did that make Cynthia the first jealous ghost I ever met? Why would Cynthia care about me? She never did when she was alive.

CHAPTER 15

For some reason Mom kept the cereal boxes on top of the refrigerator. It was a trick because the top was rounded so they fell off easy.

While staring at the Cheerios, I thought about how Mrs. Glass' house had sat empty for longer than anyone could remember. It was at the end of the row across the street, the house next to the alley. Why nobody ever thought of sneaking in was a mystery, too.

Caution, rather than fear, killed my desire to enter that haunted house. Don't misunderstand, ghosts scared the crap out of me, especially if one of the ghosts was my old friend Cynthia or worse, my brother Alan, so there was some fear in that. But ghosts alone wouldn't keep me out. What if Freeman the Cop came along while we hung out in that house?

Bob, on the other hand, was on a mission. Johnny Bruce almost ran him over with his father's car. We both saw him do it. He didn't even stop or nothing. Since Alan died, Bob had been afraid Johnny Bruce might kill Penny. He thought Johnny Bruce may have killed Cynthia, too. Or Menoitios killed her. Depended on when you talked to Bob. We all had our little fears.

While stretching for the Cheerios, a new thought hit me. How hard could it be to plant my feet on a sturdy chair and place my hands on top of the refrigerator? I could swing around and park my carcass up there. A guy could see the world from there.

It didn't appear hard to do. You had your liftoff, the swing and, oh no, the oops as my right side slithered down where the refrigerator door handle stuck out. The handle was one of those long metal jobs that bent out and up. The top of the handle pushed my tee shirt out of the way and took a one-inch wide scrape of skin off my right side.

The damage ran from my waist up to almost my arm pit. On the way to the floor, I ran into Mrs. McGillicutty who must have wanted my chair.

"Don't be so noisy down there," Mom yelled. She was upstairs so she did more to wake the little ones than I did sliding down the refrigerator.

On the floor, ain't nobody thought about crying. Not me, not Mrs. McGillicutty. Nobody. Ain't happening.

Mrs. McGillicutty hightailed it for the dining room. After a few minutes, I sat up. I worked hard to stand through the pain. I couldn't bend over without hurting which was why I planned to stay stiff from the waist up.

In my fall, the boxes of Cheerios and Wheaties ended up on the floor. I squatted down and picked them up. None of the cereal fell out so I didn't need a broom. But the discomfort made me perform an Irish jig where my feet moved like crazy but the rest of me remained motionless.

Bob dropped by while I chomped and danced. "What's wrong?"

"Fell off the refrigerator."

"Hurt bad?"

I pointed. "Lift my shirt."

"Ain't lifting your shirt."

"Neither am I. Not for a while. So if you want to see the blood and guck, you have to lift my shirt."

Bob reached for my shirt.

"Not that side. Over here on the right." I pointed again.

Bob lifted my shirt and dropped it. "Wow, what happened to you?"

"Refrigerator door handle jumped out and bit me."

Bob headed for the cabinet next to the sink. "I'll find the iodine."

"No way."

"Can't let it become infected, Tommy."

"I'd rather have puss ooze out than the pain."

Bob pointed to the front door. "Come outside with me. Bring Danny and Banning."

"They're not up yet. Are you getting a game together? I can't pitch, at least not this morning."

Bob came back so his face was up close to mine. "Better than a game. I have the whole neighborhood outside. We're about to check out the inside of Mrs. Glass' house."

I tilted my head to one side. "That's never been done."

"First time for everything."

"The other kids will sneak in with you?"

"Yep." Bob shrugged.

"I'll watch."

"You don't want to bust in?" Bob leaned into my face again.

"Somebody has to keep watch for the cops."

Bob pounded a fist into his hand. "Yeah, like the movies. Wounded guy waits outside when you break into the bank."

I gawked at Bob for a second like he was crazy.

"What?" he asked.

"Nothing. Except you talked about cops and robbers."

"I know. I can't let Dad and Mickey ruin my life forever. Besides, this isn't cops and robbers. We're explorers after long lost treasure."

"Treasure in Mrs. Glass' house?"

"Maybe she was a pirate. You never know."

***

95

Bob ran across the street to the alley.

I hobbled after him. I didn't want to stretch my right side. I motivated like when you pretend to ride a horse. "Hey, Bob."

He stopped at the entrance to the alley. "You need help?"

"No, check out the sign."

The front door to the old house had little glass panes. You could see through into a dark hallway, but not beyond. A sign was posted on the inside. I tested the doorknob. "It's locked."

"Figures," Bob said. "What's on the sign?"

"Says the borough locked the house up back in nineteen-oh-six. Think about it. You'll be the first person inside in more than fifty years. Must be a reason nobody ever broke in."

"Ghosts?"

"Or how about the plague? Some disease has waited fifty years to cut loose and chomp on your blood."

"We're breaking in. Period." Bob ran around to the alley with me galloping behind in slow motion. He had rounded up Jamie Bordeaux, Donna, who lived next door to Mrs. Glass' house, Dickey and Chiamaka. Coleman, a colored kid from down on Minor Street, was there, too. Coleman was fifteen years old and all muscle. He was a head taller than Alan. I mean a head taller than Alan used to be, and they were about the same age since Alan turned fifteen in June.

Alan would have climbed right into this house. He wasn't afraid of anything. When we were four and six, Alan would charge into places I was afraid of. We still lived in the country then, and I once dropped my shoe off a bridge on a country road. Wasn't more than a five-foot drop, and you could walk around to a path at the end of the bridge to get down into the meadow below. My shoe landed next to the crick. Alan ran down and retrieved it. I was too scared because, well, the cows might eat me. What do you expect from a tyke?

You wanted to be on Coleman's side. He was a likeable, pleasant guy. None of us had ever seen him fight because nobody would be stupid enough to stick around if Coleman was mad at them.

Coleman said, "Bob, everybody's here. You want me to rip these boards off the window, now?"

The windows on the side of Mrs. Glass' house had no panes, thanks to children taking firing practice with stones. The boards Coleman mentioned were a foot wide and an inch thick. They were nailed up on the inside of the house and stretched across the window so you couldn't climb in. The wood shrunk over the years, and you could peek in through the cracks between the planks, like the way Coleman did right now.

"Wow, check out the dishes and stuff on the table like they're about to sit down for dinner," Coleman said.

This set everybody off for a turn at the window. It was too high so Coleman lifted them up.

"Hey, you're busting into the house. You can see it when you're inside." They ignored me.

When everybody finished, Coleman glanced my way. "Come on, Tommy, it's your turn."

Bob said, "He hurt his side so don't touch him."

Coleman approached. "Must have hurt it bad. Can I see?"

Everybody gaped at me so I slowly lifted my right arm in the air. The brand new scab tore. My side pain felt like fire. I reached over with my left hand and raised my tee shirt. This started a round of "Ewws" from everybody. I dropped my shirt and made a slow arc in the air to bring my arm down with a minimum of pain.

"I'll rip these boards off," Coleman said.

Jamie Bordeaux said, "Wait. Freeman the Cop might come after us for breaking and entering."

I whispered in Bob's ear. "He's starting to think like Alan."

Bob whispered back, "Because he doesn't have Alan to think for him anymore."

Jamie Bordeaux fished around for another way in. We followed him to the backyard. No fence remained on the alley side. The yard was a mess of weeds and tall grass. The huge cherry tree in the middle of the yard attracted Jamie Bordeaux who shimmied up the trunk to the bottom branch. He climbed higher where he made his way out on a big limb that stretched towards the house. The branch reached into a small porch built over the back shed.

The houses in our neighborhood have these little rooms behind the kitchen. Dad said they used to be the back porch but the people enclosed them to make an extra space. Everybody called it their back shed.

"Come on," Jamie Bordeaux said, "We can climb in up here. The backdoor is not locked."

Coleman started to help the kids clamber up the tree.

I scrutinized Bob. "That door has been unlocked for fifty years and nobody has broken in. Tells you something."

"What, Tommy?" Bob asked.

"Plague," I said.

Bob glared at me like I was crazy. He let Coleman help him climb the tree. When Bob achieved the first branch, he reached down so Coleman could grab his hand. Bob didn't have the strength to pull Coleman up. Coleman dug his big feet into the side of the tree the way Jamie Bordeaux did and pulled himself up.

The kids were not as sure on their feet as Jamie Bordeaux, so they sat on the big branch like cowboys riding a horse and shimmied their way over to the porch.

While I gawped up at the kids in the tree, somebody kissed the back of my neck.

CHAPTER 16

"Don't they know this house is haunted?" Penny stepped around so she could smile in my face. "What are you kids up to?"

"They're breaking into Mrs. Glass' house," I said.

"Like Coolville."

"You can see into the house from down here if you want to."

"You can?"

"Sure, follow me." I made like the haunchback of Notre Dame while Penny sauntered beside me.

I placed my left hand on the lowest of the cracks between the boards in the old window. "Grab hold where you see a lot of space between the boards and pull yourself up."

Penny reached up to take hold of the board and lifted off the ground. She stared into the house through the crack between the boards. When she couldn't hold on anymore, she dropped down. "They left one day and never came back for their stuff."

Penny stepped back. I reached up with my left hand and then my right so as not to disturb the scab under my shirt. The plan was for my left hand to do the work while my right hand helped out as needed. I pulled hard with my left hand, but my right side proved useless.

"Let me help." Penny hugged me around the chest from behind and squeezed my sides. My scream was the loudest since the last time my older brother Eddie went on a rampage right before he joined the Army. Bob ain't the only one with an older brother he hopes never comes home.

Penny released me. I tumbled to the ground and rolled back and forth on my back while clutching my injured side.

"What's wrong?" Penny shouted. "Tell me what I did."

I turned on my left side and lifted my shirt so she could see.

"I didn't know." She dropped on her knees and kissed my face and kissed me and kissed me and somehow forgot to stop.

When she came up for air, we gawked at each other. I breathed funny and felt strange inside. Maybe she squeezed me too hard.

She kissed me again, long and sweet this time, and then sat back on her bottom. "Guess I sort of got, you know, carried away."

I made with the silly grin while struggling to sit up through my side pain.

"I'm sorry, Tommy. I didn't mean to cause you pain."

"I know."

"I guess you understand that I like you a lot."

"I know."

"You like me, too, don't you?"

"I know."

"But you're just a kid."

"I know."

"I can wait."

"I know."

She took my right hand which made my side hurt worse. "You won't be a kid much longer."

"I know."

"Then, I won't be too old anymore."

"I know."

She leaned into my face and kissed me again. She held the kiss on my lips. I tried to pucker up and return the kiss, not because Penny felt great, which she did, but because I liked

Penny Durkin. Yet, what I felt at that moment was stronger than like.

We sat together on the ground in the alley. I leaned against the haunted house while Penny rested against me. We held hands. I closed my eyes to squeeze out the pain. I opened them. Penny wore those wonderful Bermudas, which held my attention.

Penny stopped talking which she never did before. My heavy eyes closed. Penny held my hand on top of her left hand which was now on top of her lap. My left hand was the thickness of a girl's left hand from all the secrets of the universe.

I thought about our hands intertwined and the possibilities for a thirteen-year old boy. With my eyes closed, my mind sailed off into the blackness. Soon thunder rumbled in, but the sound evolved into the stomp of footsteps. My eyes popped open, and the whole crowd glared at Penny and me.

"You're holding hands!" Chiamaka pointed at us like a teacher scolding a student.

I started to pull my hand away, but Penny held on. "So?"

Bob glared at me weird like a smoking gun was pulsating in my hand and a bullet hole was parked in his forehead. His words came slow and filled with rage. "You're holding hands with my sister."

Penny released my paw and stood up. To Bob, she said, "I wanted to lift Tommy up so he could peek into the window. I didn't know he was hurt. He fell to the ground in pain. I soothed his pain. Besides, you know darn well Tommy and I like each other."

"Oh" came out of several mouths.

It was time to change the subject. "So what did you guys find?" I asked.

Donna said, "Guess what we found. Jamie Bordeaux wants it, but I found it first so it's mine."

She held out an old book with a green cover with black print that read "Twenty Years After" at the top and "Dumas" at the bottom. It was thick.

"Twenty years after doom," pronounced Jamie Bordeaux in a solemn voice.

"They spelled 'doom' wrong," I said.

"Probably the way they spelled doom in the old days," said Coleman.

Everybody nodded, "Yeah."

"So who reads it first?" Bob asked.

"I do," said Jamie Bordeaux.

Where did Jamie Bordeaux learn to take charge? His job was to come up with crazy stunts and then do them. And get away with them. It was Alan again, but why say anything?

Jamie Bordeaux took the book from Donna. Donna stared at her empty hands. She became sad like she might cry. She glanced at me and Penny. A sly grin slithered across her mouth, which meant nothing but trouble.

"Tommy McConnell loves Penny Durkin," she hollered. Before we could say anything, the other kids picked up the chant. "Tommy McConnell loves Penny Durkin."

Penny said, "Stupid kids." She hugged me and planted a big kiss full on my lips, which resulted in a round of squeals from the kids. She ambled off towards home.

That grin I always get when I think about Penny Durkin wiggled onto my face.

***

One of the fun things about the kids in our neighborhood was they became bored fast. The gang ran off to do other stuff. I was left on the ground in the alley with my stupid grin. Bob stayed with me.

"Find any signs of Johnny Bruce?" I asked.

"Never mind that," Bob's face turned red and his lower lip pouted. I thought he was about to bop me. "What's with you and my sister?"

"Nothing."

"Are you guys in love?"

"Bob, I'm thirteen years old. Think about it. Are you in love with girls?"

"Yech, we had this conversation before so don't be stupid." Bob's hands were now firmly planted on his hips.

"See."

Bob went from hand-on-hip to pistol-shaped finger in my face at the speed of Wild West gunslinger. "See what? Just because I'm not in love doesn't mean you ain't. Tell me what you two are up to."

I told Bob what happened including the kisses on my face.

"She didn't lick you again, did she?"

"No."

"That licking part is freaky. Now, tell me the truth. Are you two in love?" Bob's eyes shot rays of hate enough to make my eyes boil.

"Yeah, maybe. When she finished kissing me, I grinned this silly smirk."

"I know. You're still beaming."

"She held my hand."

"Eww, sicko."

"I know, but I was like, you know, liking it."

"Eww. Then what happened?"

"We talked for a while."

"What about?"

It was my turn to shoot ray guns out of my eyes. "Stuff. She said she was too old for me and I was a little kid."

"She's right."

"Then she said someday I would be older, and we could be together." Why was I saying all this junk?

"Yech. Penny said all that?"

"Yeah."

"She must be nuts." Bob shook his head.

"Yeah, but I like her. Maybe I love her."

Bob had a funny expression on his face, like he wasn't sure about something. "You do?"

"Bob, what's wrong with me?"

Bob held his left elbow in his right hand and stroked his chin with his left hand. I almost heard the rumble of the wheels whirling behind his eyes. "My sister must've brainwashed you."

"Like the Russians?"

"Yeah."

"Didn't think of that. Makes sense."

Bob pointed his index finger at my chest. "Are you still brainwashed?"

"I don't think so."

"Then why are you smiling?"

"I am?"

"Yeah."

"Must be from watching you get mad because your sister loves me."

Bob knocked me to the ground, flopped on top of me, and held me down.

"Oww, Bob, my side, not today." I did my best to keep from screaming in agony.

Bob rolled off and we gazed at the sky. It was blue with tiny clouds dancing by.

After a while my side cooled off so I sat up. "Did you run into Johnny Bruce in Mrs. Glass' house?"

Bob continued staring at the sky with his hands behind his head. "No. We discovered about an inch of dust all over the place. No footprints. Nobody's been in that house for fifty years, like you said."

"What about the ghost of Cynthia Matting?"

"No ghosts."

"Not even Alan?"

"Nope."

"Hope you don't come down with the plague."

"Think I could?"

"Let me put it this way, Bob. Today's Saturday, ain't it?"

"Yeah."

"Bath night, right?"

"Yeah, so?"

"When your mom tells you to take your bath tonight, take it, don't fake it."

Bob went home to do his Saturday chores. I started back to my house to work on my cleaning responsibilities the best I could with a sore side. As I passed the front of Mrs. Glass' house, I gaped in through the front door. Cynthia Matting stood about ten feet inside. She smiled and waved for me to come into the house. She wore the red blouse with the green stripes they found scraps of when they dug up her bones.

CHAPTER 17

"You guys ever smash cars?" Jamie Bordeaux asked. We sat on our bikes at the north end of town where the rich people lived in their old Victorians.

"No." Bob adjusted the handlebars on his bike.

I gawked at Jamie Bordeaux. "What are you talking about?"

Jamie Bordeaux gave Bob's bike a hard shake. "Alan and I invented this game last summer."

"Alan didn't tell me about smashed cars." I grabbed Bob to keep him from falling over.

"Bet he wanted to keep your butt out of jail," Jamie Bordeaux said. "What you do is find a one-way street and go to the corner where no one can turn into it."

"Why can't they?" Bob turned his handle bars towards Jamie Bordeaux's bike like he wanted to ram him.

"As I said, it's one way." Jamie Bordeaux pointed up the street. "Check out the cross street there at the corner? Car coming down can't turn up this way 'cause it's one way. They can only turn the other way. Get it?"

"Yeah, they can't chase us because we're on a one way street. Like coolville, daddyo." Bob punched me on the arm to see if I got it.

"The street we're on is perfect if somebody was chasing us in a car, right?" I asked.

"A method to my madness, Tommy. We need a car to come along that can't follow us up this one way street."

"Why do we want a car?" Bob asked.

"So we can bash it." Jamie Bordeaux smiled.

"With what?" I asked.

Jamie Bordeaux climbed off his bike to poke around in some rich person's flower beds. Bob and I stared in disbelief as he yanked out three humongous green plants, each with a huge wad of dirt and roots on one end. He gave one to Bob and one to me, keeping the third.

We didn't have to wait long for a car to come along the cross street. Following Jamie Bordeaux's lead, we tossed the giant plants up so they landed on the windshield of the passing Ford. The car screeched to a halt. It backed up. I started to speak but noticed that no one else was around.

The driver hesitated for a few seconds to figure out the best way to trap us. The black Ford screeched rubber and hauled butt after me. The driver had no problem with travelling the wrong way up the street to kill us. In a panic, I skidded my bike into an alley and swung into the first backyard. I added a bunch of new scratches when I scrambled through some bushes before I could stop my bike.

The bushes ripped my shirt and tore off the big scab on my side. New cuts formed across the old wound. Up to this point, the big scrape on my side had been healing.

I stayed behind the bushes as the car roared down the alley. My side needed to cool down from the pain as I breathed hard and tried not to scream.

Sure enough the Ford came around the block again, slower this time. When it came by a third time, the driver stopped next to the yard. By this time, I had tossed my bike over a white picket fence, crossed the second yard and over the next picket fence into the third yard. I was staked out behind a big bush wishing bike tossing didn't have to hurt my injured side so much.

The guy stepped out of his car with all the patience of someone with nothing better to do than kill three teenagers starting with me. He strolled around his car and stared into the first yard, lighting it up with a flashlight. A loud horn cracked the night air. My guy swung around. He was lit up by somebody's headlights, which revealed him as a crew cut, broad-shouldered monster.

"All right," the guy's voice was as deep as his barrel chest. He clicked off his flashlight and meandered slow-motion style around to his driver-side door. "Keep your shirt on," he said.

He climbed into his car and drove off. The other vehicle turned out to be a pickup truck that continued down the alley.

After several minutes of waiting, I walked my bike out of the backyard and around to the front of the house. I climbed aboard being careful about my side. Keeping the bike steady while crossing the street kept my mind off the pain. It was safer to pedal down the alley on the other side rather than stay on the street where the Ford driver might change his mind and come back.

Alan used to ride his bike along these streets and back alleys, so it was like following in his footsteps, except I planned to live longer, despite my wounded side.

On the cross street at the end of the alley, I stopped under a streetlight and waited to see what would happen. My side didn't hurt so much now, and the guy must have given up. After a while laughter chirped from across the street and down the next alley.

"Hey, you guys." Not too loud because I didn't want to attract attention. Bicycle wheels squeaked when Jamie Bordeaux and Bob appeared out of the darkness.

"Close call," Jamie Bordeaux flashed one of his trademark smirks.

Bob asked, "You okay, Tommy?"

"He couldn't find me." I checked my torn shirt. Blood made it stick to my side.

"I never had anybody chase me before," Jamie Bordeaux said.

"Bob, do you think Jamie Bordeaux lies sometimes?" I asked.

"Could be," Bob said.

"Screw you guys. That was too close for comfort," Jamie Bordeaux said. "Let's head down to the golf course."

"Maybe we should head home so I can clean up my scabs." I lifted my arm so the guys could see my bloody and torn shirt in the streetlight.

"Nah, you'll be okay." Jamie Bordeaux headed north on the side street towards West Chester Country Club which was a few blocks away at the edge of town. Once we caught up, Jamie Bordeaux drifted behind us. Sure enough, when Bob and I crossed over to the club parking lot we heard a loud thud on a car.

"Ride!" Jamie Bordeaux roared.

We high tailed across the parking lot and out onto the fairway for the third hole because it was downhill. My scabby side complained about this bouncy jaunt.

"That car will never come out on the fairway," Jamie Bordeaux shouted.

West Chester Country Club was a nine-hole golf course on the north edge of town. My older brothers caddied there. They said the golfers played two rounds so they could get their eighteen holes in. The course was easy except for the sixth hole which was a steep uphill hole from the tee. Most golfers weren't strong enough to jolt the ball with an uphill arc high enough and long enough to reach the green on the first shot. Usually the ball zoomed into the side of the steep fairway. Bob and I knew the sixth hole as one of our sledding hills in the winter. So did Jamie Bordeaux and the rest of the gang.

Meanwhile on the third hole, the car gained on us.

"Split up," Jamie Bordeaux screamed. "Whichever one of us they catch says he doesn't know the other kids. You ran into them on the street."

We followed Jamie Bordeaux's order to split up like he knew what he was talking about. A steep embankment dropped down splitting the fairway as you moved towards the green. It was about a five-foot mini cliff. The trick was to hit the ball off the tee and onto the green in one shot.

Jamie Bordeaux hit the embankment first and flew over. He landed on both wheels and kept on riding. Bob flew over in imitation of Jamie Bordeaux, but when he landed, his bike wobbled like crazy. Bob regained control and followed Jamie Bordeaux. But he rode slower. I worried that Bob may have clobber-busted his boy parts.

An old tree stood where the fairway met the rough on the right side. The car's driver wouldn't want to smash into the tree and he wouldn't want to fly over the embankment, which continued behind the tree. The embankment was more like a sharp downhill ramp at this point, still too steep for a car. I slowed down to take the embankment and then pedaled hard at the bottom.

The remaining scab on my side ripped open, and more blood oozed through my shirt. As I pedaled for my life, I pictured Alan under that bloody blanket outside of the Royal kitchen.

The sound of the car engine faded behind me. The driver was forced to halt at the embankment. I angled uphill along the fifth hole fairway. When I arrived at the big hill for the sixth fairway, my side pain was as bad as could be. About halfway up towards the green at the top of the hill, I stopped to catch my breath and give my side a break. After a few minutes, I walked my bike the rest of the way. I glanced back. The car hadn't moved. The man must be on foot. I ran through the pain in my side hopping to beat him to the top of the hill.

***

A large sand trap in front of the green at the top of the sixth hole hill provided a place to hide. The guy could walk right past in the dark and not see me, if I kept my mouth shut, which was a challenge because I was out of breath. There was no moon, but I could see stars.

If the guy found me, I could race the bike back down the hill, and he wouldn't be able to catch me on foot. I'd cut across High Street, head up the first little street on the other side and disappear on that end of town. By the time the guy drove his car off the golf course, I'd be history. A kid has to have a plan.

At the sand trap, I tripped over something and fell with my bike on top of me. A scream started from deep in my throat when the handlebars tore at my injured side.

"Quiet," whispered Jamie Bordeaux.

I slapped my mouth, biting down hard to muffle my scream to a hushed, "Hunh" before asking, "Where's Bob?"

"Don't know."

I stayed down in the sand. Jamie Bordeaux crawled over to the edge and peeked out. I started to lift my torn shirt, but it was still stuck to my skin.

"The car lights are out."

"He wants us to think he left." The pain made me gasp for breath.

"Whoa, careful," Jamie Bordeaux stood up and pointed toward the clubhouse parking lot where we came in. I stood up in slow motion with my shoulders hunched over because of the pain in my side. A big red jelly bean was flashing on top of a car in the country club parking lot. We watched the police cruiser drive down the third hole fairway and park behind the guy's car. In the police car's headlights, we spotted the man standing by his car. I couldn't tell from this distance, but it appeared to be a Buick or Olds.

I exhaled slowly. "He turned his lights out so the cop wouldn't see him."

"Yeah," Jamie Bordeaux replied. "Somebody must have called the cops on the jerk. He has no business driving on the course, and tearing up divots."

"We better wait here until the cop leaves."

Jamie Bordeaux said, "Let's move north. They're building some new houses. We can explore them."

"We have to find Bob and I have to tend to my side."

"Maybe he's hiding in the new development."

"Listen. Do you hear it?" I asked.

"What?"

"Shh."

"What?"

"Sounded like a popping noise," I said.

We both glanced around. There was some kind of glow from the direction of the housing development.

"Let's move," Jamie Bordeaux said.

As soon as we crossed over the hill leading out of the golf course property, we spotted the fire in the construction site.

"Be careful, you might fall into a hole dug for a basement," I said.

"You better watch out for the night watchman."

"This way." Bob appeared as a silhouette in the distance with the fire behind him.

In the light of the flames, we saw a macadam street about twenty feet in front of us. Following the winding street, we arrived at the flames which shot out of a hole in the ground. The hole was the kind the construction people dug for the basement of a house.

A police car, with red light flashing, pulled into the development from High Street.

"We can get away across the golf course," I said.

Jamie Bordeaux said, "No, wait here. We'll be fine."

A guy squirted water into the basement hole fire with a garden hose hooked up to a pipe sticking out of the ground nearby. I've seen grownups who look scared in movies but never this scared in real life. He stared at us for a few seconds. "Somebody's down there."

In the hole the flames outlined a Cadillac. What remained of the rear fender was fire engine red.

"Let's stay longer," Bob said.

Jamie Bordeaux said, "They won't yank the body out until they lift the car out of the hole. Could take all night. The car has to cool off. They didn't even send for a tow truck yet."

"Bet Johnny Bruce is down there," Bob said.

People gathered around, many from the houses across the street. Turned out Freeman was the cop in the police car on the golf course. He pushed everybody away from the hole and the fire.

Three fire trucks pulled up and the firemen yanked their hoses and hooked them up to a pumper truck. They squirted water, but they didn't have to for long. The security guard had accomplished the heavy work with his little hose.

More cops came and shooed people away. Jamie Bordeaux said we'd better head out because it was getting late. Without Alan, Jamie Bordeaux had become more responsible even though he was always the reckless one and Alan was… no, he wasn't responsible either, but Alan was more responsible than Jamie Bordeaux.

My bloody side ached as we rode back through town, but Bob and Jamie Bordeaux maintained a slow pace with me. On north Walnut Street a block away from the Y building, we heard a familiar voice. "Why are you boys out for a bike ride this late at night?"

"Loco, loco, Will Barnes!" I hollered.

"You're learning to see in the dark, Tommy McConnel, 'cause you have no light on that bicycle. Seeing when it's dark will come in handy for you later with Penny Durkin."

My face heated up.

Bob said, "What are you talking about?"

Will replied, "Tommy McConnell and Penny Durkin better be good in the day time or the dark. Is your sister a good girl, Bob Durkin?"

"Yeah." Bob's lower lip stuck out in a pout so far that we could see it even in the dark. His face must be about red right now, but I couldn't tell without light.

I yanked Bob's arm before he forgot Will Barnes was twice as big as him and had an advantage fighting in the dark. Jamie Bordeaux seized hold of him, too.

While Bob shook us off, Will Barnes said, "Does Tommy McConnell respect your sister, Bob?"

"Of course I do." I said.

It was the only answer to give to an adult, but Bob busted up laughing at me and then gave me a light punch. "You were joshing us, Will. Will? Will?"

"Will Barnes rode off into the sunset or moonrise or whatever he rides off into because he is nowhere to be seen," Jamie Bordeaux said.

Bob glanced my way. "How did he know your bicycle light wasn't working?"

"How's Will know anything? He's got the power." Jamie Bordeaux punched his arms out straight on the word power.

At the Bordeaux Restaurant, Jamie Bordeaux parked his bike and headed up to his family's apartment. Bob and I walked our bikes the half block to his place where we parked our bikes in the little hall at the bottom of the steps. Bob locked the door behind us and we headed up the steps with me struggling on each step with my sore side.

"You ready to be yelled at?" I asked.

"Mom's working. Penny won't give me grief."

"Your mom will not like the dust and dirt we're leaving on the stairs. You're supposed to keep them clean."

"Yeah. We're tracking dirt from the construction site."

"Somebody else tracked it, too." I pointed out the mud on the steps above us.

"Where did Penny get the dirt from?"

114

CHAPTER 18

With my left hand holding my right side scrape together, I hobbled behind Bob into his apartment.

Penny splashed wet splotches of mud around the sink and counter where she scrubbed her sneakers. Soil and dust coated the bottom of her blue jeans.

"Where you been, Penny?" Bob asked.

"I was here. You're the one coming home at eleven-thirty. You know I could tell Mom."

"Don't worry," Bob said. I'll clean up the mud and guck in the hall. Can you scrub my sneaks, too?"

"Right." Penny's sarcasm made it clear she planned to clean no more than one pair of sneaks tonight.

"Mom will want to know how come you have mud-covered jeans and sneakers," Bob said.

"Give them to me." No sarcasm this time.

Penny flashed me a smile. "Take 'em off, buster."

I smiled back and stripped off my sneaks.

Penny pointed a wet sneaker at us. "Where were you guys, anyway? In case Mom asks."

Bob ignored the question. Instead, he snatched a broom and dust pan and tramped out into the hall.

Penny asked, "What's wrong?"

"Ripped open that scrape down my side, see?" I held my right arm up to display the wet blood squishing through my shirt.

"Let me help."

"Don't touch."

"I won't." Penny dried her hands. "Leave your arm up one second." She kissed me a good one and pulled my shirt up the way Mom likes to rip a band-aid off in one quick pull.

"Oh." It was a simple, no nonsense oh. I expected excruciating pain, but there was none. Instead, the joy of a kiss remained on my lips.

"The scab is torn off, Tommy."

"Yeah. It'll dry up soon."

Penny stared at me the way Bob does when he has his doctor's kit out.

"Now what?" I asked.

"Iodine."

"No way!"

"Don't wake the neighborhood, Tommy."

"No iodine," I whispered.

"Don't worry. I was kidding. We have hydrogen peroxide."

Bob came back in and noticed I wasn't wearing my shirt. Penny walked into the bedroom on her way to the bathroom medicine cabinet.

Bob said, "What's with you two?"

"I was ripping your friend's clothes off," Penny bellowed from the bedroom. I think she forgot about the neighbors.

"No, you're not," Bob replied.

Penny popped her head out of the bedroom door. "When I'm finished, he'll rip my clothes off. Want to watch?" Penny disappeared back into the bedroom.

Bob's pout grew as large as I've ever seen it. "Yech. You guys better behave or I'm telling Mom."

"She's helping me with my broken scab, Bob. She's teasing you."

"That's not something to joke about, you guys." Bob planted his hands on his hips.

"She's getting hydrogen peroxide. Want to watch it ooze." I wiggled my midsection.

"Yeah." Bob planted himself on a kitchen chair.

Penny returned with the hydrogen peroxide and a box of cotton balls. She sat next to me and grabbed some of the squishy little spheres, wetting them with the open bottle. As she swabbed my side injury, the hydrogen peroxide bubbled and oozed.

"It's ice cold," I squealed.

"Cool," said Bob. "Do some more."

Penny gave us both an evil grin and wiped down the rest of the long wound. "Are you cold, Tommy?" Penny asked.

"Y-y-yes."

She placed a hand on my bare chest. "That warm you up?"

"Yes." My nerves crawled up and down my spine not knowing which way to slither.

"Bob, why don't you finish cleaning the dust in the hall while I finish up here with Tommy?"

"Do I have to?" Bob headed for the door with his broom and dustpan.

"Mom will be home soon."

Bob closed the door behind him.

Penny caressed my cheek. "Tommy, do you feel okay?"

"Yeah."

"Stand up. Let's see if you pass out."

I stood without fainting.

Penny stood up and stepped in close to me. She crept around my neck with her hands in a gentle, slow way that tickled and raised goose bumps. I could feel the twin towers on her chest against me as she leaned in closer.

"Feel better now?" she whispered.

"Yes." My voice shook.

"Perfect." Penny yanked my face into hers and planted a huge kiss with that yucky licking thing, except this time it was pleasant. While she tickled my lips, I heard the front door open. Penny didn't pay any attention. Instead, she held my face clamped to hers and continued to kiss and lick. My eyes were closed so I opened them. Penny's eyes were closed.

"Stop," Bob shouted.

Penny opened her eyes in a soft, slow way. They were wet, smooth and so deep and blue I wanted to stare into them forever. But they were red around the edges. Penny ignored Bob as she continued to kiss me with her eyes open.

"Penny," Bob shouted.

Penny pulled her face back and made a heavy sigh. She kept her hands around my neck.

"That's called making out." Penny's voice came from a deep place. "Next time, try to work with me. It's not fair to make the girl do all the work."

I licked my lips to take in the taste of her presence left behind. At the same time I inhaled her breath as she exhaled.

Penny dropped her hands from around my neck and slid them down my bare chest to my waist. She gazed into my eyes and smiled one of her mischievous smiles before taking her hands away.

"Don't do that stuff," Bob complained.

"Don't worry," Penny said. "I was teasing your friend, wasn't I, Tommy?"

"Yeah." My voice came from far away.

Penny twisted away from me. Over her shoulder, she asked, "Bet your side doesn't hurt anymore, does it, Tommy?"

"No, Penny." Our eyes locked.

Bob came over and spun me around to face him. "Did she take away the pain?"

"Yes."

"Okay." Bob turned to his sister while releasing my arm. "Penny, don't ever do that junk to Tommy. He's my friend. We're too young for making out."

"Are you both too young for girls?" Penny asked.

Bob shouted, "Making out is going too far."

"Making out is what you're supposed to do with girls." Penny returned to the sink.

"Shut up, Penny," Bob stamped his foot.

"I'm waiting for Tommy to get big, Bob."

"Didn't look like waiting," Bob whined.

"We were practicing so Tommy wouldn't hurt so much, right Tommy?"

"Uh-huh." My side still hurt, but at least it was cleaned up.

Penny's expression changed from liking me to the little mom expression she sometimes gave us. She was about to change the subject. "So where did you guys say you were until eleven-thirty at night?"

I had my breathing under control now. "On the north side of town. We hung out with Jamie Bordeaux."

"Ritzy section, huh?" Penny asked.

"We rode our bikes around the golf course." No reason to tell her about smashing cars.

"Where'd you get the dirt?" Penny asked.

"You know the new houses they're building north of the golf course?" Bob asked.

Penny lifted Bob's sneakers from the counter and scrubbed them. She faced the window above the sink. Her voice rose to a higher pitch. "No, what development?"

"Not important," I said. "A car fell into one of the basements they're digging and caught on fire."

"Anybody hurt?" Penny asked with her voice normal again.

"Afraid so," I replied. "The police and fire company came, but the security guard had the fire almost out by the time they arrived. It was a red Caddy. Bob hopes it was Johnny Bruce."

Penny raised her head up to face the ceiling with her back to us. She dropped her head, picked up something in the sink, put it back down, and in a soft voice said, "Him and half of West Chester."

"Where did you find your dirt?" Bob asked. "It's the same color as our muck."

Penny continued to face the wall. Her voice remained soft. "Not so exotic a place. I hung out with high school friends. You know the big field near the college campus south of Walnut Street Park?"

"You mean the one behind the houses where they have a bunch of practice fields?" I asked.

"Yeah." Penny came over to me and caressed my cheek with her wet hand. Her face was damp. Her blouse was moist around the neck. She must have rubbed dishwater on her face.

"Those are grass fields," Bob said. "How did grass make you muddy?"

Penny yanked a towel off a chair. She turned around for a moment while she dried her face. When she gazed my way again, she brought her lips up close to mine. This time I kissed her. It was supposed to be a quick peck, but she pressed in tight and stayed there.

"Hey!" Bob complained.

"Relax," Penny said. "The area around the edge of the field was muddy. Anyway Michelle, Jenny and I hung out with the guys."

"What were you doing?" My voice was far away again.

"Making out." Penny shrugged.

"Oh." My face glared at the floor.

"Are you jealous, Tommy?" Penny lifted my chin.

"Were you kissing a guy?" I asked.

"Kissing is what making out means, that and more," Penny said.

"More? What kind of more?" I asked.

"You know, like more." Penny shot her hands up in the air like she was frustrated at the way I responded, but I couldn't help my feelings. What's a kid supposed to do when he had a crush on his best friend's sister, and she was the make out queen of West Chester?

"Then I'm jealous." I spit out the words.

Penny smiled. She rubbed my cheek in that gentle way of hers. Her eyes turned to silky pools of blue. "I'm waiting for you to grow up. But you don't want me to become out of practice do you?"

"Do you need practice?" I touched my nose to her nose. I peered into her gentle blue pools of delight, but it made me feel cross-eyed and dizzy. Her eyes were red and puffy like she'd been crying.

"Don't you think one of us should know what we're doing when you get big?" Penny blinked a bunch of times.

"Guess so. Are you catching a cold?" I asked.

"No. And the odds of you knowing how to make out with a girl are what, zilch and none?" Penny asked.

"Everybody starts somewhere. You're doing a great job of teaching me," I said.

"That's one of the things I like about you. You have a head on your shoulders. Now, let me scrub your sneaks for you." Penny headed back to the sink.

Bob dumped a load of dirt clumps and dust into the trash can. He swept up more dirt around the living room. After he dumped that dirt into the trashcan, he pulled three cold sodas from the refrigerator. He handed one to me while passing another to Penny.

"Nothing like an ice cold Pepsi to make you feel great on a hot night," I said.

"Ahhhh." Bob said before belching a big one.

CHAPTER 19

Will held up my gray penny between his forefinger and thumb. "This is a steel penny you gave me. Sure you want to?"

"It's a penny, ain't it?" I shrugged.

"Sure, but I thought you might want to save it. Not many steel pennies around, you know." Will added the penny along with the other nine cents I had given him to his paper funds.

Bob thumbed through the paper. "They find Johnny Bruce in that car that burned on Saturday night?"

Will yanked another paper from his pile and folded it for the next customer. "Scoot over to page three where you'll find what you want to know. Police think they found what they sought, too, but if they did, then who did Johnny Bruce? Something fishy is going on is what I think. When something fishy is in the air, I start itching for fishing. Couple of catfish out of the Brandywine crick will taste mighty fine."

I leaned back with giant question marks popping out of my eyes. "How do you know it's on page three, Will?"

"I see with my other senses. Told you about that, didn't I?"

"You heard somebody say it was on page three?" I asked.

"Yes sir, fishing sounding mighty good, right now." Will folded his arms and rocked back and forth. He covered his face with a giant, toothy grin.

"Who takes you fishing?" Bob asked.

"Oh, I have brothers and sisters, don't I, Tommy?"

"Yep. Will's a Catholic, Bob. His sister is in my class and he has a brother or sister in most of my brothers' classes. A lot of Barneses attend St. Agnes."

Bob cocked his head to one side to let some question marks out of his eyes. "Are you Irish, Will?"

Will roared with laughter. "I'm what you call 'Black Irish,' Bob. Am I Irish? That do beat all. Down south where my people come from the one thing worse than being colored is being Catholic and colored."

"Not a good thing is it?" Bob asked.

"Not down south. Steel pennies down there don't like either one of them kind of folks and when you put 'em together, it's awful. Colored folks don't much like Catholic colored folks neither, not no way. Explains why we're up north now. Up here, nobody cares. Leastwise, not so Will Barnes heard about."

Bob had page three open and we spread it across the marble platform at the base of the big columns.

"Johnny Bruce was killed," Bob said. "The police have closed the case on his father's murder. See, I told you Johnny killed his father."

"Closing the case and proving somebody is guilty are two different things," Will said.

"If the paper reports it and the police agree, I don't need to hear no more," said Bob. "Besides, who else could have done it? We saw Johnny speed away from the crime the day he almost ran me over. Johnny Bruce was a dirty rotten coward."

Will said, "Driving his dad's car fast and almost running you down doesn't mean he killed anybody, not even his father. Man, whether he's white or colored, deserves his time in court. Now dying like he did, the court that counts is up in heaven for Johnny Bruce."

"He did it, didn't he? Why talk about it anymore?" Bob parked his hands on his hips and pouted.

Will leaned against the marble bank. "Supposing Johnny didn't do it. Then somebody else killed his dad. That somebody else could be killing somebody else again someday. The same person maybe killed your friend Cynthia Matting."

Bob dismissed Will with a hand wave. "Ah, you worry too much."

"Maybe so, Bob Durkin. Maybe not."

"They say how Johnny Bruce died?" I asked to change the subject.

"Not yet. Let me finish," Bob said.

I jumped to the end of the article over Bob's shoulder. "Says he was killed in the crash when the car flipped over. Crushed his head."

"Too much head chopping and head crushing around here," Will said. "Does it say why his car ended up in a basement hole in the first place?"

"They think it was an accident pending further investigation," said Bob.

"Farmers have reported seeing a red Caddy running around late at night along the back roads. He may have been driving into or out of some woods and thought he was crossing a farmer's field when he smashed into a basement hole," I said.

"Tommy, he'd have seen the street and the other houses under construction," Bob said.

I backed up a step. "Not if he was speeding and slid on the loose dirt. He could have been hiding in the development, but didn't see the hole."

Will Barnes jumped in. "Maybe too many maybes. Man only driving at night. He needs gas somewhere. He needs food somewhere. And like you say, Tommy, he needs to hide somewhere in the daytime. More people helping to hide Johnny Bruce than Johnny Bruce. Lots more work for some police investigators."

"Nope, says his dad's murder case is closed." Bob folded the newspaper over. "They're done. Nothing left but the accident investigation."

"Ain't that something?" Will closed his eyes and started the contortions he liked to do with his face screwed up for about three minutes which can feel like a long time to a kid waiting for him to return from consulting with the spirits. He snapped back to us. "Tommy McConnell loves Penny Durkin, alive or dead."

CHAPTER 20

The sun continued to bake West Chester as the old town approached the dog days of summer. Every Saturday the Warner Theater ran a special where they showed 25 cartoons along with a continuing movie serial. Anytime you can watch Looney Tunes and sit in an air-conditioned theater, you're having an excellent day. Doesn't matter if it costs your entire thirty-five-cent allowance. I hoped Bob could join me.

I jumped off my porch and took a gander as screeching tires grabbed my attention. Penny was in another brand new Chevrolet. This one was black, but it had two doors instead of four like the one at Alan's funeral.

The passenger door creaked open. Penny poked her head out. "Get in."

She checked me out. "March back inside and put on dress slacks and a nice shirt with a collar."

"You don't like my shorts and tee shirt?"

"Don't argue. I'll drive around the block. When I return, you be here or else."

While jumping out of the car, I considered what "or else" meant. If one of my older brothers said "or else," it meant a black eye. I charged up to the second floor back bedroom I used to share with Alan and changed clothes.

Mom was at the bottom of the steps carrying a load of clothes when I came down.

"Why are you wearing long pants?" she asked.

126

I fumbled for a few seconds. "It'll be cold in the movie theater."

"Don't forget your chores when you come back. I need all the help I can get."

I ran past her and out the door as Penny squealed the tires in front of the house.

"That's better," she said.

"Where we headed?" I climbed in the passenger side.

"Church."

"Today's Saturday." I pulled the door closed.

"So?"

"So church is Sunday."

"Not where we're off to."

On the northeast side of town we arrived at a rundown wooden church covered with faded and peeling white paint. The sign said it was Baptist. There was a parking lot in back, but Penny drove past it and parked on a side street under a tree.

I tapped Penny on the arm. "Can't walk into that church because I'm Catholic. You're supposed to be Catholic, too."

"Shut up." Penny removed a bobby pin from of her hair and poked around in a tiny hole in the chrome around the place where you stick the key into the ignition. The whole lock mechanism came out of the dashboard. Penny pulled another key mechanism out of her purse and stuck it into the dash. She put the one she yanked out into her purse along with her key with the rabbit foot.

"What are you doing?" I asked.

"Never borrow a car for more than two hours. You have to have rules. Another one is always return the car a block away from where you found it. Listen when I tell you these things because they're important."

She gave me a wide, blue-eyed stare with the smooth smile. I leaned into her as she pulled me close with her left hand wrapped it around my neck. It was a long kiss and I caressed her cheek with my right hand. It felt soft and squishy like a marshmallow. I liked touching her.

Penny pulled back and took my hand. "Another rule – never pass up an opportunity to make out. By the way, you did better this time. I like when you caress my cheek. Ready?"

Penny exited the car so I climbed out on my side.

"Lock the door," she said.

I locked it. "What about fingerprints?"

"You ever been fingerprinted, Tommy?"

"No."

"Don't ever get fingerprinted, and you'll be okay."

"So how will we drive home?"

"I'll get you home. You worry too much."

Penny fumbled with my arm and pulled me to a stop. She stood in front of me. "Gentleman should always wear their hair slicked down nice and neat, Tommy. It's another rule" She licked her hand and wiped down my cowlick which never stayed down no matter what you did. "That's better."

"It is?" I touched the back of my scalp and found no cowlick. "Wow, you can plaster my cowlick down anytime you want."

"Spit is the all-purpose stick'em," she said.

"Another rule?"

"Naw, a fact."

Colored people were walking around to the front door of the church from the parking lot in back.

"Why are we visiting a Negro church?" I asked.

"Remember Johnny Bruce?"

"Yeah?"

"Let's just say you weren't my first boyfriend."

The colored folks were kind to us as we walked up to the church, like they were glad we came. One was dressed in a brown suit with a red tie and a gold shirt. He said, "Why, Penny Durkin, I sure am glad to see you, baby. Who's your friend?"

"Tommy McConnell meet Pastor Baines," Penny said.

Pastor Baines held out his hand and we shook. He had a firm grip. He was a strong man who seemed pleasant.

"Tommy McConnell? Haven't I heard your name somewhere? Of course, he's your new boyfriend. Appears a mite young for you though, Penny." Pastor Baines laughed.

We left him at the steps and walked into the church. Penny held my hand. Hers felt sweaty and shaky. I was scared, but figured it must be okay to attend a Protestant church on special occasions.

When our eyes adjusted to the light, I spotted open seats in the back so I started to walk us into one, but Penny yanked me back.

She led me up to the front pew, almost to the casket. Chiamaka's grandmother, Mrs. Davis, saw Penny and smiled. Mrs. Davis was also Johnny Bruce's grandmother and Johnny was Chiamaka's cousin. Mrs. Davis slid over pushing her entire family down the row. Penny pulled us in and sat next to Mrs. Davis. Once we were settled, Penny leaned her head on Mrs. Davis' shoulder and began a soft audible weeping.

Down the row Chiamaka smiled at me, and we waved to each other. She stuck her tongue out and made a fist. Then she smiled again.

I fiddled around with my hand down on the floor.

"What?" Penny whispered.

"Where's the darn kneeler? How do these colored Baptists pray without a kneeler?"

"Sit still and shut up or I'll use spit to plaster your pants bottom to the pew." Penny said.

Sitting still can be fun. Everyone else sat with little or no movement, so I froze in place and prayed for the happy repose of Johnny Bruce. Every now and again I peeked out the corner of my eyes to make sure Penny didn't spit on nothing.

I leaned over to Penny and whispered, "Which mystery of the rosary do Baptists use at funerals?"

"Shhh."

The sorrowful ones worked for me but when I reached into my pockets, my hand came back without my rosary beads. So now what? Rattling off Hail Maries got me onto Bob and how he would kill me if he knew I was praying for Johnny Bruce. He'd kill Penny if he knew she had been Johnny Bruce's girlfriend.

If you're white, you can't date colored kids in West Chester. If Chiamaka and I hung out too much, some white kids would take me aside and beat the crap out of me. Colored girls would band together and beat the tar out of Chiamaka. Wouldn't matter that we like each other or are friends. So this whole Johnny Bruce thing must be tough on Penny. It takes a lot of courage for a white girl to love a colored guy, especially an older colored guy. Johnny was a senior and Penny's a junior.

Penny continued to hold my hand. She noticed me watching our hands and took her head off Mrs. Davis' shoulder. The tears streamed down her cheeks, but she managed to smile at me.

I loved her, even as she cried for Johnny Bruce. She picked up my hand and kissed it. This must be her way of telling me she was glad I came with her. And it sure beat spitting to glue my butt to the pew.

I was glad I came, too. If you love someone, you should help them through the tough moments. That's a rule, too, isn't it?

I gave Penny my best grin. She smiled at me a bit longer and then planted her head back on Mrs. Davis' shoulder.

I picked up Penny's hand, aimed for the back of it but ended up kissing her on the fingers before parking her hand back on her lap. All the mysteries of the universe were right under a few layers of cloth in church. Didn't matter if it was a Baptist church. The mysteries bear no prejudice and trek off to wherever your girlfriend travels.

Pastor Baines came to the front of the church where he talked.

And talked.

He preached on and on about things in the Bible and about what a fine young man Johnny Bruce was and how his father's death was a tragedy. "But I don't want anyone thinking Johnny did evil work. He was an upright child who loved his dad."

When he finished, Pastor Baines sat down in the pew across the aisle from me. Somebody walked to a piano up front and banged on it. The tune was sad and happy at the same time. Everybody stood up and sang, "Amazing Grace."

The words were about how wonderful God was because he saved your butt from hell, but Jamie Bordeaux's version of the hymn at Cynthia's pretend funeral popped into my mind. This made me crack a smile and chuckle. Penny turned my way so I straightened up and made sure she was not reaching for spit. She gave me a love smile, and I grinned back.

The nuns should sing this hymn because they were always telling us kids what wretches we were. The hymn talked about how God saved wretches. He gave us a chance. Wish the nuns would tell us that once in a while. The cool part came at the end as we sang about when you are in heaven 10,000 years from now you'll still have as many years left as when you first arrived. I guess song writers don't have to know their arithmetic.

Tears wanted to spill out of my eyes, but I wouldn't let them flow. Were the waterworks for the beautiful hymn or for Johnny Bruce? Or were they for Penny? It pained me knowing my Penny hurt so much. Wow, she was my Penny now. The love pouring out of me for her was so great I could break. Glad Penny brought along her spit. Might need it to put my carcass back together again.

Penny didn't deserve to lose her boyfriend because he was colored. Maybe Freeman the Cop was right. He said he thought Johnny's father was killed by some kids who broke into their house. What if it was a gang of white kids who wanted to kill Johnny because he dated a white girl? What if that was why Johnny was running away the day he almost ran over Bob? And why he was hiding out in the woods until he had that accident? Or was it an accident?

But why kill Johnny's father? His dad should have stopped Penny and Johnny from loving each other. What if instead of stopping it, he encouraged it? You would encourage somebody you love to be with the one they loved, wouldn't you? I'd be happy for Penny if she still had Johnny Bruce, wouldn't I? Well, maybe not, but not because Johnny was a colored guy. I loved Penny and didn't want her to have some other guy for a boyfriend.

While this stuff circled around inside my head, Penny was squeezing my hand and weeping. She about died when they sang "Amazing Grace." The whole place took to weeping for Johnny Bruce.

I had to talk to Bob. We had to figure out who killed Johnny Bruce and his father because Johnny was in love with a white girl. Johnny's death was no accident like the police said in the newspaper.

Then it thumped me like a light bulb. You know, when your big brother chucks a light bulb at you and it smacks you on the head and makes that exploding sound?

What if somebody in this church did in Johnny Bruce?

CHAPTER 21

"Penny, you're like my own granddaughter now." Mrs. Davis patted Penny on the cheek, black hand against white face. We were at Mrs. Davis's house for some family dinner after visiting the cemetery. "It doesn't matter that you and our Johnny never married. You're family. Remember that in the hard days ahead. And you will have them before you see good days, child."

I gawked at Mrs. Davis like she was crazy. Penny held onto me and she appeared crazy, too, with her teary eyes and turned-down mouth. Reminded me of Bob when he becomes angry. How can my steel Penny be part of Mrs. Davis' family?

Chiamaka brought chicken in from the kitchen, while her mom carried in mashed potatoes. Her father carried a bowl of vegetables in one hand and a cardboard carton holding six bottles of Schmidt's beer. Her Aunt Edna limped in leaning on a cane with one hand and carrying a large glass pitcher of iced tea with ice cubes and lemon slices floating on top in the other.

Mrs. Davis put her arm around me. "You take care of Penny. She needs a man. You're not ready, but sometimes you have to be all set even when you're not. Do you understand me, young Tommy McConnell?"

"It's like when you're General Custer and you're surrounded by a million Indians. Doesn't matter if you're not prepared to fight, you have to battle 'em anyway." I hugged Mrs. Davis in return.

Mrs. Davis shook her head. "You have the general idea. Sometimes you have to keep secrets even when you're dying to tell them. You have to protect the person you love no matter what she may have done."

I nodded. "Penny's secret is safe with me, Mrs. Davis. White boys would try to beat her up if they knew she was Johnny Bruce's girlfriend."

"Sometimes people have bigger secrets to keep, young man." Mrs. Davis wiggled a finger in my face.

I nodded one of those head bobs where you squish your lips together for emphasis. "Penny can tell me anything she wants me to know. Her secrets are safe with me. Besides I already know."

"You do?" Mrs. Davis asked.

"Sure," I said.

Penny stared at me like I was nuts.

Now, it was my turn to squeeze her hand. "Don't worry, Penny, I'll never tell."

Penny and Mrs. Davis appraised each other with big question marks on their faces.

A small foot made a large impact on my backside. I spun around to discover Chiamaka lowering her foot to the floor.

Mrs. Davis laughed. "I guess thirteen-year-old granddaughters aren't too young to be jealous now are they, Chiamaka?"

Chiamaka rose up in a haughty pose. "I ain't jealous of Tommy McConnell, Grandma. It doesn't matter to me who he makes an idiot of himself with."

"Is that so?" Mrs. Davis asked.

"Of course it's so, Grandma," Chiamaka said.

The long dinner table, made by combining three tables together, was set and the food spread out. We sat down, and while grabbing food, I noticed everybody but me had their head bowed. I let go of the chicken.

Pastor Baines and his wife sat at the table. He asked the Lord to bless the food and the people to God's service. He asked God to bring peace to this poor family that had lost a son and a grandson to violence. He asked God to forgive anyone involved in these evil events. Then he asked God to bless his servant, Alan McConnell, and raise him to the resurrection in Jesus' name, Amen.

I blessed myself but I was blown away. "How'd you know about Alan?"

"I read the paper, son," said Pastor Baines.

Chiamaka piped up, "Grandma, tell us about how you came north when you were a young girl."

Mrs. Davis wiped her mouth with a napkin. "Our company doesn't want to hear that old story. It's been told and told again."

Pastor Baines laughed. "Yes, we do, Grandma."

"I told this grandchild of mine maybe I would and maybe I wouldn't." Mrs. Davis chomped a forkful of potato salad.

"Tell it, Mom," Chiamaka's Aunt Edna said from across the other end of the table.

Mrs. Davis shook her head like she meant no, but said, "You won't be leaving me alone 'till I do. Listen, Chiamaka, when I was ten years old, I worked the farm and went to school down south."

"I know that part, Grandma. You lived in Alabama."

"Yes, and I did well in school. My mother wanted me to have an education. She saw how I loved to read and I was a whiz with numbers. Still am to see me counting change at the A&P. My father thought a girl didn't need an education. He believed his children didn't have to know any more than he did, which was just about nothing except farming.

"My mother and father were discussing this. Note I say 'discussing' because they never argued. But they were right fine at discussing things and if they raised their voices sometimes, why that was only to make a point. Anyway, they were fighting, I mean discussing, over this when Ted Ashland, a local white boy, came around to see me. I think he

135

was thirteen or fourteen, just a bit older than our Chiamaka and Tommy here. And a bit younger than our Penny."

Penny blushed as Mrs. Davis put her arm around her. Everyone gazed at Penny and smiled and bobbed their heads up and down, so Penny was "their" Penny although she belonged to the Durkins. I decided to ask Penny about this later.

Mrs. Davis started back telling her story. "Ted Ashland is carrying a couple of fishing poles along with a can of worms. He asks if I'm of a mind to go fishing. I allow as I am because I don't like sticking around when Mamma and Papa are having one of their loud discussions."

Chiamaka leaned her head to one side. "I didn't know you liked fishing, Grandma."

"I did back then, but that was the last time I ever went fishing, I'm here to tell you."

"Why, Grandma? What happened?" Chiamaka asked.

Mrs. Davis wagged a finger in Chiamaka's direction. "If you hush up, I'll tell you. See, Ted Ashland was a fine boy when he and I were little, but when he turned twelve he hung with that cracker bunch down in Buford. They put some wild ideas in his head. We went fishing all right. He gave me a worm and I hooked it and threw it in the water. Then Ted asked me if I ever saw a boy naked and I said no. Then he asked if I ever let a boy see me naked and I said no. Then he said it was time to do both and grabbed at my clothes. He about had my dress half tore off before I could kick him where boys don't like to be kicked and then scurried on home. That cracker never could outrun me."

"Were you scared, Grandma?" Chiamaka asked. The rest of the table, including me, stared on like it was happening right in front of us.

Mrs. Davis chomped a chicken leg. After eating it, she drank half a glass of lemonade before picking up the story. "When I returned home, I was crying and trying to talk to my parents and my words came out garbled and my whole body shook. Took my father and mother a few minutes to calm me down enough to tell them what had happened. Papa said, 'No cracker is about to violate one of my own and live to tell the tale.' He took off out the door.

"Papa didn't come back till late. I was in bed. I snuck out and peeked and saw Papa covered in blood. Them crackers, Ted's Dad and uncles, whipped my father something awful and then they threatened to come around and have their way with me. That's what Papa told Mamma. He said, 'We have to get her out of here and hide her away somewhere.'"

"Were you scared, Grandma?" Chiamaka asked.

"Was I scared? Child, it was all I could do to not pee my pants and I wasn't wearing no pants being as how I was in my nightgown. I ran to the back of the shack where I shared a room with my sisters, and I flung myself under the bed and stayed put. I wasn't coming out for nobody nor nothing."

"So then what happened, Mrs. Davis?" I asked.

"I told you. I stayed put until morning. My father sat on the floor in front of the bed holding onto his double-barrel all night, too. Come morning, Mamma came in and made me put on my best dress which was easy to find because I had but one Sunday dress and it belonged to my sister, Ella, which she had outgrown. Then Mama made me kiss everybody goodbye. My brothers, my sisters and my Papa. And everybody's crying so I'm crying, too, except I don't know why everybody thinks of crying all at the same time. Then Mama walked me into town and bought me a one-way ticket up north and so then I knew why everybody was sad and carrying on."

"She sent you up to Pennsylvania by yourself, Grandma?" Chiamaka asked.

"She did. You have to understand, child. Mama emptied every coin out of the cookie jar to buy my ticket. My brothers and sisters didn't get no shoes that fall for me having to be sent up north."

"How'd you know where to go?"

"I climbed aboard the northbound train and showed my ticket to the conductor, like Mama said to do. The conductor said to stay put until we pulled into Birmingham. When the train arrived in Birmingham, the conductor asked me if I knew where to go next. I said, 'No sir, I do not.' He took me by the hand and led me off that train and put me on the one bound for Atlanta. He told the conductor of the Atlanta train to do the same for me in Atlanta so I could catch the train north to Philadelphia. That conductor was a white man, and he took good care of this little colored girl. I praise the Lord and thank him every day for sending that conductor to take care of me. Otherwise I'd be wandering around Atlanta or Birmingham someplace to this day trying to figure out which way to go."

"Then what happened, Grandma?"

"I traveled up north. I didn't have any baggage either. All I came with was the dress Mama put on me that day. I remember kissing my Mama goodbye at the train station and her crying all over my dress. She cried fit to make me almost miss the train. I didn't realize till a long time later I was never going to see my Mama 'til Jesus comes and raises the dead."

"You never saw your family again?"

"I did not. When I came to Philadelphia, I told the conductor I needed to get to West Chester, Pennsylvania, to my aunt's house. That conductor took me by the hand and put me on what they called an el train. He said when I get to a place called Sixty-ninth Street Station, I was to look for a trolley car headed to West Chester and that would be my ride."

"Did you find the trolley car, Grandma?"

"How was I supposed to know what a trolley car looked like? I was an ignorant farm girl from Alabama."

"Then what did you do, Grandma?"

"I saw a colored man dressed in a fine suit of clothes and wearing a tie, so I figured he must be the preacher or the undertaker. I walked up to him and told him what I needed.

He asked me where I come from and I said, 'Jethro, Alabama. Came in this morning on the train.' He roared with laughter like he never heard anybody say something so funny. Then he said, 'Come with me. I'll show where to meet the trolley.' He took me to the platform and said to wait there until the Red Arrow trolley came for West Chester. He said it would say 'West Chester' on the front. Then he smiled and asked did I know how to read. I told him I was ten years old, and so I better know how to read or my teacher will tan my hide. He laughed again and said, 'Reckon your hide already be tan, girl.' He was still laughing when he walked away. I waited for the trolley and in time it came. I climbed on board and the man said you have to have a dime for this ride to West Chester. I said I would pay him at the other end because I was out of money and my aunt would give it to him."

"And he let you stay on the trolley?" Chiamaka asked.

"No, Chiamaka, he did not."

"So what did you do?" Chiamaka asked.

"I waited until the next West Chester trolley came. I climbed aboard and sure enough the man said I needed to give him a dime. I said I would pay at the other end and he said it doesn't work that way and I have to remove myself from his trolley. A white lady was sitting near the front. She said, 'You can't kick a little girl off the trolley. She has to get home. She'll miss her dinner.' The man said it didn't make any difference to him. He had to have a dime before I could ride the trolley. Don't you know the white lady dug a dime out of her purse and paid my way? I prayed the Lord bless her and hers everyday of my life. Know what her name was, Chiamaka?"

"I don't suppose it was Chiamaka, was it Grandma?"

"No child, it was Patricia Josephine Durkin."

While attempting to pull my jaw off my knees, I glanced over at Penny and she stared back at me. She won because her jaw was about a foot lower than mine. Mrs. Davis gave Penny another hug. "I believe if you ask at home, you'll find out she was your great-grandmother, Penny. Her friends called her Patty Jo."

Penny smiled while lifting her napkin from her lap and twisting it. "I can remember Grandma saying how she remembered her mom's friends calling her Patty Jo, but she died a long time ago."

"Mrs. Durkin invited me up on the bench seat next to her. We talked all the way to West Chester, which is about a twenty mile trip on the trolley with some stops. She asked me about Alabama, and she told me about West Chester and what a charming little town it was. I told her I was glad to hear it was small because I was from a tiny town back home and didn't believe I'd take to the city. When we pulled into West Chester, it was like a city to me compared to Jethro, Alabama, and I became scared. Mrs. Durkin asked if my aunt was planning to meet me, and I said my aunt didn't know I was coming. All I had was an address. Mrs. Durkin seemed puzzled so I told her about Ted Ashland and my father getting beat up and that wonderful white woman gave me a hug and shared the love of the Lord with me. She was so warm and welcoming it made me feel I was coming home by the time I arrived in West Chester."

"Did you find your aunt without any trouble, Grandma?" Chiamaka asked.

"Chiamaka, how I wish the wonderful people from those days had lived long enough to know you. You are my pride and joy, child. Mrs. Durkin took the old envelope with my aunt's address and walked me right to her front door. Said it wasn't one bit out of her way, even though it was in the colored section of town. She knocked on Aunt Flora's front door for me and when Aunt Flora answered, she about fell back and fainted to see me standing on her front steps. She said, 'I know you're one of my nieces because you look like your mama when she was ten years old. Come on in, child and introduce yourself. And please introduce your friend to me, too.' So I made the introductions, and Aunt Flora insisted Mrs. Durkin please stay for a cup of her tea and a piece of peach pie, too. Mrs. Durkin did and we all became friends. Aunt Flora took me in and I became the daughter she and Uncle Ned never had."

"I never knew any of that," said Penny.

"Neither did I," said Chiamaka.

"When you and Johnny began seeing each other I knew two things, Penny Durkin. One was I had to treat you like my own child, like my own granddaughter, Chiamaka here. You look like a young version of your great-grandmother, you know. The other thing was this dating between you and Johnny was bound to lead to trouble. I prayed for the Lord's blessing upon you, child, because more trouble waits for you up ahead."

CHAPTER 22

Bob parked on the stool at the soda fountain in Fuller's Restaurant on Gay Street. A twirl of my hand spun the red plastic seat of my stool. I sat down to brake it. Penny's friend, Jenny, worked the counter and her other friend, Michelle, waited tables.

"When can Penny come out to play, Bob?" Jenny checked behind her to make sure Mr. Hipplemeyer was out of sight in the back. He was. She poured us both a free cherry cola.

"Anytime she wants."

"Tell her to expect a call from me," Jenny said.

Michelle smacked Bob on the back of the head. "Hey, tell your sister not to be such a stay-at-home."

"I will." Bob rubbed his head.

"Tell her Jenny and I had a ride to the shore the last couple of weekends. She can come with us next time if she wants. We have a place to stay in Wildwood."

"Mom won't let her go to Jersey." Bob shook his head from side-to-side.

Jenny smacked Bob on the shoulder. "Yeah, it'd be tough for Penny to sneak out with you around, right?"

I plopped a straw into my soda. "So what happens at the shore?"

Jenny threw the small towel she was holding over her shoulder. "What do you think? We hang out under the boardwalk with the big boys."

A glint formed in Michelle's eyes. "You boys staying out of trouble?"

Both girls giggled.

Jenny placed her arm around my shoulders. She whispered loud enough for Bob and Michelle to hear, "Tommy McConnell loves Penny Durkin."

Stupid smile crept across my face.

"Who told you?" Bob shouted.

My face felt hot as Jenny answered me instead of Bob. "Little birdie told me, Tommy. Want to know what else I heard?" Jenny raised her voice.

"What?" Bob's lower lip quivered.

Jenny sauntered back around to the other side of Bob and planted her arm around him. She leaned over him to gawp in my direction. "Penny Durkin loves Tommy McConnell."

I spun my stool to face away so I could ignore her, but my smile was too big to hide.

Michelle leaned across the counter with her face right up to mine. "No sense denying it. You two are the talk of the town."

I spun back to face Bob. "You ready to split?"

"Yeah, these girls are just yapping."

Michelle gave the counter a quick wipe with a towel. "Bob, Tommy will be your brother-in-law someday." She grinned.

"Come on, we have better things to do." Bob stormed out of the restaurant. Over his shoulder, he called, "Thanks, girls."

"You're welcome, boys," Michelle hollered back.

Outside I latched onto Bob's arm. "Why did you thank them?"

"Our drinks were free, you know." Bob shook off my grip.

"They repeated what everybody else says."

"You mean you and Penny are in love?"

"Yeah. You're okay with that, right?" I nudged Bob on the arm.

"No. A guy shouldn't date his buddy's sister."

"I really care for her."

Bob stopped. He flashed his index finger in my face. "She looks out for me. It's my job to keep her out of trouble."

"I wasn't planning anything bad."

"You're a kid, ain't you?" Bob resumed drifting down Gay Street east towards High with me beside him. No clouds hid the sky and the temperature soared close to a hundred.

"Penny likes me." I stepped around a big wad of chewing gum on the sidewalk.

"I know. I can see the way she gawks at you."

"She didn't always though, did she?" I whirled around a parking meter.

"No, you used to be a little kid to her." Bob twirled the parking meter knob.

"Why do you think she likes me?" I stared at Bob with the parking meter between us.

"I don't know. Could be a combination of being the little mother to us and her wanting a boyfriend."

"Why do you think she lied to us?" I backed away from the parking meter so I could mosey down the street with Bob beside me.

Bob shoved me on the shoulder. "My sister doesn't lie."

"She said she was with Jenny and Michelle on Saturday night, but the girls said they were at the shore." I tramped down Gay Street with one foot on the curb and the other in the gutter.

"She probably didn't want to say where she really went." Bob strolled on the sidewalk.

"Which was?" My foot struck a storm drain so I checked for dropped coins in the bottom.

"If she told us, we'd know." Bob stopped to take a gander down the storm drain.

"You have to watch out for your sister." I kicked a crumpled cigarette package from the gutter out into the street.

"I know. Dad's coming home. So's Mickey."

"When?"

"Soon. Depends on the paperwork. Once the government gets you, you come and go when they say, not when you want to."

"I wasn't thinking about your father and brother, Bob."

"Who else is there? Menoitios?" Bob shrugged.

"Not sure I should tell you." I wiped sweat from my forehead with my shirt.

"You better tell."

"Promise you won't become angry?" The Pontiac parked on the street in front of me jumped up and bit me. I sat on the curb to rub my sore kneecap.

"Why would I get mad at you?" Bob asked.

I reached down into the gutter under the Pontiac's rear bumper to pick up an empty pack of Pell Mell cigarettes "Whoever killed Johnny Bruce might want to hurt your sister."

"Why would they want to hurt Penny?" Bob took the empty pack from me.

"Can you keep a big secret, Bob?" I stood up to resume our stroll.

"Tell me." Bob flipped the empty pack. It sailed into the middle of Gay Street where a Buick ran over it.

"She dated Johnny Bruce."

The first polio shot, which was the most painful needle injection I ever had, came to mind as I flew across the sidewalk and bounced off a parked Buick.

While rubbing my shoulder and glowering at Bob, I became amazed. First, who knew Bob could hit so hard? Second, I never, ever saw him so angry. Not only was his lower lip in a quiver, but also his whole lower jaw. His chin was pulled back in a mass of wrinkles like an old man.

I made a fist with my right hand. "What?"

"Don't ever say that about my sister."

"Sorry. Told you it was a secret."

Bob's face was like a television set with words streaming on the screen except the words became angry. He still had a red face and pouty expression, but he wasn't glaring anymore. He took off down the sidewalk. "I'll kill her."

Bob ran with a mission. There was no way to catch up, but I tried. At the big bank on High Street, I stopped.

"You boys are in a mighty hurry," proclaimed Will Barnes.

"Trying... to... catch... Bob."

"Sounds like your breath needs catching first. Bob ran by here like lightening was chasing him."

"He's... going... to... kill... his... sister."

"Don't that beat all? He should wait for his Dad to come home. He'll kill them both for sure or their brother Mickey will. They're big men. Bob is small. Penny Durkin eats his kind for lunch and spits out the bones. No, you tell Bob to wait for his Dad if he wants somebody to kill his sister."

While staring at Will like he was about three-quarters bonkers, and trying to think of something to say, my breath returned.

"You better be getting' on. Bob is in for a heap of trouble if he finds his sister before you get to him. Go on, now."

I rounded the corner onto Market Street too late, but kept running. At the Durkin apartment, I tore up the stairs two at a time. Bob's apartment door hung open, so I stuck my head in.

Penny straddled Bob on the couch. She pinned his hands down while staying out of range of his kicking feet, Bob kicked up into the air in an attempt to nail her on the back of the head. Bob's hatchet was on the floor within easy reach of Penny's free right hand.

"You guys all right?" I asked.

Penny cold stared me. "I thought you could keep a secret?"

"He needed to know," I mumbled.

"Telling was my decision. Johnny Bruce was my secret." Penny growled.

I entered the apartment. "You need us, Penny. You may be in big trouble. Somebody had a reason for killing Johnny Bruce and the reason might be you."

"Paper said his death was an accident." Penny continued giving me a pouty, cold stare.

"Ever think you might have an accident?" I asked.

Penny studied the ceiling for a few seconds and then dropped her head down. She shook it like she was saying no to somebody. She gazed over at me. "For a stupid little kid, you're smart."

Penny glared down at Bob. "If I let you up, will you promise not to kill me?"

"Maybe." Bob's lips both stuck out in a pout..

"Cool off, Bob," Penny said in a sweet voice.

Bob's face fell into something approximating his normal look. "I won't kill you. at least not yet. But you have to listen to Tommy. He's right, you know."

Penny glanced my way. "I know. So what should we do?"

I gestured with my palms up. "Talk to Freeman the Cop."

"No way." Penny climbed off Bob.

"Why not?" Bob rolled from the couch to the floor.

Penny picked up Bob's hatchet. "Freeman the Cop will tell Mom. Mom will tell Dad. Dad will murder me for going out with a colored kid."

"Did you date a colored guy?" Bob stared up at Penny the way a doe gazes at a car's headlights.

"Yeah, little brother. I'm sorry if I've brought shame to the family name." Penny flipped the hatchet end-over-end once before heading into the bedroom.

"Why?" Bob's eyes went from doe to cold steel.

"He asked me," Penny called from the other room.

Bob's eyes softened. "Did you like him?"

Penny returned. "I guess. He treated me nice."

"Did you love him?" I asked.

Penny patted my cheek in that loving way of hers. "He was fun, Tommy. Treated me better than my father and Mickey. He was almost as nice as you."

Something in my chest melted into a puddle.

"We can't let them find out." Bob pounded his right fist hard into the palm of his left hand. "The secret stays here with us three. Don't tell Mom."

"I didn't plan to tell anyone. Big mouth did the talking for me." Penny slapped my face a good whack.

"I need to know about stuff like this," Bob said. "I have to watch out for you."

I rubbed my face and tried lifting my jaw off my chest.

Penny folded her arms across her chest. "Great, my safety depends on two thirteen-year olds."

CHAPTER 23

The cowlick would not glue down so my spit wasn't as sticky as Penny's. But with more water, my hair stayed put. I buttoned a short-sleeve, green plaid shirt and tucked the tails into my church khakis. I dipped my toes into my brown school shoes and tied the laces. Before giving up the bathroom so Mom could bathe the little ones, I brushed my teeth, and it wasn't even bedtime.

I headed down to the front porch where Jamie Bordeaux sat on the railing with a big grin on his face.

Bob's face held his angry pout. He leaned against one of the porch columns. "It ain't right, Tommy."

"Why not?" I asked.

"You know why." Bob's lower lip quivered and his face reddened.

"Maybe you better tell me anyway." I shrugged and held my palms upright.

"You're supposed to be my friend." Bob gave me a little shove.

"I am your friend." I smiled.

"Yeah, he's your friend," Jamie Bordeaux said.

"Friends don't date each other's sisters." Bob stamped his foot, which surprised me. I doubted girls stomped anymore and the boys stopped a long time ago.

Jamie Bordeaux planted a hand on Bob's shoulder. "Bob, Tommy loves your sister. Penny loves Tommy. Get over it already. They make a cute couple, what you call a May-December thing, except they're more like April and May."

Penny squealed the tires of her mom's powder blue Chevy to a stop in front of the house.

While I made googly eyes at the car, Bob punched me hard on the shoulder. I turned around. "What?"

"You better treat my sister right."

"Bob, don't worry." I removed Bob's finger from in front of my face.

"No making out, okay?" Bob asked.

Jamie Bordeaux slapped Bob on the shoulder while flashing me his smiling eyes. "Don't make any promises you can't keep, Tommy. Have a good time. I'll make Bob happy."

Penny blew the horn on the Chevy. I shook my head and slapped Bob's other shoulder before hopping into the car.

"Didn't steal a car tonight?" I asked.

Penny glared at me. "It's another rule. Never borrow a car for a date without permission. Cops are always on the lookout for teenagers joyriding on Saturday night. Odds are they'll catch you. Now, tell me about up on the porch?"

"Bob doesn't like the idea of us dating."

"I know. He told me. He'll live." Penny had her hair in a ponytail as usual, this time with a powder blue ribbon.

"So where do you want to go?" I asked.

Penny faced forward with a bounce of her ponytail. "You're the man so you decide."

"Are you hungry?"

"Do you have money?" She wore a white blouse with a light blue skirt that almost matched her ribbon.

"Yeah. I've been helping my dad in his carpenter business."

"In that case, I'm hungry." Penny released the emergency brake.

"Good, because I am too. Want to eat at Fullers?"

"Are you sure you're okay with the high school kids seeing us?" Penny asked.

"Don't you want the kids to know we're together?"

Penny spun her head in my direction so she could stare into my brown eyes with her deep blue ones. "You don't know how proud I am to be seen with you, do you?"

I rubbed her cheek with my right hand. She leaned into my hand while puckering her lips. Right in front of my house, she planted a big one on my lips. Flames shot out my ears.

From the porch, we heard a loud "Hey" from Bob.

Penny pulled back and grinned. Jamie Bordeaux laughed on the porch behind me. I dropped my hand away from Penny's face. She shifted the car into Drive and hit the gas.

I waved to Bob and Jamie Bordeaux.

Penny headed north on Walnut, cruised past Market and hung a left at Gay Street. When we crossed High Street, she found a parking space on the right side of the street.

She squeezed my hand. "Here we are."

"Yeah.".

We climbed out of the car and promenaded up to the corner of Gay and Church Streets where we crossed to the south side of Gay Street. We made our way back up Gay a short distance to Fullers in the middle of the block.

On the way through the crowd of teenagers, a guy grabbed Penny by the arm. "Who's the pipsqueak, honey?"

I was ready to duke it out and didn't care that he was a head taller than me.

Penny shook off the intruder. "Buzz off, buster."

We found a booth in the back of the crowded restaurant. I slid onto the bench on one side while Penny slipped onto the other.

"Don't pay any attention to the riffraff," Penny said.

We both ordered a hamburger and French-fries with root beer. A tiny machine on the end of the booth table against the wall showed the songs on the jukebox. You played tunes by dumping coins into the slot. Penny asked for a nickel, and when I gave one to her, she slid it in. Her fingers danced across the red and white buttons at the bottom of the machine before she pushed the letter B and the number seventeen, an Elvis song called Love Me Tender.

It didn't play right away because other kids had shoved their nickels into the little machines in their booths.

Penny smothered ketchup over her fries and burger. When she passed me the bottle, Elvis sang. While dumping ketchup out of the bottle, I splashed some on my shirt. I jerked my hand away and knocked over my root beer.

Penny laughed. She stuck her feet up on the booth bench to keep them off the sticky, root beer-soaked floor. Darlene, our waitress, arrived with a rag for the table. Some kid carried a mop for the floor.

"Sorry, Darlene." I stepped away from the booth to give them room to work.

"Don't worry, Tommy. This is how I earn the big tips."

The kid with the mop flashed me the same gawk he probably saved for the cockroaches in the kitchen.

I decided then and there to give Darlene a tip of two quarters instead of one.

Once the table was straightened out and I returned from the restroom where I washed my face and wiped the ketchup off my shirt, I was able to eat my hamburger with no more problems. My shirt mostly dried as I ate.

"Are you okay?" Penny asked.

"I am now that my face and shirt are clean."

"It's okay to be nervous, Tommy. This is your first date, isn't it?"

I tried to dip a French fry into a glob of ketchup on my plate but missed. It ended up in my second glass of root beer.

"It becomes easier over time," Penny said.

I parked my elbow on the table, rested my chin on my hand, and gazed into Penny's little blue sparkling spheres across the table from me. Her eyes captured mine. I leaned over the table to kiss her. She reached to meet me halfway, but instead two more root beers splashed around on the table and dripped onto the floor. Some landed on Penny's skirt. She dabbed with napkins as she stood next to the wet booth.

After Darlene wiped the table and seats, the mop person mopped up the floor. Darlene handed me the check. I plucked down three quarters and headed for the cashier to pay up.

Outside, Penny stepped toward the car.

I tugged her elbow. "We can walk if you want. Warner's around the corner."

"Good idea." Penny reversed direction so we could stroll east on Gay Street. "Your shirt will dry by the time we arrive at the movies and so will my skirt."

We headed north at High Street towards the Warner Theater. They were playing a movie called Because They're Young which starred Dick Clark, from the American Bandstand television program, and Tuesday Weld.

"Doug McClure and Duane Eddy are in the cast," said Penny. "And James Darren makes a cameo appearance. He's such a dream."

I bought two tickets.

Penny held onto my arm as we walked into the theater. I started for the auditorium, but Penny yanked me to a stop. She leaned in close to my ear and whispered, "Balcony."

I froze.

She dragged me to the staircase that led to the make-out hub of West Chester. We parked in the third row near the center. Most people preferred the late show at the Warner Theater, but a few early birds were scattered around the balcony for this one. Penny and I had the front section to ourselves.

Besides the red velvet seats, the main color of the theater was gold. When I was a little kid, I thought the theater was made out of gold. Now, I knew the gold look was accomplished with lights and gold paint. The ornate trim ran from the floor to the lofty ceiling, which was painted in a blue and gold pattern.

Soon after the movie began, Penny whispered in my ear, "I'll be back. Have to powder my nose."

"It looks fine to me."

"You're sweet, Tommy. Don't ever change." Penny disappeared into the darkness behind me.

I watched the movie for a while before sensing that special female warmth next to me. I thought about placing my hand on her lap near the center of all the secrets of the universe but didn't have the guts. Instead, I settled my paw on the armrest. She parked her hand on mine. My heart raced because she wanted to touch me, but she must have used the cold water in the ladies room.

"Your hand is frozen, Penny."

Penny didn't respond, so I spun my noggin to see if she was okay except I was not sitting beside Penny. I was holding hands with Cynthia Matting.

She wore her red and green blouse with a grey skirt. I slid to the far side of my seat away from her while my mouth hung open. I figured I better not scream because they would kick me out if I did. I dragged my hand away from under her mitt on the armrest.

Cynthia smiled so I smiled back, but my heart pounded, and I tasted sour hamburger wanting to explode out of my stomach. She leaned in to kiss me. When she pursed her lips a maggot crawled out.

I leaned back as far as I could the other way.

Cynthia mouthed a word, but no sound came out. It looked like "boo."

"B-b-boo b-back at you, Cynthia." What do you say to a ghost?

Cynthia smiled the way she used to when we were younger and before maggots hung out in her throat. Even in death, Cynthia was still the same as when she became too old to play with us anymore. As I watched, she faded into the darkness.

A few minutes later, somebody shook my right shoulder so I opened my eyes to see Penny pushing me and smiling. I jumped about a foot above my seat.

"What's wrong?" she asked.

"Cyn-Cyn-Cynthia…"

"No, I'm Penny. Remember? You fell asleep." Penny gave me her wonderful smile.

"Cyn-Cynthia was here."

"Cynthia who?" Penny whispered so I spoke softer. A container of popcorn flew by my head from somewhere behind us.

"Cynthia Matting."

"You saw Cynthia Matting?"

"Ye-ye-yes."

"You do realize she's dead?"

"Yes, I know."

"Tommy, watch the movie. Tuesday Weld is much prettier than Cynthia ever was."

"You're prettier than Tuesday Weld."

Penny planted a big one on me, and somehow, Cynthia Matting no longer mattered. I was busy making out in the balcony of the Warner Theater with my girlfriend. I couldn't wait to tell Bob.

CHAPTER 24

"Ouch, ooch, ouch, ooch, ouch, ooch..." Bob sat on his bottom under my kitchen table praying the ancient chant of the newly injured. This followed his hurried backdoor entrance into my kitchen and the dive beneath the table, where he had cracked his head on one of the chairs and banged an elbow on another.

Mrs. McGillicutty jumped off the table to answer Bob's prayers with a few "feed me" rubs.

I poked my head under the table. "You okay?"

Bob finished his chant. "Yeah."

"Want to tell me about it?"

"Dad and Mickey are home." He petted Mrs. McGillicutty.

"So?"

"Dad came in this morning and I went over to greet him. He picked me up like I was a stick of gum and threw me on the floor next to the couch. He said he was glad to see me because he hadn't had a chance to whip my butt in more than a year. Mickey came in behind him and said, 'Me neither.'"

"So what did you do?" I shoved the salt shaker around the table.

Bob thrust his face in my direction. "Scampered out the backdoor, never mind Menoitios. I'll hide out under your kitchen table. Think they'll rummage around here?"

"Hope not. They'd kill us both."

"I wouldn't mind if they were quick." Bob blinked a few times to block some tears trying to sneak out.

"What if you moved in here and slept on Alan's bed?"

"Like Penny says, 'Coolville.'"

"I'll ask Mom." I ran upstairs where she was busy scrubbing the toilet.

"Can Bob live with us? He could sleep on Alan's bed in my room. Can he, Mom?"

"Does he clean toilets?"

"Don't know. He helps his mom clean the apartment at home."

"Then his mom will want to keep him. Who'd help her if Bob moved out?"

"His dad and Mickey are home."

Mom leaned her toilet brush against the outside of the tub. She scrunched up her face the way she does when us kids bring home our report cards and she doesn't expect good news. "Where's Bob now?"

"Under our kitchen table."

"Let him stay here today if he wants, but he has to go home at supper time. He's their kid. We can't take in somebody else's kid. There are laws."

I felt let down, but Mom was right. Anybody Freeman the Cop ever had to drag home, like Bob and me on numerous occasions, knows about the law.

Back downstairs. Penny sat in my place with her face over a bowl of Cheerios.

I patted her shoulder. "Hi, Penny."

Penny raised her head and both sides of her face exhibited large welts.

A big lump formed in my throat, but no tears. Instead, anger and frustration roared their ugly heads in my heart. I stroked with my fingertips under her chin where her skin felt soft and warm. "Penny, what can we do for you?"

Penny pulled her head back. "Don't shout for one thing. My ears are still ringing from Dad's greeting.

"Why'd he smack you so hard?"

"Said it was down payment on the bad stuff I did while he was away."

I heard Bob's voice from under the table. "What bad stuff?"

"I've been a bad girl while Dad was away. Just ask Tommy. Dad doesn't need a list of the things I did to know I was bad. Nobody's perfect, you know."

Bob stayed under the table. "What did you do bad with Tommy?"

Penny chuckled. "Nothing, little brother, except make out with him in the balcony of the Warner Theater."

Bob said, "Other than messing around with my best friend, how bad could you have been?"

Penny smiled so I jumped in. "You've always been good to me, Beautiful."

"You mean before I got my face knocked around?" Instead of a smile, she wore her scrunched-up-about-to-cry face.

"You're still pretty, Penny. My smile proves it," I said.

"No, I'm ugly now. Dad wouldn't hit me if I was pretty." Penny covered her face with her hands.

Mrs. McGillicutty hopped up on Penny's lap.

Bob climbed out from under the table. His placed his hands over his ears. "Penny, the guys say you're pretty. That makes it so. Dad hits you because he's bad, not because you're bad. They stuck him in jail. It's a shame they let him out."

Penny petted the cat. "But you don't realize how dreadful and appalling I am, Bob. By the way, you have to go home. Dad sent me to get you so he could finish greeting you. Mickey wants to say hi, too."

Bob stormed out of the kitchen. "I'm never going home. Moving in with Tommy and sleeping in Alan's bed."

I took a deep breath before calling out the bad news. "Mom said you can play over here 'till supper time, but then you have to go home. She said it's the law. You can't move into somebody else's house unless your parents give you away."

Bob poked his head into the kitchen. "Why's Mom always at work when I need her?"

Penny dumped the cat on the floor. She made her way over to Bob at the entrance to the dining room where she placed a hand on his shoulder. "She has to."

Bob dropped his head. Penny and I watched as he moseyed through the house and out the front door.

Penny grabbed my hand and led me out to the backyard. She pointed up to the window of my bedroom. It opened onto the roof of our back porch. "Can I sneak into your window at night and sleep in your bed?"

"You have to climb up to the porch roof somehow."

Penny walked to the rear of the yard by the fence and gawked at the roof over the back porch. "The window up there?"

"Yeah?"

"All I have to do is climb up those wooden fire escape steps to the second floor apartment next door, scramble over the railing, and jump." Penny checked out the house between my house and the alley. It had two apartments, one up and one down.

I could see that Penny was right. "Hmm, funny how a kid can look at something for most of his life and never make the connection. Anyone could climb over the little railing to break into my house."

"Tommy, I bet you guys never lock your front door, do you?"

"Naw, eleven kids and two parents would make for a lot of lost keys. Let me ask you one question before you leave."

Penny pushed her face close to mine and surrounded me in her arms. "Anything."

"Why does Mrs. Davis call you 'her Penny' as if you're part of the Davis family?"

"You don't want to know." Penny backed away. She stared down, no longer meeting my eyes.

"You said anything."

Penny glanced around the yard. She paced. She came up to me. "She thinks ..." Penny stopped and dropped her head again. She spun on her heels and lumbered away.

"Thinks what?"

Penny sloughed back to me with a troubled expression on her face. Suddenly, a mischievous smile crept across her mug. She hugged me and planted a huge, wet kiss on my lips. I kissed her back. She smiled and patted my chest before meandering out of the yard.

Scrutinizing her cute little butt as it bounced up and down made me glad. I loved her so much, no matter what she did or didn't do. But the neighborhood kids would razz me about loving Penny Durkin so I took pleasure in knowing that no one saw her kiss me.

"She be a mighty fine kisser, ain't she?"

Oh, no. I spied the front yard of the house behind us where Chiamaka flashed a big grin on her face.

"You don't have to shout, Chiamaka."

Chiamaka breezed out of her yard into the alley and around to my backyard. She checked out my bedroom window. "Yeah, breaking into your steel penny bedroom be easy, especially while you're sleeping at night."

She grasped me by the ears and planted a huge, wet kiss on my lips. When she pulled back, she wore about as big a grin as a girl can grin.

My eyes felt huge, about the size of half dollars. I couldn't figure out a way to close my mouth. Do all girls kiss this good? "What was that for?"

"Didn't want you to think colored girls can't kiss. Matter of fact, colored people might have invented kissing. It's too cool for steel pennies to have discovered by their selves." Chiamaka strutted out of the yard with her little bottom bouncing.

I hung out with my younger brothers and sisters for the rest of the morning so Mom could get her work done and not bother me about cleaning my room.

About lunchtime, Bob charged through the front door without knocking. Tears streamed down his red face. His lower lip quivered. "Tommy, come quick."

"What's wrong?"

"They killed Penny."

CHAPTER 25

"No!" I screamed.

Bob took hold of my wrist and yanked me out the door. We ran up Walnut Street and around the corner on Market Street to where some people had gathered in front of the Royal Restaurant. An ambulance pulled away from the curb.

I couldn't breathe and fell to my knees. Weird thing was I didn't cry, but I yelled, "Bob."

He came back and helped me to stand. "We don't have time." Bob pulled me along by the hand while pushing his way through the crowd.

Three police cars were double parked on Market Street. Two cops yacked to each other and smoked cigarettes. The people hung around the sidewalk and in the middle of the street. The action was over and so everybody buzzed with each other instead of watching. Some wandered off in different directions.

I spotted blood on the sidewalk. "Bob."

"Ain't nothing. Wait till you go up."

We tore off skipping half the stairs to Bob's apartment. McCarty, one of the cops, yelled "hey" at us, but we ignored him. At the top of the steps Bob slammed into Freeman and I plowed into Bob. We both tumbled to the floor on the upstairs landing in front of Bob's apartment. The door stood open. Big splotches marked the carpet in the living room area by the stuffed chair, but I didn't notice a chalk outline. Two cops in uniform and somebody in a suit worked inside the apartment. They had a confab going and one of them took notes. They ignored Bob and me.

On television and in the movies, they always chalked an outline. Alan got an outline chalked. So did Cynthia Matting, except hers was painted.

"Bob?" I asked.

Bob didn't get a chance to answer before Freeman jerked us both up by the back of our shirts. "You boys headed somewhere?"

"Into the apartment, Freeman." Bob's face was tight. Tears flowed down his cheeks.

"Not yet, boys." Freeman released us and then pulled an honest-to-Abe-Lincoln five-dollar-bill out of his wallet and handed it to me. "Tommy, take Bob out and buy him lunch. Take your time. Come back in a couple of hours."

"You want the change?"

"Nah, see a matinee. Buy some candy and popcorn. Get lost for a while. Let us take care of things here."

"Freeman?"

"Yeah, Tommy?"

"Is she…" I can't bring myself to say it. I wasn't about to cry no matter what, even if I was choking 'em back at that moment.

"No, boys." Freeman placed his hands on Bob's shoulders and stared at him man-to-man, eyeball-to-eyeball. "Bob, your sister is still alive."

Bob cocked his head sideways. "Huh?"

I figured Bob thought Freeman needed a few screws tightened. Bob's head and shoulders shook. His lower lip quivered.

"I know that's hard for you to believe, the way we found her. I thought she might… you know… too. But you tore out of here before you let me check her for a pulse. She's been knocked around something fierce, but she's alive. Your father beat the living crap out of Penny, but I think we found her in time, thanks to you."

163

Freeman patted Bob on the back of the shoulder and gave him a little spin toward the steps. That was my cue to snatch Bob's arm and make ourselves scarce. I peeked into the apartment again to make sure the splotches were big blood stains on the carpet. Freeman caught me staring.

"Will she survive?" I asked.

Freeman rubbed his chin with one hand and planted the other on his hip above his pistol. "Don't ask me. I don't have any answers for you. You boys will have to wait until you hear from Bob's mom. And Bob, I want you to stay at Tommy's house until your mom calls or comes for you."

"I can sleep in Alan's bed."

Freeman winced at Alan's name but covered up and whispered like we're in church, "Will that be all right with your mom, Tommy?"

"Guess so. I'll ask when we return from the movies."

"If she has any problems with Bob staying over for a few days, have her call me at the police station so I can make other arrangements."

"Other arrangements?" Bob's eyes widened like when his Dad was about to clobber him. I'd be afraid, too, if I didn't know anything about the other options.

I took Bob by the arm and dragged him down the steps. "You don't want to know, believe me."

A few of the stragglers watched us come out of the apartment house. One asked, "What's happening upstairs, kids?"

"Nothing," I said. The two cops glared at us, but they didn't say anything.

The man stepped in front of us, blocking our way. "What did you see?"

"Leave us alone," I said.

"Come on, you can tell me." The man pushed his hat to the back of head.

I called to the two cops. "McCarty, can you help us here?"

McCarty strolled over like he owned the street. His buddy, a rookie I didn't know, followed him. "Leave the kids alone, Duffy. They don't need any guff from a reporter."

"Yeah, but I'm on a story, McCarty. Give a guy a break here." He turned from the cop and gaped at me.

I glared back. "Talk to Freeman when he comes out. He knows everything." I held onto Bob's arm above the elbow and took off, pushing my way past the reporter.

Down the street, we slowed to a crawl. Bob asked, "Who's the dunce?"

"Dumb reporter wanted to interview us."

"We don't know nothing. No big deal talking to him."

"You talk to him, and he quotes you in the paper. Your name spreads around. Kids think you're a hero. Girls want to kiss you and make out…"

Bob smiled. "Oh, yeah?"

"Yeah, and then some wise guys hate your guts 'cause you're a squealer."

"Ain't no squealer."

"Doesn't matter. The next thing you know, whoever did it kills you because the newspaper blabbed about you to the bad guys."

Bob frowned. "The bad guys will kill me anyway."

"What do you mean?"

"Don't you know Dad and Mickey are the bad guys who killed Penny?"

"She ain't dead yet!"

As we passed Will Barnes at his newsstand, he overheard us and joined in, "Course she ain't dead yet."

"How do you even know who we're talking about, Will?" Bob asked.

"You boys are talking about Penny for sure. I see it in your voices. What did somebody do to our poor little steel Penny?"

"Mickey and Dad about killed her," Bob said.

"Lord have mercy, when a child ain't safe in her own home. Lord have mercy, I say."

I patted Will on the arm. "I agree."

"Tommy is taking me out to lunch." Bob gave Will a little hug and backed away. Guess he was still half crazy about Penny being almost killed.

Will patted Bob on the head, but he gazed my way like his eyes worked. "You must have hit a gold mine, taking your friend out to lunch, Tommy McConnell. Where have you been panning because I've never seen gold in the Brandywine? No sir. Of course I've never seen any other color in that crick either."

Will laughed at his little joke. "You better save some of that money for Penny so you can take her out or buy her things. Girlfriends like when their beaus buy for them. Lord have mercy. Amen."

Bob smiled and pumped his chest out. "Freeman gave him five bucks to feed me."

"Freeman the Cop gave Tommy McConnell five bucks?" Will scanned out on High Street with his dead eyes. He shouted, "Loco, loco, cop gives citizen money. Loco, loco!"

CHAPTER 26

Bob and I moved up to the corner and turned left on Gay Street, leaving Will Barnes to hawk the local paper and mingle with the spirit world.

Bob's smile vanished and his chest no longer puffed out. "Tell me about those 'other arrangements' Freeman mentioned."

I covered my mouth with my hands. "Orphanage."

"No way." Bob threw his arms out to his side like he had to or he'd pop for all the built up stuff brewing inside.

I grabbed Bob's shoulder. "It's where they send you if no one else will take care of you."

"My granddad would take me in." Bob shook his head like his grandfather does when he says no. "He's old though."

"Mom will let you stay with us, don't worry."

We stopped at Fullers on Gay Street.

"Let's sit in a booth." Bob slid into one without waiting for my reply.

Jenny wiggled her butt over in her yellow and pink waitress uniform. She wiped her hands on her apron while snapping her bubble gum. "You boys plan to eat or just take up space?"

Bob ordered a hamburger with French-fries. I asked for the hoagie. We both opted for black and white shakes.

Jenny headed for the kitchen with our orders.

I flipped through the song titles on the juke box control parked on the end of our tabletop. "So what happened?"

"Remember when I left your house?" Bob pointed his finger at the ceiling like a teacher about to make a point.

"Yeah?"

Bob placed both hands on the table. "I was on my way home, but decided to hide under Chief Hanson's desk in the police station instead."

"You what?"

Bob smiled for the first time since he told me about Penny. "I was under his desk for about an hour minding my own business. Chief Hanson wasn't around. Then Freeman found me."

"What did Freeman do to you?"

"Yanked me out fast, and it wasn't even his desk. Said Chief Hanson wouldn't be back 'till Monday. Said I'd have a long hide under Hanson's desk and asked why I was there in the first place."

"What did you say?"

Bob pulled his head back like he was dodging an invisible fist. "I told him the truth. You always tell the truth to the cops, particularly Freeman."

"And the truth was…"

Bob picked up the salt shaker and poured some on the table. "Tried to tell him I was playing Hide and Seek. Guess I came across as too old and scared. He said to tell him the truth, and this was the last time he would ask. He pulled out his blackjack, Tommy. And he meant it, too."

"So then what did you tell him?"

Bob tried to stand the salt shaker on edge in the little pile of salt he made. "What could I say? Told him the actual truth. He was the one holding the blackjack. I said I was hiding from my father and brother. He asked if they were home. I said they arrived this morning and weren't wasting any time beating the daylights out of me and Penny. Told him Penny was about dead by now."

"Wow, you said all that?"

Bob smiled as he let go of the salt shaker. It stood on edge in the salt pile. "Sure. The more I talked, the better the truth sounded. You should have seen the look on Freeman's face. Man, was he getting ticked. I shut up because I didn't want him fuming at me. Turns out he wasn't mad at me at all."

"So then what happened?" I gave the booth table a little bump but the salt shaker didn't fall.

"He grabbed my wrist and marched me out the front door of the police station up to our building. He stormed up the stairs dragging me behind and didn't bother to knock. Barged right on in."

"He allowed to?"

"Yeah. Freeman told me about it the time he chased me home from painting bases on the parking lot. Said he can break into your house if he is in hot pursuit of a bad guy. Tommy, my dad and brother are bad guys and besides what I told him had given him something called 'probable cause.' Freeman explained it to me the time I tried to chop down old Mrs. Glass' cherry tree."

"You whacked Mrs. Glass' cherry tree?" I grasped the pepper shaker.

"Long time ago. Miss Blitz at school talked about George Washington and the cherry tree. Figured if George could take one down, then I might as well, too. I got one chop with my trusty hatchet, though, before Freeman chased me home."

Jenny brought our order and sat down in the booth next to Bob.

"So where's your sister?" She snatched the pepper out of my hand before I could make a pile on the table.

"He was coming to that part." I slurped from my thick chocolate and vanilla shake.

"What do you mean?" She sprinkled pepper on Bob's french-fries.

"You ain't heard?" I asked.

"If I heard, I wouldn't be sitting with Bob and talking to you." Jenny snagged a fistful of Bob's fries. Bob twisted his straw and popped it in and out of his milkshake.

I wrapped my mitts around the hoagie. "Bob's about to tell how, oh never mind, tell her what happened, Bob."

Jenny poured ketchup on Bob's fries while Bob poked at his burger with a straw. "I've been waiting for you two to shut up so I could talk. Anyway, Jenny, I was over in the police station and told Freeman my brother and Dad were beating up on Penny and..."

"Crap. They out of jail?" Jenny grabbed Bob's arm.

Bob dropped the straw on the table. "Mickey's out of reform school. Dad's out of jail. Anyway, Freeman and I headed up to the apartment and Freeman opened the door..."

"He allowed?" Jenny asked.

"He's a cop, ain't he? Anyway, listen. He busted open the door and Penny was dead on the floor." Bob dragged a fry through the ketchup Jenny poured. He bounced it up and down on his plate.

Jenny jumped out of the booth seat and bent back over towards Bob like she didn't know which way to go. "No!"

Bob checked out Jenny with his eyes big like a doe's. "I thought she was dead..."

Jenny sat back down and smacked Bob hard in the upper part of his arm, making the ketchup fly off the fry in his hand. "Don't ever do that to me again, Bob Durkin. You scared the bejeebers out of me. How is she?" Tears welled up in her eyes.

I made myself busy by rotating my hoagie. The secret of eating a hoagie is to turn the meat to the outside and the lettuce and stuff to the inside so nothing will leak out.

"We don't know," Bob said. "I tried to hug and kiss her and make her better but she was busy looking dead with big pools of blood around her face and ... her head ... and... and... her mouth ... and her nose, too." Bob collapsed into

Jenny's arms. I checked to see how close Bob's face was to her boobs.

"What did Freeman do to your dad and brother?" Jenny sniffled.

"Nowhere to be found. Penny was in our apartment... by herself... bleeding." A tear dropped out of Bob's left eye, rolled down his cheek and plopped onto Jenny's blouse.

"Is she like okay or what?" Jenny pulled herself together. She pushed Bob into an upright position.

Bob wiped his cheek. "Took her away in an ambulance while I chased after Tommy. Don't know why I wanted him, except I was scared and Tommy should help me with stuff like this."

"So is she still alive or dead or what?" Jenny stared at Bob and then at me.

Bob gawked at me like he had more tears wanting to gush out of his eyes.

"She's or what, Jenny." I eyed my hoagie, but the long sandwich stared back, not wanting me to chomp.

Jenny glanced at me and then back at Bob. "So like tell me, how is Penny now?"

"Don't know." Bob rested his head on his arms which he folded on the table. His shoulders shook. Jenny pulled him close for a hug. The salt shaker fell over.

I swallowed a chunk of hoagie. Okay, when you're from a big family you eat. Food is scarce at my house. I jumped back into the conversation. "Freeman couldn't tell whether or not she would recover. You know why, don't you?"

Bob and Jenny stared at me. Bob's tears streamed down his face. Jenny snatched Bob's burger and chomped despite the tears in her own eyes. If they didn't stop gawking at me soon, I'd cry too. Instead, I pushed ahead to speak before I burst. "She's almost dead and Freeman doesn't think she'll live. Otherwise, he would have said she would be fine. If Freeman doesn't tell you somebody will be fine, they are not going to be fine. She'll be dead like Alan."

I was about to bust out crying so I turned away from Jenny and Bob.

A voice from the kitchen cried, "Jenny." I turned back.

Jenny hopped out of the booth and ran towards the kitchen with Bob's burger still in her hand. She tripped over a chair on the way, which she straightened. "Wait till you hear this, Mr. Hipplemeyer." Her voice faded away as she disappeared behind the kitchen door.

***

After the movie, Bob and I headed back to my house. Don't ask what movie we saw. Mostly we stared at the screen. Some Army flick, I think. We climbed up to my room so we could worry about Penny without a bunch of little kids hanging around.

Bob napped on Alan's bed with Mrs. McGillicutty curled up next to him. I tried to read my Huckleberry Finn from the library but I kept missing Alan and thinking about Penny.

Around five the phone rang downstairs. Bob and I jumped a foot. After a while, Mom came up and said Mrs. Durkin called. Bob would be sleeping over tonight. She said Penny has to stay in the hospital, and Mrs. Durkin was staying with her because she was a nurse and received special permission.

Bob started again with a few sobs and Mom said not to worry. They were keeping Penny to be sure she didn't have any serious injuries. Bob smiled. I wondered if Mom was making stuff up so we wouldn't worry.

CHAPTER 27

Bob stuffed a gun into his waistband. "If Dad kills Penny, I'll have to kill him. I swore to protect her."

We were out in my backyard after dinner. I held onto my pistol and sat on the top step of the back porch. Bob paced the tiny yard before sitting next to me.

Our weapons were cut from Dad's leftover pine from carpenter jobs. He sometimes made us machine guns, but they always broke pretty fast. The handguns held up longer. They were shaped like Army forty-fives. You could stretch rubber bands along the length of the wooden barrel to the handle. Then, bam, pick off a girl's skinny leg as she walked by in a dress. Or you could shoot each other.

I aimed at the steel drum Dad used to burn the trash. "Your Dad's way too big for you to tackle."

"I'll run away. Come back when I'm big." Bob pulled the gun out of his waistband to feel its heft. Being a pinewood gun, it didn't weigh much.

"You'll never be big enough." I popped off a pretend round.

"Why not?" He lifted his pistol to eye level and aimed at something over in Chiamaka's yard.

"Look at you. You take after your mom. You're huskier than me, but not like your Dad and big brother. They're broad shouldered and barrel-chested. You'd have to shoot them." I hoped Bob aimed for Chiamaka's rooster that crowed every morning.

"Pachool!" Bob blew the smoke off his barrel. "I wanted Freeman to shoot them this morning. Now, Penny is in the horsepistol. Dad and Mickey are out drinking beers."

I watched a pretend creature bite the dust. "Mickey's eighteen. Too young to drink."

"Dad will buy quarts. They'll hang out in the woods. They're probably sitting under that big oak at the top of Will Barnes's hill chugging beers right now. They'll toss the empties onto Cynthia Matting's pretend grave." Bob brought the gun up to eye level again and squeezed off two pretend rounds. "Pachool! Pachool!"

I followed Bob's aim into Chiamaka's yard where her rooster perched on top of a grey rotting doghouse. "Maybe they're tossing the empties onto Cynthia Matting's old grave. It's just a pile of dug up dirt now."

"What you steel pennies shooting at?" Chiamaka opened the gate to my yard.

"Aiming for your rooster, but Bob keeps missing." I patted Bob's shoulder.

"No, I killed the sucker with the first shot," Bob said.

"Better not shoot old Booker T. Washington, Jr. the fourth." Chiamaka looked at the rooster.

"Booker T. Washington, Jr. the fourth?" Bob smirked.

"It's what Dad named him and that's what we call him. Booker T for short. Mama says she will call him to supper one day, but I don't want to eat old Booker T. He don't bother nobody except early in the morning. Dad says he helps the hens lay eggs, but the hens do the work. Roosters just hang around and crow about it. 'Ain't that just like a man,' Mama says."

Coleman came up the alley past Chiamaka's house. We watched him walk into my yard. He wasn't smiling.

"Whatcha doing?" I asked.

"Never mind me. What have you been up to?" Coleman sounded angry. You don't want Coleman mad at you because he is the strongest fifteen-year-old anybody ever saw.

"Hmm, so what are you talking about?" I asked.

"You know what I'm referring to all right." Coleman folded his arms across his broad chest.

Bob said, "He and I both don't."

"It's about Tommy here, who everybody in West Chester knows is in love with your sister." Coleman softened his glare as he turned his attention to Bob. "By the way, how is your sister? Is she out of the horsepistol yet?"

"How'd you know about my sister?" Bob planted his hands on his hips.

"Everybody knows about Penny. Thought you were the only kid who didn't."

"Didn't know what?" Bob asked.

"She's in the horsepistol, and she's in love with Tommy McConnell." Coleman glared my way and I backed up a couple of steps. "Now then, Tommy, why are you kissing colored girls when you are in love with Penny Durkin?"

A cold, slithery snake named Fear crawled up my leg and was about to sink its fangs into my back. The fiend wanted to suck out all the colors from my spine except yellow. My older brothers, Sean and Leon, might come to my rescue if I shouted loud enough and remembered to remind them to bring a baseball bat. "Didn't kiss a colored girl. She kissed me."

Coleman smiled from ear-to-ear in his big friendly way. "Yeah, I was joshing you. Chiamaka is supposed to be sweet on me, but she's sweet on you instead. Now, you have two girlfriends. Which one do you plan to marry?"

"Coleman, shut your big mouth." Chiamaka had that look on her face that lets you know she is about to punch your lights out.

I planted my eyes on Coleman. "I'm thirteen years old. Penny is way too old for me, but we like each other, and when I'm older, who knows? By then, Penny may be married to some older guy."

Coleman peered at Chiamaka who back stepped towards the gate. "Chiamaka, come here, girl."

"Whatcha want, Coleman?" Chiamaka closed in on the back gate.

"Listen to what Tommy said. He's too young for Penny. She might marry some older steel penny before Tommy is big enough to be a real boyfriend to her. He is plenty available for you, but you have to wait your turn. Get in line, girl."

"Coleman, back off. I kissed him because I didn't want him to think colored girls didn't know how to kiss a steel penny. If you'd have seen the whopper Penny laid on him, you'd of figured you better look out for your interests, too."

Coleman threw his hands up. "Ain't no way I would have kissed Tommy McConnell. I don't care if the queen of Sheba kissed his butt."

Bob wore his pout. "Tommy, since when do you run around kissing my sister whenever you want?"

Bob didn't wait for an answer. I smacked into the dirt with a sore jaw before thinking about what to say. Coleman and Chiamaka laughed their heads off. Bob didn't laugh. I got up.

"She kissed you?" Bob asked.

"Penny and I are like boyfriend and girlfriend. We had a wonderful make-out session in the balcony on our date last Saturday."

I smashed into the ground again with two sore jaws or one jaw with two sore spots. I was dizzy and not sure which. Bob was not smiling, both of him.

"You liked it, didn't you, Tommy?" Bob's voice sounded far away.

My head buzzed but now there was only one Bob. "What?"

"Said you liked it." Bob's hands were on his hips which was a good place for them. I hoped they stayed there.

"I liked it. And if she wants to make out again, I'll like it again." I stayed on the ground seeing as how that was where Bob wanted me for this conversation.

"And you tell her she's pretty," Bob said.

"She's the prettiest girl I ever saw."

"Prettiest steel penny you ever saw," Chiamaka planted her hands on her hips.

"And you tell her you love her?" Bob asked.

"I... yi-yi."

"Admit it, Tommy," Coleman said. "Everybody already knows you two love each other. Go on. You'll feel better."

"I... what the heck. I love Penny Durkin. Now, are you satisfied?"

"I ain't satisfied," Chiamaka said.

I gazed up at Chiamaka. I wasn't sure if she wanted to slug me or kiss me. "Chiamaka, you are the prettiest colored girl I know."

"Too late now, Tommy McConnell. I'm through with steel pennies. Come on, Coleman, you can walk my butt on home." Chiamaka grabbed Coleman by the arm. She turned back to me with a stern expression. She pointed her finger at me. "No sense us staying here. They don't be needing colored folks hanging around when they in love with their steel penny girls."

"I ain't in love with nobody," Bob shouted.

Chiamaka had Coleman spun around and the two of them walked out of the yard. Chiamaka glanced back over her shoulder again. "Good, then you and I can hang together sometime."

Paul R. Lloyd

CHAPTER 28

"Let's hire Elvis." Bob flopped on Alan's bed.

"Bob, what does Elvis have to do with finding killers? The Hardy Boys would be digging up clues by now." I stretched out on my bed.

"Nah, Elvis might be too expensive," said Bob.

Mrs. McGillicutty curled up next to Bob's bare tummy.

I focused on the Hardy Boys. "Who would want to kill Johnny Bruce? That's the question we need to answer. Same guy might want to kill Penny."

Bob and I had our arms folded behind our heads. We were stripped to our underwear to stay cool in the dog-day heat of a July evening. I wished there was a breeze blowing in through the open window.

"We'll hire one of the bands from the Italian Social Club," said Bob.

I became excited. "That's it, Bob. There are bands of bad kids all over town. You got your Italians on the west side by St. Agnes. Your Irish down in Rig town. Your colored kids on the east side and some on the west side. Any one of those crowds could be involved in this."

Bob's voice sounded happy for the first time today. "So we'll book the band. We'll have the reception at the Italian Social Club, too."

"And the Greeks. We can't forget Menoitios. Where do the Greeks hang out anyway?" I watched Mrs. McGillicutty stretching by Bob.

178

"The Knights of Columbus Hall. Yeah, that could work. The Italian Social Club won't do. You're not Italian and Penny sure ain't Italian."

"We can't." I rolled over to face Bob.

"Sure we can. They make tuxedos for thirteen-year-olds, don't they?" Bob patted Mrs. McGillicutty between the ears.

I rolled back over to count the cracks on the ceiling. "Yeah, you're right. We have to find out who's after Penny without getting killed ourselves."

"Of course you two will have to talk to the priest about this stuff." Bob petted Mrs. McGillicutty who soaked it in with a purr.

"We can't talk to them, they'd kill us, Bob."

"Nah, once he gets over your ages, he'd be cool."

"Wait a minute. I have an idea."

"Good, because I'm about out of them. I know I'm the best man, but who will be the grooms? Your brothers? Means a lot of grooms." Bob watched Mrs. McGillicutty roll over.

"Every one of those older kids has little brothers or sisters in Catholic School or Public."

"Yeah, I see your older brothers in this. I'm not sure about your younger ones. And your sisters are way too young." Bob scratched Mrs. McGillicutty on the belly.

"I'll cover the Catholics, and Bob, you cover the publics."

"Wait. You lost me, Tommy."

"You cover the publics."

"What about the publics?"

"Some of the older kids in town who want to kill Penny have younger brothers and sisters. We'll find out who wants to kill Penny by talking to their kid brothers and sisters. We already know most of them."

"What does this have to do with planning your wedding?"

"I'm not getting married!"

"Hey, buddy, you can't fall in love with my sister without marrying her. What kind of friend are you, anyway?"

179

"Bob, I'm thirteen years old."

Bob rolled onto his side. "Yeah, like me. Don't worry. You'll be at least fourteen by the time we can plan a wedding."

"I'm too young to get married!"

Mom screamed up the steps, "Hey, you boys quiet down. The little ones are trying to sleep."

Bob sat up. He whispered, "You said you loved Penny."

I sat up to face Bob. "I have strong feelings for Penny. Is it love? How does anyone know for sure when they're in love? What is love anyway? I want to kiss your sister's sweet lips, hear her syrupy voice, feel her arms around me, be wherever she is, hold her in my arms, touch her soft cheeks..."

Bob was on top of me with a fist poised to smash my face.

I held up my one free hand and pointed one finger up. "But should your sister marry when she's seventeen and broken to pieces in the horsepistol?"

"She'll be eighteen by the wedding and all better long before. She's a tough girl. Don't worry." Bob climbed off me and back onto Alan's bed where the cat stretched and resisted Bob as he pushed her out of the middle of the mattress.

"Bob, are you listening to me?" I asked.

"It'll be like the kings of England. Didn't they get married when they were little kids so they could make treaties with other countries? Isn't that how Henry the VIII married eight times so he could make eight treaties? Then he broke them all and started World War I. Don't you remember nothing from history?"

"Look at me, Bob. Do you see a king? Can you imagine getting married as a kid? When I grow up, I'll marry your sister."

"That's a long time away."

"Yeah, so?"

"I can't wait that long for you to marry my sister. You guys would be doing too much kissing and hugging and not enough marrying."

"Bob, what are you talking about?"

"I don't know. Marriage stuff. Making babies. Do you want to wait until you're twenty years old to make a baby?"

"Sure, why not?"

"That's old, Tommy."

The window screen clattered. Dad put wooden screens on the windows in our house. They had a hook-and-eye latch to keep them from falling out, but they rattled in the wind.

We heard a voice in the darkness, "Ooooh, I'm the ghost of Alan and I want my bed tonight. Who be sleeping in my bed?"

"What was that?" I asked.

"Sounded like Alan's voice."

I landed on the floor between the wall and my bed. Bob was out of sight. He might have been under Alan's bed.

I thought I would be seeing Cynthia Matting again as I peeked over the side of my bed to the window. "That wasn't Alan."

"Yes it was," Bob said from somewhere out of sight beyond Alan's bed.

"Sounded too girlie, Bob"

A girlish giggle floated in on hot, dark, stale, still air.

"Did Cynthia giggle like that?" I asked.

Bob poked his head above the mattress. He was stuck between Alan's bed and the wall. We gawked at each other, and neither of us moved.

A voice said, "Ain't you letting me in?"

"Chiamaka!" Bob said.

We pulled sheets off the bed to cover our underwear.

I meandered to the window, unlatched the screen and pushed it out at the bottom. Chiamaka climbed in.

"Be careful the screen doesn't fall out," I said.

Chiamaka's thin summer pajamas covered her top and bottom but not her long, skinny chocolate legs. She wasn't wearing shoes.

Mrs. McGillicutty snuck out the window.

"What are you steel pennies up to?" Chiamaka asked.

"Talking," Bob reached around for his clothes.

Chiamaka handed Bob his pants, "Appears to me like you be flying off the beds and scurrying on the floor in your underwear. You boys ready to have a midnight adventure?"

"It's not midnight, yet." I grabbed my pants before Chiamaka could reach them.

"You ain't on an adventure yet, either, Tommy. I'm in the middle of one myself. Ain't every night a little colored girl climbs into a steel penny's bedroom."

"What do you want to do, Chiamaka?" Bob buckled his belt.

"I told you I climbed into a steel penny's bedroom so the question is what do you boys want to do? You can't have an adventure staying around here."

"What kind of adventure would you like?" Bob asked.

I rubbed my jaw. "Don't know." Then the answer came to me. "Bob, where would you like to visit tonight more than anywhere else in the world?"

"You kidding?" Bob's eyes were about to pop.

"Where do you want to go, Bob?" Chiamaka plopped on Alan's bed next to him.

I smoothed my pants over the sheet that covered my lap. "He wants to visit Penny in the horsepistol."

Chiamaka shook her head. "Ain't no adventure for me. Sneaking into the crazy house, now that would be an adventure."

I smiled at Chiamaka. "The horsepistol is way on the other side of town."

"Okay, Tommy. Let's take off," said Chiamaka.

Bob put his shirt on. I realized I was still holding my pants and hadn't been worrying much about the sheet.

Chiamaka said, "Your legs be mighty white, Tommy. Don't they ever see the sun?"

I ignored her.

While we pulled our shoes on, Chiamaka said, "I be needing some pants, too."

I reached into Alan's bureau and removed a pair of his blue jeans. "Try on Alan's pants. Nobody else is wearing them."

Chiamaka raised her hands in protest. "I ain't putting no dead steel penny's slacks on my butt."

I dumped the jeans on her lap. "He wasn't wearing this pair when he was murdered, Chiamaka."

"I have confidence in you, Tommy, but I'm not sure I trust these pants. Give me some socks and sneaks, too."

I found a pair of white socks in Alan's sock drawer. Bob reached under the bed for Alan's sneaks.

"Are these Alan's?" Chiamaka asked.

"Not anymore." My head hurt but I wouldn't cry.

Chiamaka pulled on the socks and sneakers. She tied the sneaks as tight as she could, but they were still loose.

"Wait a second." I snatched a couple of big globs of toilet paper from the bathroom. "Here, stuff these up where your toes go. Advantage of a big family is you learn how to make your big brother's shoes fit."

Chiamaka stuffed the toilet paper into the sneaks and they fit better, but still looked like clown feet. She rolled the pant legs up several folds so they didn't drag. I handed her one of my old belts I outgrew to hold up her pants.

"Better let me borrow a shirt, too," Chiamaka said.

I withdrew a tee shirt from Alan's drawer. Chiamaka tried smoothing the oversize shoulders which came down to her elbows. Her puffy pajama top made the tee shirt extra fat.

She smoothed the tee shirt down the front. "These be adventuring clothes borrowed from a dead steel penny. Life don't get much better. You boys will have to do with what you have. A colored girl wears a dead white boy's clothes, she

Paul R. Lloyd

automatically on an adventure, and if the dead steel penny comes chasing after his clothes, well, that beats all, don't it?"

I shook my head. "Doubt if we'll run into Alan tonight."

"Could happen," Bob said. "Be fun to see what a steel penny ghost does to a poor colored girl who borrowed his clothes."

Chiamaka gave Bob the glare she used when she didn't know whether to kiss you or slug you.

I climbed through the window to hold the screen in place at the top.

The moon was full and a billion specks lit the summer sky. We took turns jumping from the porch roof outside my window into the darkness below.

CHAPTER 29

Two white boys and a colored girl wandering around the ritzy north end of West Chester late at night might be in big trouble if a cop happened by.

On our way to the north side, we passed the Bordeaux Restaurant. It was closed but the neon sign cast a purple haze over the corner of Walnut and Market streets.

"Let's kick Jamie Bordeaux out of bed." Bob pointed to a second floor window above his family's restaurant.

"Don't know how we can. His building has straight walls with no porch roof or anything to climb up," I said.

"Bob, let's save Jamie Bordeaux for another adventure," said Chiamaka.

We crossed Gay Street despite the busy traffic. High and Gay Streets had cars and trucks passing day and night. Walnut Street ran downhill north of Gay. We walked past the YMCA building in the middle of the first block. Its big sign was turned off for the night. The Y was a great place because they had swimming and showed free scary movies at their annual Halloween party.

I thought about Bob in swimming class one time when we were both about eight. He slipped off his swim trunks to change back into street clothes, and his entire butt was black and blue. I asked him what happened and he said his dad had whipped him proper. I said he must have done something awful bad to warrant such a beating. He said no, his dad just loved to whoop on him.

185

"Loco, loco, Love's not always a safe game to play."

"I hear him, but I don't see ol' Will Barnes," Chiamaka latched onto Bob's arm while moving in close to him.

"Where you at, Will?" I faced Bob and Chiamaka. "Sounded like up in the tree."

"What's he talking about?" Chiamaka asked.

"He's always saying weird stuff and predicting what will happen." Bob untangled himself from Chiamaka's grip.

Chiamaka said, "I know and he ain't never been wrong according to my grandma, and she ain't never been wrong neither."

I checked out the tree tops, but couldn't see a thing in any of them. "He's doing an outstanding job of hiding."

"He is, boys. He floated off somewhere with the spirits. He can see with them blind eyes when he's with the spirits." Chiamaka grabbed hold of Bob's arm again.

"Can't hang around here all night. I want to visit Penny," Bob yanked away from Chiamaka and tore up Walnut.

"I'll stay with you steel pennies, but this appears to be a mighty fine adventure right here exploring where Will Barnes went." Chiamaka jogged ahead to catch Bob. She took his arm again.

We continued north on Walnut Street past big old houses and huge horse chestnut trees. Most of the trees around town were horse chestnuts with a few walnuts, oaks and whatevers thrown in.

We cut through the midnight dark alley behind the horsepistol.

"What are you kids doing out?" Mickey Durkin blocked our way. Bob grabbed my arm. His hands shook.

Chiamaka stepped between us and Mickey. "Don't you bother these steel pennies, white trash, or I'll call out the Midnight Colored Patrol on you. The MCP be right around the corner. Look for yourself if you don't believe me."

"Nah, I believe you. Always something new when you leave town for a while. You kids better get home. Bob,

Freeman the Cop can't protect you forever. Dad and I are biding our time."

"Wh—wha—what do you want here?" Bob asked.

"Did you think a stupid hospital was a safe place for Penny to hide from me and Dad? He's sneaking in now to finish whooping her. When he's done, it's my turn. She can't go around with colored boys and expect to not be beat. Yeah, Dad and I heard about her running around with Johnny Bruce." Mickey folded his arms. He reminded me of the genie from Sinbad the Sailor.

"No!" Bob charged Mickey like a tackle in football, knocking him into a rose bush. Chiamaka and I knew when to cut out, so we were right behind Bob as he charged for the loading dock at the back of the horsepistol. The bay doors were down and locked. At the end of the building, the regular entry door for workers was locked, too. Footsteps rang out behind us.

We took off around the building where Chiamaka ducked behind a row of big trash barrels, the kind made from old steel drums. Bob and I squeezed in beside her so we were out of sight.

We spotted another entry door, but before we could check it out, Mickey stormed around the corner of the building headed our way.

CHAPTER 30

Mickey Durkin scattered several of the trash barrels, spilling bloody rags and other hospital junk in the alley. He kicked one of the cans and hopped on one foot like that steel trash barrel was harder than his foot. He drifted to the entrance door on this side of the building. "Stupid jerks," he muttered.

After a minute of waiting to see if Mickey would return, Bob nudged me on the shoulder. "We better find Penny before Mickey does."

He crawled over me and made his way to the side door. Chiamaka was right behind him, and I followed. Inside, we discovered a concrete stairwell.

"Which way?" Bob asked.

"She in the second floor ladies ward in the back," Chiamaka said. "Follow me."

"How do you know?" I asked.

"Cops parked Aunt Edna in one of the beds when she crashed her Buick last year. It's where the accident ladies end up so they stay away from the sick people and don't be catching no diseases."

We reached the top step to the second floor when Mickey charged down from the stairwell to the third floor.

"Going somewhere, you little twerps?" Mickey pounded his fist into his hand.

Chiamaka pushed in front of us. I stepped up beside her. We heard Bob take off through the doorway to the second floor.

"Your brother be getting away, white trash," Chiamaka said.

Mickey pushed Chiamaka hard against the wall. He punched my chest, sending me towards the steps. As Mickey closed in to bash my face, my foot tangled up with his, and we both stumbled. Chiamaka kicked Mickey behind the knee. He fell over the top step and rolled past me to the bottom. I saved my butt by grabbing hold of the railing. Chiamaka placed a death grip on me so I wouldn't fall.

"I told him not to be messing with me." Chiamaka pulled me up into a hug. We gazed at each other weird for a moment. Chiamaka planted a quick kiss on my lips and giggled.

"You kiss nice," she said.

"Let's find Bob." I shook my head.

"He's with your girlfriend by now. Let's see how messed up she is."

At the big double doors to the ladies ward, Bob was crying. "Where is she?" he asked. "Did she die?"

My stomach felt like it dropped out of my body. I fell to the floor and put my head between my legs. Bob took hold of one of my arms while Chiamaka snatched the other to pull me up.

"Okay?" Bob asked.

"You really do like her, don't you?" Chiamaka asked.

That smile crept across my face, the one that always pops out when I think of Penny. "Yeah, Chiamaka, I do. Bob, don't ask if she's dead when she ain't."

"Don't you boys know nothing about no horsepistols? She ain't in the ward for one of three reasons." Chiamaka counted on her fingers. "One, they sent her home because she been faking. Two, she's dead and down in the morgue. We can sneak in later and check the bodies. You'll be happy,

Tommy, 'cause if she's dead, they be stripping her naked. Dead people don't need no clothes no more."

I caught Bob's arm as he was about to unload on Chiamaka.

Chiamaka glared at Bob for a second like she couldn't figure out what his problem was. "Third, they gave her a private room on the third floor because she's messed up so bad they don't want to scare the other patients, or she needs to be protected from somebody, or they arrested her and she's off to jail after she's done here."

We ran up the stairwell with Bob in the lead. At the top, Bob peeked out the door into the hallway. I spied over his head. Chiamaka squeezed in under him to peer out.

"Bunch of rooms," Bob said.

"Better hope she's at this end of the hall," Chiamaka said. "Be tough sneaking past the nurse's station. You steel pennies better wait for me. I'll signal when I find her room."

Chiamaka disappeared into the first room, ran across the hall, checked the next one, and then worked her way down the long corridor until she peeped out of the last door.

My head started to spin.

Chiamaka strolled past the nurse's station to the passage on the other side. No one noticed her this late at night.

"What if Penny is dead?" I asked.

"She can't be dead," Bob said.

"Yes, I know. But what if she is?"

"She can't die from a simple beating."

"Right, but what if she died anyway?"

"If you're still alive when they get you to the horsepistol, you don't die from a beating."

"But Will Barnes said I loved her alive or dead."

"She can't be dead."

"But what if she is?"

"Yeah, what if she is dead?" Bob screamed down the hall.

I followed him while screaming at the top of my lungs. "Aaaaaghhhh!"

***

Chiamaka was in the middle of the hallway ahead of us. She pointed into a room. We stopped screaming. People were making noise behind us, and the noise grew louder as they headed in our direction.

Bob stopped at the door and let out a huge breath. "Don't ever scare me again."

"Hey, you're the one who took off running and screaming." I breathed deep from the run.

"You made me think she was dead." Bob punched my shoulder.

"She was dead, wasn't she?" I gazed into the room.

Penny sat in a chair. She held a heavy paper coffee cup to her lips. It was the kind restaurants give you for takeout. She tried to smile over the cup, but stopped as tears came out of her good eye, the one half open. After a few sniffles, her half open eye filled with love. My heart broke as I fought back the tears.

Bob reached out to embrace Penny. She handed her coffee to Chiamaka to hold while she tilted her head a little and lifted her arms enough to notice. Their mom grabbed Bob before he reached Penny. "Oh, no you don't. Your sister is in a lot of pain right now."

Penny gazed over at me, shrugged slightly and waved her fingers to show she wanted me to come to her. I entered the room followed by several orderlies and a couple of nurses.

Penny's legs were covered with bandages.

Mrs. Durkin said, "They're with me, now."

"But, Bonnie, we have rules," one of the nurses said.

"I know, Mildred, but my daughter almost died today. She can have time with her brother and her boyfriend." Mrs. Durkin had wet eyes, but she smiled.

"Boyfriend?" the nurse asked. She herded the orderlies and the other nurse out of the room. "It's Tommy McConnell. Too young if you ask me." She left the room. We heard her voice from down the hall. "But nobody around here ever asks me because I'm only the night duty supervisor."

I had never been called anybody's boyfriend, especially by their mother. This thought made me happy.

Penny held my paw in her limp right hand. She held Bob's the same way in her left.

Chiamaka sipped Penny's coffee. "Yech, how can you drink this stuff?"

"She needs to stay awake," Mrs. Durkin said.

"How do you feel?" Despite myself, I gawked at Penny's swollen face like she was a monster from a Saturday matinee.

Penny smiled at me and then turned to her mom.

Mrs. Durkin said, "It hurts too much for her to speak right now. She has stitches in her mouth that you can't see and has to drink her coffee in little sips."

"Why is she drinking coffee?" Chiamaka snatched some sugar packets off a tray on top of Penny's nightstand. She ripped them open and dumped the sugar into the cup.

"She has to stay awake all night in case she has a concussion," Mrs. Durkin said.

"Why?" Bob asked.

Mrs. Durkin said, "So she doesn't slip into a coma."

"A comma?" I pictured Penny sitting next to a word in the middle of a sentence with her legs hanging down. She wore her pretty white blouse and white Bermudas. She smiled and had no bruises or injuries.

"A coma," Mrs. Durkin repeated. "It's when you fall asleep and can't wake up. You can stay asleep for days, weeks or the rest of your life."

My knees buckled, but I caught myself. Penny gazed up at me and then rubbed the side of her head against my arm. It must have been the one spot not in pain.

I pictured the back of the closet in Mom and Dad's bedroom where they hide the Christmas presents every year next to Dad's double-barrel.

Penny tugged on Bob's hand.

Bob smiled at her. "What?"

Penny moved her head from side to side a tiny bit.

Mrs. Durkin pointed to the nightstand. "Give her the pad of paper with the pen so she can write."

Bob moved the tray aside and spotted some paper and a pen. He handed them to Penny.

Chiamaka held the paper cup to her nose and sniffed. "Penny, you be drinking this coffee? Because if you ain't, it's starting to taste mighty sweet over here." This was followed by a loud slurp.

While we laughed, Penny half smiled and tried to hold her laughter in. Now, she appeared like she was in pain from the laughter.

Penny released my hand and wrote in slow motion. When she finished she gazed at Bob with her one good but tear-filled eye.

Bob took the note. "It's all right, Penny." He wiped tears from his eyes.

I took the pad and read "My hero."

Penny pointed to the nightstand. Bob asked, "What?"

Their mom said, "She wants a tissue, Bob. See the box in the space down below."

Bob handed a tissue to Penny. She dabbed at her mouth. The tissue came away covered in blood.

Her mom knelt down next to her. "Let me see, Penny."

Penny opened her mouth a tiny bit and groaned. Her mom took hold of her bottom lip and turned it out. We saw where the doctor had to sew her up. Blood trickled around the stitches.

Mrs. Durkin released the lip. "It's only a tiny leak."

We laughed, including Penny who tried to ignore the pain.

Mildred, the night duty supervisor, returned. "Bonnie, they need you in Emergency."

"I'm not working tonight, Mildred. I'm caring for my daughter with Doctor Blue's permission."

"Yes, but they brought your son into Emergency. They found him at the bottom of the stairwell. He has a broken leg. You'll want to see about him."

"Serves him right," Mrs. Durkin said. "You children wait here while I take care of Mickey. If Penny needs anything, push the button by her bed to call the nurse. And don't let her fall asleep. Call the nurse if you have to."

"We'll keep her awake, Mom. Don't worry," Bob said.

Mrs. Durkin kissed Bob and Penny on the head. Penny winced.

"Sorry, honey," Mrs. Durkin disappeared out the door.

Penny stared at Bob and then me with as nice a smile as you're bound to see from someone with a mouth full of stitches and a swollen face.

Chiamaka said, "Taught your big brother not to mess with me."

Penny snuck a glance at Chiamaka with what might be a questioning face given her condition.

"Penny, let me tell you what happened to Mickey," I said.

"Tommy, ain't nothing for you to tell. I kicked Mickey down the stairs is what happened." Chiamaka planted her hands on her hips.

I explained what Chiamaka and I did together to cause Mickey to fly down the stairwell.

Chiamaka folded her arms as her eyes tightened. "You lucky you didn't soar down those stairs yourself, Tommy. You were working on it, but you grabbed hold of the stair rail when I kicked Mickey in the back of the knee. With his big bottom, gravity did the rest. I may be just going into eighth grade, but I know my science. A big butt properly kicked goes down easy."

Penny rocked back and forth to indicate yes instead of nodding her head. She smiled. She picked up the notepad and added to the message which she handed to Chiamaka.

Chiamaka read, "My hero 2."

"See, you're a hero, Chiamaka," said Bob.

Chiamaka stared at Bob like he was nuts and then turned to Penny. "We be women so I'm your heroine. But don't think I won't steal Tommy McConnell from you one of these days."

Penny smiled.

"Thought you liked Bob, now?" I said.

"I like Bob fine. He's handsome. Tommy, you be looking like Howdy Doody."

Everyone laughed except me, so I grabbed a tissue for Penny to wipe the blood leaking from her mouth stitches.

Things quieted down until Penny made a chirpy bird noise at the back of her throat and waved her hand in front of her face.

"She be eating hot chili peppers," Chiamaka said.

"She be needing more hot coffee." I winced as Chiamaka punched me on the arm.

"She can't stop yawning. Must be painful." Bob took off out the door. Chiamaka shook her head a few times and pushed the nurse's button.

Later, Bob returned with a nurse who carried a tray. On the tray sat a cup of coffee in a heavy paper container.

"Let it cool, Penny," said Mildred the nurse. Penny nodded from her waist in her full body way. The nurse left.

Bob sat on the side of the bed. Penny was in her chair. I was in the other chair. Chiamaka fell asleep on Penny's bed with my brother's oversized clothes billowing around her.

Later, Mrs. Durkin returned. I popped up in my chair from somewhere far away and glanced over at Penny. She sipped her coffee, which gave me a sigh of relief.

Bob said, "Don't worry, Tommy. I kept Penny company. We were planning ways for you and me to protect her."

"Good."

Mrs. Durkin said, "I forgot about you children. You better head for home. It's close to one o'clock. Bob, stay at Tommy's until I can bring Penny home from the hospital. In the meantime, I'll be here at nights."

"Penny's coming home tomorrow, ain't she?" Bob asked.

"No, Bob. It may take a few days. The doctors will decide."

"But, Mom, you need sleep," Bob whined.

"I'll be able to sleep when the doctors say Penny can sleep," said Mrs. Durkin.

"Okay, Mom," Bob said.

"Don't forget to wake your little friend," said Mrs. Durkin.

Bob turned to Chiamaka sleeping on the bed. She was on her side facing away from us, curled up and making a perfect target. Bob slapped her hard on the behind. Chiamaka popped awake and glared at us. Bob reached the door where he wore a big grin on his face.

"Bob Durkin, I'm gonna throw your sorry but handsome butt down the stairwell," Chiamaka said.

"Tommy did it." Bob had a satisfied grin on his face. "I was way over here. Besides, my mother raised me to be a nice boy."

"Then you the nice boy who slapped my behind."

"You don't think Tommy's guilty?" Bob asked.

Chiamaka was off the bed with her hands on her hips. "Nope. Tommy don't be slapping no girls on the behind. He don't be slapping no girls no ways. His Dad brung him up to respect a lady and I be a lady."

"Young lady and you two gentleman, how about leaving now?" asked Mrs. Durkin.

"Will Mickey be waiting for us?" Bob asked.

Mrs. Durkin placed her hand on Bob's shoulder. "He's on crutches. I sent him home in a cab some time ago. Be careful walking home. You'll be okay."

"Yeah, let's take off. I'm pooped." At least my yawns didn't hurt like Penny's.

Chiamaka gave me a cold stare. "Whatcha tired about? You didn't do nothing. I beat up a giant white boy, threw him down a stairwell, and I'm ready for another adventure. I say let's skedaddle out of this place."

We said goodbye to Penny and her mom before we skedaddled.

CHAPTER 31

"Those be ghosts." Chiamaka leaned her head way back as she checked the tree tops. We were on our way home after our midnight visit with Penny in the horsepistol.

"Not ghosts," Bob said. "Just the breeze."

"I hear your brother calling your name, Tommy," Chiamaka said.

"Not funny," I said.

"Oooooo!"

"Who said that?" Chiamaka grasped Bob's left arm with both hands.

"Tommy." Bob tried to yank himself away from Chiamaka.

"Didn't say nothing." I was not about to sound scared. Instead, I contemplated which of the two wise guys with me had made the noise.

"It be Alan," Chiamaka whispered.

"Oooooo!"

I said, "It's not Chiamaka. Sounded like a guy. Bob, it must be you."

"I can't go oooooo." Bob garbled a sick ogoowwhggeeee sound.

"Ain't Bob 'cause I watched every move his lips made," said Chiamaka.

"Oooooo!"

I pointed up. "It's from the tree."

"Where?" Bob's head swung back and forth as he gazed into the tree above.

"Oooooo!"

"It's an owl," I said.

"Alan, you be up in that tree scaring your poor brother and his friends?" Chiamaka wrapped both arms around Bob.

"Yeeeesss."

"Ain't no Owl," Bob said.

"Not Alan either," I said.

"Sure sounds like your Alan," Chiamaka said.

The branches on the huge walnut started low. Rich summer foliage meant the owners were hosing it, despite the drought. Although the moon was still out, the thick layers of leaves made it easy for someone to hide.

"Let's climb," I said.

"You nuts?" Bob asked.

Chiamaka leaped up to take hold of the lowest branch. "Tommy, sometimes you be having great ideas for midnight adventures."

I followed.

"I'll wait here to catch the bodies," Bob said.

"Doooonnn't cliiimmbbb the treeeeee."

"We be coming up to catch your butt, Alan McConnel, then you be doing our will. We be sending you to haunt Mickey Durkin so he be running away to Cleveland."

"Noooooo."

When I reached the third branch from the bottom, I took a gander up. Chiamaka disappeared into the foliage above me on the left. We heard laughter from the other side of the tree away from Chiamaka.

"Jamie Bordeaux, climb down here," Bob called.

"I'm noooot Jaaaammmiee Bordeauuuux."

Chiamaka imitated the sound. "Yeessss youuuu arrrre."

Chiamaka and I climbed back down.

"Let's throw rocks," Chiamaka said.

Jamie Bordeaux dropped out of one of the lower limbs and landed at our feet in a squatting position. He straightened up. "So what are you guys up to?"

"We visited Penny in the horsepistol," Bob said.

"Explains why you weren't home when I dropped by to scare you." Jamie Bordeaux's teeth glimmered in the moonlight.

"I be beating you to that old trick by a couple of hours," Chiamaka said. "I done scared them steel pennies, too, didn't I?"

"Did not," Bob said.

"Bob was the one under Alan's bed. I scrambled as far as the floor under mine. Chiamaka did a good job."

"You be doing a fine job up in the tree, Jamie Bordeaux," Chiamaka said. "I thought sure you be Alan come to haunt us poor children to death."

I peeked up into the tree. Cynthia Matting waved to me from one of the branches.

"Look!" I cried.

"What?" Bob asked. Everyone stared up into the tree.

"I see Cynthia." I pointed at her.

"Yeah, right," Jamie Bordeaux said.

Cynthia faded away.

"Scared the crap out of me." I rubbed my jaw to figure out what I saw.

"Cynthia is not up a tree," Bob said. "Remember, I'm the guy who watched as you yanked her skull out of the earth. Shouldn't go around digging up dead people, Tommy."

Chiamaka raised her hands and waved them about while pretending to be a ghost. "Yeah, she not be liking when you tickled the inside of her skull. She is haunting you for sure."

"It was your imagination, Tommy," Jamie Bordeaux said.

"The heck with dead girls. What are you doing out here in the middle of the night, Jamie Bordeaux?" Bob asked.

Jamie Bordeaux waved his arms about. "I told you I snuck into Tommy's bedroom. You guys should hook the screen when you leave. Of course you'd have to rip a hole in the screen first."

"Not the best idea in the middle of mosquito country," I said.

"Not many mosquitoes in the drought," Chiamaka said.

"Then I covered for you boys when your mom knocked on the door," said Jamie Bordeaux.

I took hold of Jamie Bordeaux's arm. "Mom never bothers with my room."

"She did this time. I pretended she woke me up and said, 'We're sleeping, leave us alone.'" Jamie Bordeaux made his voice sound like an old man's.

"You didn't," I said.

"Yeah I did. Your mom said, 'You feeling okay, Tommy?' so I said, 'Shhh, don't wake Bob up.'" Jamie Bordeaux used his tired old man voice again.

"We talking all night or going home?" Chiamaka asked.

"Home." Bob yawned.

We hiked down Walnut Street past the Y and then across Gay Street. I thought about why Cynthia's ghost bothered me. "You'd think Cynthia would thank me for finding her missing body so she could have a proper burial."

Chiamaka smacked me on the arm. "She's haunting you because you found her dry bones, Tommy. She wants to thank you with a ghost kiss. She's hot for you now. Maybe she'll tell you who done her in."

"No sense asking her about it. Ghost testimony won't hold up in court," said Bob, our resident expert on the law.

Gay Street was empty, but we saw a couple of trucks cross Gay at High Street down the next block. We followed Walnut south to the parking lot behind the Bordeaux restaurant.

Jamie Bordeaux said, "Let's get some booze."

"Let's get some sleep," Chiamaka said.

"This won't take long." Jamie Bordeaux meandered over to the trash bins and fiddled around with some boxes. He pulled out a whiskey bottle. "They're supposed to be empty, but sometimes the lazy bartender throws them away with a little whiskey left in them. This one has a couple of shots."

Jamie Bordeaux offered the bottle to Chiamaka.

"Don't ask me to drink whiskey out of the trash bin," she said.

Jamie Bordeaux handed it to Bob.

Bob took the open bottle and sniffed. "Smells like piss to me."

Jamie Bordeaux said, "Ain't piss. Take a sip. It'll put hair on your chest."

"Nah, too tired to climb into Tommy's room drunk as a skunk." Bob handed me the bottle.

I remembered my Uncle Jack and his Irish whiskey as I took in the rye smell. I tilted the bottle up. The booze burned my throat. It left a taste worse than the Irish booze. "What awful crap did you give me?"

Jamie Bordeaux tapped the label on the bottle. "Cheap bar stock for making whiskey sours and other mixed drinks. Ain't so bad once you dump in orange juice or something else sweet."

"Have anything sweet?" I smacked my lips like I ate a lemon.

"Let me take a look." Jamie Bordeaux rummaged around in the trash bins again.

"Ewww!" Chiamaka grasped her stomach.

"Never mind." I tilted the bottle again. The whiskey burned but not as bad as my other swallow.

"You're drinking your whiskey straight," Jamie Bordeaux said.

"I can wash it down with water or iced tea at home." My next swallow was a big one, hot on the back of my throat.

"Hey, save some for me." Jamie Bordeaux yanked the bottle away and upended it. He dumped it back in the trash. "Let's get out of here."

Bob pointed to Jamie Bordeaux's back door. "You're home."

"Yeah, but I left a note for my mom saying I was spending the night at Tommy's house. Said I'd be home by dinner tomorrow." Jamie Bordeaux encircled Bob's shoulders with his arm.

"We have but one extra bed," I said.

"One's enough." Jamie Bordeaux pointed a finger in the air.

"Tommy gave it to me." Bob popped a tiny pout.

"Yeah, just kidding. I laid out my sleeping bag on your floor."

I shook my head. What would Mom think if she found three of us asleep in my room? I could hear her saying, "I'm not feeding extra kids. You send those boys home this minute. I don't care if it is the middle of the night and Bob has nowhere to go." But Mom wasn't talking at the moment.

We headed across Market Street by Rubenstein's where we continued south as far as the alley. Chiamaka crossed Walnut and sashayed down the alley. We kept an eye on her until she arrived at her house. She waved to us in the moonlight to let us know she was okay. We watched until she snuck back into her house.

We shuffled off to my house and discovered Mrs. McGillicutty on the porch. She meowed at the door. We tried to be quiet with the front door, which we never locked. Jamie Bordeaux tripped over Blair's tricycle in the living room.

Bob said, "Shhhhhh."

I closed the door as quietly as possible. "You guys sneak upstairs and don't make a sound. I'll get a drink from the refrigerator. If Mom or Dad wake up, they'll think somebody got up for a drink of water or something to eat."

They disappeared into the darkness of the stairs while Mrs. McGillicutty and I made our way through the living room and dining room to the kitchen. Moonlight shone through the windows.

From the refrigerator, I grabbed a glass pitcher half-filled with iced tea. I snatched a jelly glass from the cabinet, filled it and drank. Mrs. McGillicutty rubbed around my feet. From upstairs, I heard one of the boys bang into something in the bathroom. I kicked the stove to make a bigger noise, said "Ouch" loud and hit some stuff around the kitchen. Mrs. McGillicutty ran out of the room. I finished the iced tea and climbed the stairs.

I tripped over Jamie Bordeaux on my bedroom floor and landed on top of him. He laughed despite trying not to. This started me laughing and Bob couldn't keep quiet.

The old windup alarm clock parked on Alan's bureau said half past two. I climbed into bed and stared out the window. I thought about what would happen if I wasn't able to keep Penny alive.

CHAPTER 32

"Children heal fast," Mom said, and with eleven kids, she was the expert. Three days after our visit to the horsepistol, we heard the slow clatter of footsteps up the stairs to Bob's apartment. Bob ran to open the door. I stood beside him. Judging by the expression on his face and the way I felt, we both wore our happy faces.

Mickey stayed in his stuffed living room chair with his broken leg propped up on a kitchen chair. A pair of wooden crutches leaned against the wall nearby.

Penny reached the landing and smiled at us. Her "Herlo" sounded almost normal. Bob hugged her and planted a kiss on her cheek. She patted me on the chest and gave me a quick peck on the cheek before she entered the room.

Her faded grey poodle skirt swished as she struggled past us. It went with her pretty white blouse. Penny's face showed fading bruises, and her black eyes had transformed into a yellow and green mask. She glared at Mickey until he stared back. She hugged me and kissed me full on the lips as he watched. "Hiyer, cham," she mumbled.

I didn't know where "champ" came from, but I liked it.

Mrs. Durkin entered the apartment. She carried a small overnight case of Penny's things. Bob took the suitcase into the bedroom.

Penny lowered herself gently onto the living room couch.

Mickey's voice sounded shaky. "Hi, Penny. You feeling better?"

Penny ignored him.

In a hesitant, slow voice, Mickey said, "Penny, I want to say how sorry I am. I should not have treated you that way. You deserve better."

To my ears, it sounded rehearsed.

Penny continued to ignore him. "Tommy. Bob." She wiggled her hand at us to indicate she wanted us to join her on the couch.

Bob returned from the bedroom and sat on one side of Penny with me on the other. She lifted her arms around our shoulders. She kissed us both on the cheek.

Mickey stared at Penny like he expected her to speak to him. Penny pretended he wasn't home.

Mrs. Durkin brought a glass of water to Penny along with a handful of little pills. Penny pressed her palm full of pills to her mouth. After she dropped her hand away, Penny drank a huge gulp of water and swallowed.

The phone rang. We turned in the direction of the kitchen wall above the counter. Mrs. Durkin answered it. She listened for a moment and then dropped down so her knees were about an inch off the floor. She stood back up and noticed us gawping at her. She turned her anguished face away from us, but we heard her voice as it hardened.

"I see. Yes. Thank you. No, I didn't know. How far along? I see. Yes, of course. Thank you, doctor." Mrs. Durkin hung up the phone.

She spun around to gawk at us a moment like she might cry, but instead, her face transformed into a stone cold glare aimed at Penny.

"What, Mom?" Penny had a scared look on her face like she darn well knew what, with a bunch of scrunchy wrinkles forming little ups and downs on her face and her blue eyes wiggling around like they were lost.

"You're pregnant." Mrs. Durkin continued her frozen stare.

"No, it can't be." Penny rose off the couch like nothing hurt. She must have felt her injuries then because she limped in slow motion to her mom.

Mrs. Durkin threw her hands to her hips. Her eyes shot poison darts. "There was no mistake, Penny. They ran the test twice and with two different blood samples to be sure they didn't have a mix up the first time. You killed two rabbits, young lady, and you are pregnant."

"Mom?" Tears tracked down Penny's bruised face.

Mrs. Durkin continued her stern voice. "You want to know how long?"

"How long?" Penny's voice sounded like surrender.

No, I wanted to shout. Don't do it Penny. Hang in there. Your Mom will change her mind and you won't be sick with a baby anymore. But that was stuff that floated around inside my head while Penny tracked tears in front of her mom.

Mrs. Durkin said, "Three months. Who's the father?"

Penny dropped her eyes. "I don't…"

"Don't you dare tell me you don't know." Mrs. Durkin grabbed Penny's shoulders.

Penny read a message off the floor. "I don't want to say right now." I could barely hear her.

"Yes, you do." Mrs. Durkin gave Penny's shoulders a little shake.

Penny winced. "Send Tommy home first."

Mrs. Durkin stepped back and folded her arms across her chest. "No. He needs to know who he's in love with, don't you, Tommy?"

I was afraid to move. Penny was pregnant. Bob looked at me like he can't believe it either. His lip formed that pout of his so he must have thought I had something to do with it. I couldn't imagine how you made a girl pregnant by kissing and making out.

Alan explained to me how you do it way back when he was ten and I was eight. Not sure he had all his facts straight, especially the part about wearing rubber galoshes or rubber somthings. I was scared and missed Alan at the same time. My head spun.

Mickey remained quiet. It was the most intelligent thing he ever said.

"Mom, you win. Johnny and I... it was an accident... we got carried away one time... I'm so sorry, Mom. I knew something was wrong when I stopped having my periods... I know it was wrong. Mom, I'm so sorry." Penny dropped to the floor at her mother's feet and sobbed.

"What's a period?" I whispered to Bob.

"The little dot you put at the end of a sentence. It sounded to me like she's been talking with periods all along. How can she stop having them?" Bob asked.

"Don't know," I whispered.

Mickey smirked in our direction "Dweebs."

Mrs. Durkin stormed over to the couch and flopped between me and Bob where Penny had been sitting. I could feel her fury like when my mom is mad at me except this was ten times worse. Maybe a hundred times worse. The heat was intense.

Penny remained on the floor sobbing. She reached out with her hand. "Mom," she cried.

"Don't 'Mom' me. Go to bed. If you didn't just survive the beating of your life, I'd slap you to death myself. Now, get out of my sight."

Penny pulled herself up using a kitchen chair for support. She glanced at her Mom and then at Bob who smiled. She smiled back and gave me a little love glance.

I grinned and nodded my love. I didn't know what else to do. How was I supposed to feel? I didn't know she was married to some guy named Johnny. Who was Johnny?

Mrs. Durkin said, "Bob, it would be best if you slept over at Tommy's house one more night."

"Yes, Mom." Bob did not sound happy, but he didn't dare disagree when his mother was so furious.

Bob and I stood up to leave. My mind spun in circles.

Mickey stared at the ceiling.

As we walked over to my house, I kept my oversized mouth shut.

Bob was not speechless. "So?"

My mouth stayed shut.

Bob punched at the air like he was bashing somebody. "I told you not to like my sister."

I spit out my words slow and hard. "She wasn't faithful to me."

"She got knocked up before she started liking you."

"How am I supposed to have a pregnant girlfriend, for Pete's sake? I'm still a kid."

We remained silent as we entered my house and climbed the stairs to my room. When we were settled on our beds, Bob said, "What else?"

"What more is there?" I asked.

"You're too quiet."

I planted my hands behind my head and crossed my legs at my ankles. "She's the killer."

CHAPTER 33

Bob's lower lip stuck out. "Penny ain't no killer."

I uncrossed my legs where I lay on my bed. "She washed your hatchet the same day somebody chopped old Walter Bruce to pieces."

"You might as well accuse Chiamaka. Girls aren't strong enough to chop a guy up. Besides Johnny Bruce chopped up his old man. That was the day he stole his dad's Caddy and almost ran me over."

"Penny was at the horsepistol when my friend Sal was pushed down the steps."

Bob sat up in bed. "It was an accident. Said so in the paper."

"She was mad because she couldn't go to Cynthia Matting's pretend funeral. Maybe she didn't mean it, but she pushed my friend down the steps."

"Tommy, be reasonable. Penny's not strong enough."

"She lied about where she was the night Johnny Bruce was killed. She had the same dirt on her blue jeans and shoes as we did from hanging around that basement hole. Somebody helped Johnny Bruce into the hole, Bob."

"You're just making wild guesses about my sister. You're mad because she's having a baby."

I rolled over and faced the wall. "I'm furious."

"Doing the deed doesn't make a girl a killer."

"What does it make her?" I mumbled.

"A mother?"

I sighed as my fury sank away into the mattress. I rolled over to face Bob. "Yeah, maybe you're right. I am kinda ticked off, ain't I?"

"You're spouting crap about my sister."

"I love Penny, but … I don't know. Okay, forget it."

"You better forget it."

I didn't.

***

I woke up with the sun and the sound of Booker T, Chiamaka's family rooster, crowing out back. Mrs. McGillicutty stretched and yawned next to Bob.

"Want some breakfast?" I asked.

"Let's eat at my apartment, Tommy."

Mrs. McGillicutty meowed to join us, but we left her at home.

"Think your mom is still angry?" I asked.

"Nah. She never stays mad. She says Dad and Mickey have enough rage for everyone."

We dressed and slipped downstairs. I told mom we would have breakfast at Bob's house, which made her happy. We ran up to Market Street and around to the front of the apartment. We both avoided the back way as much as possible since Alan died at the bottom of the black iron fire escape.

"Be quiet on the stairs. I want to surprise them," Bob said.

We stepped on the squeaky old stairs as carefully as we could. Bob had his brand new key. My Dad had replaced the locks on his front and back doors to keep their father away from Penny. The hinges made a lot of noise as Bob creaked the door open.

"Won't be much of a surprise," I whispered in Bob's ear.

"Sure it will," he whispered back. "Everyone is still asleep. Let's creep into the kitchen. Fix our own breakfast."

The living room area was empty except for Mickey who sat back on the stuffed chair with his foot up on a kitchen chair. Mickey's face was a weird blue-gray-white color. I never saw anyone like that.

We moved in for a closer inspection. A huge crushed-in section marked his temple and a ton of blood had dripped down the side of his head before it dried into a scabby mess. Red gook had soaked his hair and then leaked onto the chair.

I touched Mickey's arm, but let go right away. "Ice cold."

"Mom!" Bob ran into the bedroom with me following. Bob shook his mom awake on the big bed. Penny slept on the bottom of a double bunk. The beds took up most of the room. A small bureau sat under the window.

"What?" Mrs. Durkin tried to wake up.

Bob clutched her arm to yank her up. "Hurry, Mom. It's Mickey."

I ran out of the bedroom so I wasn't in the way.

Mrs. Durkin asked, "What's wrong?"

Bob said, "Check Mickey, Mom. Is he dead?"

Mrs. Durkin came out of the bedroom with Bob tugging her along. She popped awake. "Oh my God!"

Bob tried to catch her, but she was too big and went down too fast. They both tumbled to the floor.

I ran to the phone and dialed 0. While I waited for the operator to come on, Bob ran into the kitchen and wet a dishrag. He slapped it on his mother's forehead. She woke up as a woman's voice came on the phone and said "Operator" in a funny nasal way.

"Send the police quick. Somebody is dead here," I said.

"To whom am I speaking?" asked the operator like she had a clothespin attached to her nose.

"This is Tommy McConnell. Quick, connect me to the police."

"Tommy McConnell? Why didn't you say so? Tommy McConnell loves Penny Durkin." The operator laughed and then connected me to the West Chester Police Department.

Mrs. Durkin sat on the floor. The dishrag was in her left hand. Bob tried to pull her up to her feet by grabbing her under the arms from behind.

"Wait a second, Bob," Mrs. Durkin said. "Let my head clear first."

"Shall I get Penny?" Bob asked.

"If she's awake," said Mrs. Durkin. "Otherwise let her sleep."

Bob let go of his mother and she began to fall backwards but caught herself. She sat with her head down when a rough man's voice came on the phone, "Police."

"Yes, we have a dead person here with his head bashed in. Come right away." I pointed to Mickey even though the cop couldn't see him.

"Where are you located?" the man asked.

I gave him Bob's address on Market Street.

The voice on the phone said to hold on while he dispatched a squad car. When he came back on the line, he asked my name.

"Tommy McConnell."

"Tommy McConnell loves Penny Durkin," the officer said.

"Will you please send a squad car over here?" Frustration rose through my body from my toes to my head.

"It's on the way, Tommy." The cop's voice included a smile.

I hung up and opened the front door so the cops wouldn't have to bang it down.

Bob came back from the bedroom and took hold of his mom's arm. "Penny is still sleeping so I didn't wake her."

We heard the blaze of the sirens as the police cars rolled down Market Street. I ran to the front window. The car double parked in front of the Royal. I called out, "Up here. Up here."

Freeman the Cop and another police guy in uniform ran into the building and up the steps. The other officer carried a small white satchel, like a doctor's bag. I figured it must be a first aid kit because it had a red cross on the side of it.

For the next two hours the police asked a bunch of questions. The coroner came and supervised taking away Mickey. They chalked a white line around the big chair and the kitchen chair where Mickey had been sitting with his broken leg propped up.

Penny's blood stains were still in the carpet from when Mickey and her dad beat her almost to death. The other cops ignored those stains after Freeman explained what had happened to Penny.

The cops didn't ask about Penny, who slept in the bedroom. Freeman kept asking if we had seen Bob's father. Everybody kept saying no.

Bob's mom sounded frustrated. "He wouldn't have killed his own son, Freeman."

"He almost killed his daughter. By the way, where is Penny? She still in the hospital?"

"No," Mrs. Durkin said. "She's asleep in her bed."

"She slept through this noise?"

"She's on a lot of medication, Freeman. She came home from the hospital yesterday."

"I see. Can you find out if she's awake yet for me?"

"I'll check," Bob volunteered. He ran into the bedroom and came back out. "She's asleep."

Freeman pushed his hat back to scratch his head with his stubby pencil. "Let her rest. Poor kid was beat up awful bad. Now, her brother. When she wakes up, ask her if she heard or saw anything during the night. Call me at the police station if she did."

"Will do." Mrs. Durkin sat down on the couch and sobbed.

Bob planted his arms around his mother and leaned his head on her shoulder.

Freeman said, "If I get my hands on that murdering son of a ... ahhh what's the use? But he ain't getting away with this, Mrs. Durkin. You can count on it. We'll find him sooner or later. In the meantime, have the locks changed."

Mrs. Durkin didn't respond. Bob hugged her and patted her on the back.

"My dad changed the locks yesterday." I peered up at Freeman.

"Then how did Bob's dad get in?"

"Picked the lock?" I asked.

"Son of ... that's right... he's a master at breaking into other people's homes." Freeman waved back at me as he made his way out to the stairwell. "Ahhh..." But he didn't finish the thought.

CHAPTER 34

After Mickey's funeral, Bob's grandfather invited us to lunch at the Bordeaux Restaurant. Jamie Bordeaux breezed over to stand behind my chair. I sat next to Bob and Penny plopped on the other side of me. Her hand found my lap under the table.

Penny ate regular food now, but she preferred milkshakes. Bob said it was because she was eating for two people.

"What are you guys talking about?" Penny asked.

"About how you have to dump extra food into your belly to feed your baby" I said.

Penny chuckled. "Yeah, I eat all I want. One coolville thing about being pregnant."

I couldn't wait any longer. "Penny, are you married?"

Jamie Bordeaux fell on the floor laughing. I felt my face heat up and worried I must be rolling through a million shades of red.

Penny was about as red as her pale Irish face can get considering she's covered with yellowed bruises and dime-store makeup. "No, little darling, I'm saving myself for you."

Everyone around us laughed.

"Don't you have to be married to get a baby?" I asked.

"You just have to be stupid," Jamie Bordeaux said.

Mrs. Bordeaux, who served our table, glared at him. "Jamie Bordeaux, you march right into the kitchen."

I was impressed. Even Mrs. Bordeaux called him "Jamie Bordeaux." He was the one kid in the neighborhood we called by both names. Nobody knew why. One reason may have been how he was always in trouble when he was little, so his mom would shout for him using his first and last names. But if that were true, most of the kids in the crowd would be known by two or even three names.

Penny patted my leg. "We'll talk about this later, Tommy."

"Okay," I said.

"I'm so glad you're still talking to me," she said.

"I was angry at first, but then realized getting pregnant doesn't change how I feel about you." I thought about how she might be a mad dog killer and how that fact might make me not love her anymore, but the thing I felt at that moment was love, so I decided to go with my feelings.

"You're a kind person, Tommy," Penny said. "I need someone nice in my life because Dad knows I'm so bad. Thank you." She slurped her milkshake.

"Why would anything your mean old father say matter to you?" I believed she was a good girl as long as she hadn't killed anyone. But then maybe her Dad knew something I didn't know.

Before Penny could respond, Mrs. Durkin, who did not say a word through Mickey's funeral or the meal, glanced across the table at Mrs. Davis. "Annabelle?"

Bob's grandfather sat next to Mrs. Davis on one side, but he and Father Murdoch carried on a long-winded conversation of their own.

Penny squeezed my leg under the table one more time.

"What's on your heart, Bonnie?" Mrs. Davis asked.

"Annabelle, you knew Penny was pregnant all along didn't you?"

"I'll tell you what I knew, Bonnie. When a young girl comes to me in tears and talks about she maybe made a mistake, but can't tell me about it, then that girl's done something she ought not to have done. When she sits at my kitchen table and proceeds to scoop up her chocolate ice cream and my home jarred pickles, I know what the trouble is. So I asked her did she and Johnny do something they ought not to. She said, 'Yes.' Then I knew she was carrying my great-grandchild. Later, when Johnny was gone, I rejoiced to know he left a baby behind in this world. But what did I know? I can't tell you your daughter eats pickles and ice cream so she is pregnant. Maybe she likes to mix things that ought not to go together."

Mrs. Davis sighed. Her face turned sad. "Penny needed someone she could talk to and say what was on her heart and what she had done and then not get herself into trouble for the telling. Should I have told you? I told Penny that was her job. I apologize because a mother has a right to know these things, but at the time I was worried about Penny and her baby. The baby will be precious to my family, Bonnie. It's all of Johnny we have left."

"Annabelle, we've been friends a long time. Now, I know you're Penny's friend, too. Thank you. She needs friends right now." Mrs. Durkin dabbed her napkin under her left eye.

"She needs her mother," said Mrs. Davis.

"Thank you for your thoughts," said Mrs. Durkin.

"Thank you for your kind words." Mrs. Davis pushed food around on her plate with her fork.

Mrs. Durkin stared our way. "Penny, I … Penny, what are you doing? Take your hand off Tommy for Pete's sake."

Penny jumped back on her seat and planted both hands on the table.

"She wasn't doing nothing, Mrs. Durkin," I said.

"Hush, Tommy." Mrs. Durkin turned her attention to the food on her plate.

I glanced at Penny to see if she would speak to her mom.

Tears washed Penny's makeup down her cheeks exposing her black and blue skin. "Mom." She rose out of her chair and threw her arms around her mother.

Mrs. Durkin pushed Penny's arms away. "We're in mourning here. Return to your seat."

Bob sipped Penny's milkshake through her straw until he made a slurping noise. Penny spotted him as she sat back down. She laughed, but lunch was over and everyone else prepared to leave.

At the door to the restaurant, the people gave the Durkins big hugs and kisses. I kissed Penny, which put a smile on her face and earned a punch on my arm from Bob.

CHAPTER 35

"We have five dead bodies." Bob held up the fingers on his right hand. He sat next to Chiamaka on Alan's bed in my room. Mrs. McGillicutty rested on her back in Bob's lap. She batted at his fingers with her front paws.

I sat on my bed across from them. "Take them in order."

Bob shoved Mrs. McGillicutty away and counted with his fingers. "We have Cynthia Matting and Johnny Bruce's father who happened to be Chiamaka's Uncle Walter. Then we have Tommy's brother Alan, Chiamaka's cousin Johnny Bruce, and my brother Mickey. Not to mention the attempt on my life by Johnny Bruce who tried to run me over with his Dad's Caddy."

"Don't forget my friend Salvatore Mercandante. Somebody tossed him down the steps at the hospital, wheelchair and all."

Bob rubbed an apology on Mrs. McGillicutty's belly, but he glanced my way. "That's a lot of dead people. The police don't know who killed Cynthia or why. They think Johnny Bruce killed his dad…"

Chiamaka jumped up. "No way Cousin Johnny killed Uncle Walter!"

Bob gave her a blank stare. "Didn't say I think it. It's what the police think. Read the paper."

Chiamaka plopped back on the bed, giving Bob and Mrs. McGillicutty a hard bounce. "Oh."

Bob resumed counting on his fingers. "Your school friend died in an accident. Said so in the paper. Alan and Johnny died in accidents, too. And Dad killed Mickey. Johnny Bruce tried to kill me. Leaves Cynthia as an unsolved murder. She died so long ago nobody cares anymore. And we can forget the rest of them."

"I wouldn't close the book on these deaths yet," I said.

"Yeah, the police don't have the answers to these cases," Chiamaka said. "Cynthia's case needs solving. Johnny was murdered for sure. You don't get no white girl pregnant and then die in an accident. You die in something maybe looks like an accident, but it ain't no way no accident if you be colored. Alan was kidnapped like you boys said. How can anybody think he died in an accident when he turned up dead with his head bashed in after being kidnapped? Ain't no proof your daddy murdered your brother, Bob. We have no motive, no murder weapon, no nothing. His murder is like Cynthia's. Somebody has to investigate and solve these cases, and I don't think that will happen with the West Chester Police Department in charge."

"Freeman will solve these murders," I said.

Bob wrestled Mrs. McGillicutty with his right hand. "Freeman always gets his man."

"He ain't no Mountie." Chiamaka slid her butt away from Bob and the cat. She watched the cat.

"What?" Bob asked.

Chiamaka gazed at Bob's face. "You said 'Freeman always gets his man.' Sounds like the motto of the Royal Canadian Mounted Police. Freeman the Cop be a cop."

I placed my feet on the bed in front of me and used them to push my butt against the wall. "So these murders still need solving, but we have to ask one question more important than whodunit."

"Which is?" Bob asked.

Chiamaka asked, "Who's next?"

"Who cares?" Bob asked.

"If you be paying attention, you would have noticed everyone who is dead is connected to one or more of the three of us. And except for Tommy's friend who fell down the stairs at the hospital and Cynthia, they are family to one of us. Makes for a mighty small circle."

"Could this be a coincidence?" I asked.

Chiamaka lost her smile. "Ain't no coincidences when you're dealing with murder. Someone is killing our friends and family members. The next victim will be one of us or related to one of us."

"Penny?" Bob asked.

Chiamaka asked, "Why? Her dad and brother beat up on her. Ain't nobody out to kill her."

"What if somebody was mad at Johnny Bruce and Penny for doing sex?" I asked.

Chiamaka said, "You mean fu…"

"Don't say it!" Bob screamed.

I raised my forefinger to my lips. "Shhh. Don't want Mom to come in and find Chiamaka."

Chiamaka glanced at the door. "Doorknob turns, I'm under the bed, Tommy. Don't you worry about Chiamaka. If somebody is out for Penny because she did the big 'IT' with Johnny Bruce, then we better watch out for Penny."

Bob's face lit up. "Maybe the same person killed Cynthia Matting because she dated somebody she shouldn't have. What if she had a colored boyfriend, and he killed her."

I stretched out with my hands behind my head. "She didn't like colored people, remember? We just don't know, do we? Was her boyfriend really colored? Did he kill her? Or did someone else kill her? We don't know who killed her or why. We don't even know why Johnny tried to run Bob over. Maybe Johnny sped away from his house to escape from the killer, and Bob happened to cross the street at the wrong time. We may have Johnny Bruce all wrong."

Chiamaka sat up straight and wiggled her butt to make herself comfy. "White people always be getting Johnny wrong. He was a nice cousin even if he wasn't too bright in school. And he liked dating girls. Any kind of girls. Colored girls, Puerto Rican girls, steel penny girls. He even dated Cynthia. Oops."

"What!" Bob shouted.

From down below Mom's anger roared through my bedroom door. "You boys be quiet up there."

"Johnny dated Cynthia?" I'm off the bed pacing again.

Chiamaka was nowhere to be seen. I spied the window. Bob tapped my shoulder. I spun around. He pointed under my bed.

Chiamaka's head popped out. "Sometimes us colored girls have a big mouth. Don't mean Johnny chopped her up the side of the head, though."

"How can you be sure?" I asked.

Chiamaka climbed out from under the bed and sat cross-legged on the floor. "Johnny was too nice to be bopping on people. Besides, whoever did the bopping walloped Johnny. He's dead or did you boys forget?"

I stopped pacing. "It changes things, Chiamaka. You should have told us sooner."

Chiamaka pointed a finger and cold stared me. "So you boys could think Johnny was a killer?"

I sat down on my bed again. "Don't you see? Johnny dated Cynthia and then Penny. Cynthia and Johnny are dead. That leaves Penny as the only one of the three of them left alive. Penny has to be a target because she is the other white girl Johnny dated."

Chiamaka stood up to stare sharp eyes at me. "I already said we better watch out for Penny. But who do we add to our list of who maybe done its?"

Mrs. McGillicutty rested between Bob and Chiamaka . The cat stretched her paws against Chiamaka and pushed her back against Bob.

I walked to the window. "Knowing who we're protecting Penny from would be a big help."

"We may not know who wants to kill Penny, but knowing about it gives us an advantage," said Chiamaka.

"How?" Bob asked.

"Grandma told me once she liked to read books by Mark Twain. She said he was the funniest man who ever lived. Anyway, Grandma believed Mark Twain once said the best way to invest your money is to put all your eggs in one basket and then watch that basket."

I unlatched the screen and climbed out on the roof. Chiamaka stood up and followed me. Behind her we heard Bob say, "I don't get it. What does an egg basket have to do with Penny?"

Chiamaka planted both feet on the roof and stepped over by my side. She grabbed my hand. "The saying means if you want to protect something important to you, put it in one place and then watch that place. We can put Penny in one place and then watch her. Sooner or later the secret killer's bound to show his face. When he does, we be ready."

"We be?" Bob climbed out the window. He twisted his face around to the way it appears on Saturday afternoons when we watch a horror movie at the Harrison over on Gay Street. Instead of a pout like when he became angry, he sucked his lips into his mouth like he ate a lemon.

While in mid air between the roof and my backyard, I sang, "We have to have a plan."

"What plan?" Bob sang back.

I gaped up at Bob and Chiamaka. "First we need the police. A killer is too big and mean for us to tackle alone."

"Makes sense, Tommy," Chiamaka dropped to the ground. She yanked me back out of the way so Bob could jump without clunking into us. "What will you do, cut the line and carry a phone around with you? Maybe you can stick in some batteries or one of them tiny transistor radios from Japan."

I let go of Chiamaka because one girlfriend was enough. "We have to put Penny in one place and keep her there. We should ask for police protection, too." My "I love Penny" smile slithered under my nose.

Bob stumbled to the ground in front of us. "She has police protection."

Chiamaka gazed at me like she had a question. I shrugged my shoulders like I didn't have the answer. We stared at Bob.

Bob flipped his hands palms up. "What?"

"Police protection?" I asked.

"You didn't know?" Bob asked.

"No. Neither did Chiamaka."

"Crap." Bob winced.

"What?" Chiamaka asked.

Bob's face took on a pleading look with his eyes squinty and his cheeks pulled back. "It was a secret. Please don't whisper a word to anyone. Mom will skin me alive."

"In your family, I'd be hiding the knives," Chiamaka said.

"It was a figure of speech, Chiamaka." I headed for the gate at the end of the yard. It led to a short walkway where our block stashed our crap for trash day. The walkway led out to the alley.

Chiamaka strolled behind me. "I know. I like seeing Bob's steel penny face turn red, even if it be too dark to see right now. It's how I know you like me, Bob."

"It means I'm angry with you, Chiamaka." Bob brought up the rear.

"Then why ain't your lower lip pouting like it always does when you're pissed off?" Chiamaka asked.

Bob tackled Chiamaka and held her against a trash can. She tried to fend him off, but he had her arms pinned. She squirmed but couldn't free herself.

I yanked Bob off her. He resisted at first but then stepped back on the trash way. He was pouting now.

"So you want to tell us about the police protection?" I asked.

"Yeah, start talking before I pout and kick your steel penny butt," Chiamaka brushed off her clothes.

I thought about the time Chiamaka decked me in the alley and where I might find ice this late at night just in case I needed it for a black eye. I rubbed my jaw even though it didn't hurt.

"You know the fire station across Market Street from my building?" Bob asked.

"Not what I want to hear, Bob Durkin." Chiamaka's eyes shot daggers.

"I don't want to hear about pouting lips or any other part of me, Chiamaka," Bob said.

"Is that what you call a white boy's apology?" Chiamaka planted her hands deep against her hips.

"It's my complaint," Bob said.

"Complain about this." Chiamaka socked Bob on the forehead. She brought her fist back and yelled, "Ouch!"

Bob fell against the neighbor's fence that formed one side of the trash way. He glared at Chiamaka with one hand pressed to his forehead. I cracked up, but had the presence of mind to back away a few steps out of fist range, Bob's and Chiamaka's.

Chiamaka giggled, but Bob pouted.

I reached the alley and headed left towards Walnut Street. "So what about the fire station across the street from your apartment?"

"It's next door to straight across," Bob said. "A police officer is on the second floor, day and night. If anything bad happens, we knock over a lamp on the table under our front window or turn it off. The cop can see from the fire station window. Lamp falls down or is turned off, the police come running."

"What if your dad or the secret killer sneaks in the back way?" I asked.

"You know the garage in back of the Royal?"

"Yeah, at the end of the yard." I walked next to Bob while Chiamaka lagged behind.

Bob said, "Mister Demeter installed a window in the door to the yard because he wants the cops to prove Menoitios is innocent. A cop hides in the garage watching out that window in the door. If we turn off the kitchen light, cops come running. Everyday, every night, two cops plus their backup."

"How will we sneak in and out late at night?" I asked.

"We don't. We have to make sure Mom lets me sleep over when we're gonna be out at night," Bob said.

"What happens when Penny dates one of her boyfriends?" Chiamaka asked.

"She has one boyfriend!" I folded my arms across my chest.

"Maybe we should ask those stakeout cops about that How does she get out when she visits any of her boyfriends, including Tommy McConnell who loves her like bees love flowers?" Chiamaka asked.

We reached the edge of the alley. Bob faced Chiamaka. "She rides with a plainclothes police officer in an unmarked car."

Chiamaka nodded. "Sounds like old Penny already is an egg in a basket, boys. Stop gawping at me, Tommy McConnell. You know you in love with Penny Durkin."

"Tonight, we're out for adventure," said Bob.

"What kind of adventure?" I asked.

"Sneaking past Bob's cops," Chiamaka said.

"How?" Bob asked. "They're watching all the time."

"We be kidnapping Jamie Bordeaux. He'll show us how," Chiamaka said.

"Jamie Bordeaux?" I asked.

"Tommy, he be the shiftiest steel penny I know and he be right up the street." Chiamaka pointed to the Bordeaux Restaurant.

"How are you planning to get to Jamie Bordeaux?" I asked. "His apartment is straight walls. No way to climb in."

"I'll take care of it," Chiamaka said.

CHAPTER 36

"How will we sneak past the police?" Bob asked for the fourth time in as many minutes.

"Don't know. We could do it in the shadows," I said.

"Yeah, but how?" Bob asked.

We stood in front of the yellow-brick telephone building that sat cattycorner to the Bordeaux Restaurant at Walnut and Market Streets. The entrance door was set back from the main part of the structure.

I scrunched into the corner of the setback. "Jamie Bordeaux can sneak into anyplace." The darkness of the setback made for a perfect place to hide. Of course, we had no reason to hide, but we had fun.

"What about the rest of us?"

"He can sneak anybody in anywhere." I moved forward to check the windows of the apartment located above the Bordeaux Restaurant. "Chiamaka better hurry because Jamie Bordeaux turned his light off."

Bob snuck forward to take a gander. I glanced the other way and spotted Chiamaka and Coleman making their way up Market Street toward us from the east side of town. As she passed by, I tugged Chiamaka into our hideout. Coleman followed. Even in the dark, I could see his muscles pop out of his white tee shirt. He wore blue jeans and sneakers below the waist.

"He lives over there." Bob pointed to the Bordeaux.

"We know," Coleman said. "Which window?"

"Second floor. The one in front on the right." I pointed toward the two windows on the second floor above the Bordeaux Restaurant.

"Wait here." Coleman stepped up to the corner for a close inspection. When he returned, he said, "No problem." He headed off for the Bordeaux.

We peeked around the corner to watch him.

Coleman hung in the shadows against the far side of the Bordeaux Restaurant. He leaned his back against the building with one foot raised behind him. He could have been anybody relaxing and watching the world go by in the middle of the day, except it was about eleven at night.

Coleman turned around and grabbed hold of the downspout that ran between the Bordeaux building and the apartment house next door. He pulled on the downspout to test it. He scrambled up the side of the building like a mountain climber on a cliff using a rope. In this case, the rope was a big, round metal drain pipe.

"Will it hold him?" Chiamaka asked.

Coleman reached level with the two windows at the front of the second floor of the Bordeaux Restaurant. He stepped onto the first window ledge and worked his way over to the second without falling. He braced his body in the window well with his hands.

"He's strong to be able to do that," Bob said.

"Be easier if we threw a few pebbles up to bang on the glass," I said.

Chiamaka punched me hard on the shoulder. "Shut your face, Tommy McConnell. Now's not the time to be thinking of the easy solution when Coleman's about to die doing it the hard way."

Coleman leaned down towards the bottom of the window and stared into Jamie Bordeaux's bedroom.

"I bet he's telling Jamie Bordeaux to clear a spot for him," Chiamaka said.

The little screen at the bottom of the window disappeared. The window slid open all the way.

Coleman gripped the open window with his right hand, and in one quick move, he brought his left foot over to Jamie Bordeaux's window. He clutched the open window with his left hand and squatted so that his bottom stuck out over the street. He vanished into Jamie Bordeaux's bedroom.

***

"Alan figured out who the killer was," I said.

"I didn't know," Chiamaka replied.

"No, I meant it would be a reason to kill Alan. The killers might think he knew too much."

"Menoitios killed Alan," Bob said. "We were there. He sucked him into the kitchen and killed him. Then he dragged him up the fire escape stairs and tossed him back down to fake an accident."

My head spun but I managed to hold on. Once my head cleared, I said, "Menoitios kills Cynthia because he wants to make love with a teenager. Then he backs off and figures he better be good or his buns are gonna be fried. Two years go by and he spies Penny and Johnny Bruce making out someplace around town. He decides that ain't right and he's just the man to take action. He starts with Johnny's dad out of meanness. He plans to kill everyone in Penny's family, too. But Alan finds out somehow. Maybe he sees Menoitios with an axe. Menoitios bops Alan off. Then he kills Mickey because he is big and mean and will be the hardest of the Durkins to kill besides Bob's dad. This is starting to make sense. Let's put Menoitios on our suspect list. Who else can we add?"

"Who else?" Bob asked. "We only need one killer."

"You have to put everybody on the list," Chiamaka said. "Otherwise you can't whittle the list down to the one person who did it."

Bob puffed his cheeks and blew out some air. "We have to protect Penny from Menoitios. He's a killer."

"Bob, you're guessing. It could have been a zillion other people," I said.

"Who?" Bob asked

"I don't know," I said. "It could have been Menoitios."

"I know," Bob said. "It could have been Dad."

"How?" Chiamaka asked.

Bob said, "Dad could've killed Cynthia two years ago. Maybe he was drunk and wanted to, you know, mess with her, but she didn't want to. Or she spotted him breaking into a home. Yeah, makes sense, so he killed her to shut her up. Then he gets caught stealing anyway and ends up in jail."

"How did he kill Alan while he was in prison?" Chiamaka asked.

Bob stepped back out of the setback onto the sidewalk and then back in. "Sometimes when people are in prison, they ask other prisoners to do jobs for them because the other prisoner gets out first. Then when the second prisoner is released, he has to pay off the first prisoner for the job. Dad explained it to me one time. Let's say Dad found out about Penny and Johnny somehow. Perhaps a new prisoner told him."

Chiamaka said, "Marion Carr went to jail back in April. Maybe he knew something."

Bob's eyes lit up as he stepped back into the light of the sidewalk. "Yeah, he and Dad did some jobs together. He was the one colored person Dad liked, except Mrs. Davis of course. He had to like Mrs. Davis because she was Great-Grandma Durkin's friend."

I made with the finger counting. "Okay, we have two names we can put on the list of suspects, Menoitios and Bob's dad."

"Add Marion Carr's name to the list, too," said Chiamaka.

"Why?" asked Bob.

"Wouldn't be a proper list without some colored folks and besides your dad couldn't have acted alone," Chiamaka said.

"Sounds complicated," Bob said. "But it explains why Dad wanted to kill Penny. I thought he beat on her like always, but no, he wanted to kill her the meanest way possible. Explains why he never came back. We have to protect Penny from Dad, wherever he is. And protect her from Menoitios, wherever he is. And from Marion Carr, wherever he is."

"Marion Carr is in prison," Chiamaka said. "All he did was tell your dad the tale and do in Uncle Walter. Or your dad hired somebody else to do the dirty work while he was still in prison. We may have some secret person running around we don't know about."

"Great," Bob said. "How are we supposed to stop somebody from killing Penny if we don't know who it is?"

Jamie Bordeaux and Coleman ran down Walnut Street from the back of the restaurant. They made their way across the street and met us in the setback.

"With Coleman, you don't need me," Jamie Bordeaux said.

"We need your sneaky brainpower," Bob said. "Besides, we didn't want you to miss the fun."

"So what's the plan?" Jamie Bordeaux asked.

"We want to break into Bob's apartment so Tommy can kiss Penny without the police finding out," Coleman said.

"Why would the police find out?" Jamie Bordeaux asked. "Bob has a key."

After swearing them to top secrecy, Bob explained to Coleman and Jamie Bordeaux about the police protection and how we wanted to test it.

"And who said I have to kiss Penny?" My face felt hot.

"I did. Didn't you hear me?" Coleman gave me a shove.

"We need a test," Bob said.

Chiamaka added, "We need to prove a bad guy could reach Penny and kill her without getting caught. Tommy has to kiss Penny full on the lips, and then we have to sneak out without the police ever finding out."

"Penny is the one who starts the kissing, not me." My face heated up again. "How about I tag her instead?"

"No way, Tommy McConnell." Chiamaka flashed bright cheery eyes. "You can sneak into her bedroom, pretend to tag her, and lie about it without ever touching her. If you lock lips with her and wiggle your tongue around, you'll return with that big silly grin of yours painted across your face."

"I don't like it, but she's right." Bob folded his arms over his chest "But no tongue wiggling allowed."

"But how will we do it?" I asked.

"With your lips," said Jamie Bordeaux.

Chiamaka pointed a finger in my face. "First off, you're doing it, Tommy, not us, and don't you be looking too happy either because Bob might not like you wanting his sister that way."

"I guess we can't use Bob's key?" Jamie Bordeaux asked.

"No keys. We don't know if the bad guy has a key or not, so we have to make like he doesn't," said Bob.

"Or she doesn't," said Chiamaka.

"She?" Bob asked.

Chiamaka's hands flew about as she spoke. "Sure. You could have one of Johnny Bruce's other girlfriends mad at her for dating Johnny. She might be sneaking around here right now wanting to slit Penny's throat."

Jamie Bordeaux said, "Wait here. I'll be back."

"Where are you off to?" Bob asked.

"This will take some time," Jamie Bordeaux said. "But I promise I won't sneak in without you guys."

As we watched, Jamie Bordeaux headed toward the colored section of town in the opposite direction of the Royal Restaurant and Bob's apartment.

"What's he up to?" Coleman asked.

"Wish I knew," Bob said.

***

Jamie Bordeaux disappeared for about half an hour before he returned from the colored section of town on Market Street.

"Easy," Jamie Bordeaux said.

"How?" Bob asked.

"Through Dickey Nelson's yard." Jamie Bordeaux shrugged.

"And?" Chiamaka asked.

Jamie Bordeaux explained, "The fence on Dickey Nelson's side is wire. At the garage of the Royal, twisted wires anchor the fence to a pole. We can unhook the wires and sneak in."

"Do we need pliers to undo the wire connections?" Bob asked.

"Nah, we have Coleman," Chiamaka said.

"I already undid the wires," Jamie Bordeaux said. "They were thin and about rusted through. We can slip in one at a time and then G.I. crawl so we stay in the dark. Go slow so the cop in the garage doesn't see your movement."

We followed Jamie Bordeaux back east to Matlack Street in the colored section and then south to the alley. Jamie Bordeaux explained we have to walk the long way around the block so the cop in the firehouse doesn't spot us at the corner of Walnut and Market Streets. Jamie Bordeaux said the cop may be able to see all the way to our corner from the firehouse.

We headed west in the alley past Chiamaka's house which was dark. The back of my house was dark also. At Walnut Street, we crossed to the opposite alley and passed by the side of Mrs. Glass' haunted house. Up the alley was the garage at the back of the Royal Restaurant.

The alley had no street lights. Dickey Nelson's house had a back porch light turned on, but the wattage was low. His yard didn't have a back fence so we walked to the spot where the wire fence down the side of the yard ended at a pole stuck in the ground by the corner of the garage.

Coleman checked the wire fence and it was loose like Jamie Bordeaux said it would be. Coleman moved the wire fence about a foot to give us more room to squeeze into the yard of the Royal Restaurant. The cinderblock wall on the other side of the yard was not visible. The yard was dark except for a light over the kitchen door to the restaurant by the fire escape steps.

Jamie Bordeaux gathered us into a football huddle. "We'll start the G.I. crawl as we squeeze through the opening in the fence. Stay low until you hit the concrete around the backdoor and fire escape. Then you will be in the light until you reach the second floor level of the fire escape. Climb the steps slowly so the cop isn't distracted by movement. The fire escape is black and we'll look dark in the night. We can be caught if the cop is watching close. It's late and the cop may be half asleep. If he is, the plan works. If he isn't, the cop will catch us."

"What should we do if the cop spots us?" Chiamaka asked.

Jamie Bordeaux said, "If we're discovered, and you are on the fire escape, run as fast as you can up the little brick alleyway between the two buildings and then down Market Street. Run all the way to Matlack Street. Walk around the block and head for home. Don't let the cops see you once you start to walk. If you have not entered the yard and the cop sees someone, then walk home out of the alley. Don't run. The cop can't see you here and will be focused on the person climbing up the fire escape."

"Does everybody understand?" Coleman asked.

We took turns whispering "Yeah."

Jamie Bordeaux asked, "Any questions?"

"What do we do once we make our way up to the second floor of the fire escape?" Coleman asked.

"We'll be in the dark, so the cop won't see us until we enter the lighted area streaming through the glass in the kitchen door. So sit still and don't move around or make any noise. We need somebody who knows how to pick a lock."

"I can," Bob said. "Dad taught me how, but we don't need to pick the lock on the backdoor. I need something flat, like a thin piece of metal."

"Do you have a thin piece of metal?" Jamie Bordeaux asked.

Bob said, "No."

"Does anybody?" Jamie Bordeaux asked.

Everybody whispered, "No."

"I can find one," I volunteered. "Dad keeps all kinds of parts in the basement."

"Go," Jamie Bordeaux said. "Everybody else sit down along the side of the garage and stay quiet."

CHAPTER 37

Enough light glowed through the windows to allow me to navigate the living room, dining room and kitchen without banging into stuff. At the back of the kitchen, I opened the cellar door and turned on the basement light.

The first of the wooden steps made a loud creak when my foot landed on it. I sat down and removed my sneakers.

In the basement, Dad had a workbench with lots of tools and things on the top, but no flat metal pieces. After a few minutes of scrounging around, I found one in a box in the corner that contained junk parts.

The aluminum scrap piece was rough but sharp around the edges. I returned to the bench and scraped it with a file. It made a weird loud noise, so I put the file down. I heard a quick movement from the back of the basement and about jumped out of my skin.

"Mrs. McGillicutty?" I called.

The sound rattled again.

"Cynthia?"

From the dark place, I heard a deep voice. "Tommy McConnell loves a dead woman."

"Will Barnes?"

"A dead woman may be the death of you."

"Will, I don't see you." I stared into the darkness at the back of the basement.

A light on a pull chain hung from the rafters back there, but I shook too much to venture in that direction. "I didn't love Cynthia Matting, Will. Bob did. At least he used to until she didn't want to play with us anymore. She chased after older guys to make out with. Didn't do her much good, Will. Will? Why are you in my basement?"

As my eyes took in the blackness and my knees wobbled under me, Will Barnes' face peered out at me. No body, just his face, about four times the size of a real head. It was green.

***

The group stood in a line along the side of the garage at the back of the Royal Restaurant yard when I returned.

"What took you so long?" Jamie Bordeaux asked.

I bent over to catch my breath. "Ran into Will Barnes' head in my basement. It was green and huge."

"Will Barnes?" Bob asked.

"Sounds to me like you ran into your imagination," Chiamaka said.

"You bring the metal?" Jamie Bordeaux asked.

"It has sharp edges, so be careful." I handed the piece of aluminum to Bob.

"This will work if I don't cut a finger off," Bob said.

Jamie Bordeaux gathered everyone around. "Bob will slip in first so he can be in position to work on the door. Chiamaka, you're second, because if Bob can't open the door, you can pass him a bobby pin."

"Don't have no bobby pin," Chiamaka said. "But if Bob don't know how to enter a door with a thin piece of metal, I do."

"So you're second," Jamie Bordeaux said. "I'll go third, Coleman fourth. Tommy, you come last. Keep a lookout up and down the alley in case more cops come. When you see Coleman disappear into the yard, you follow."

"What's my signal?" I asked.

"Holler anything one time. If we hear Tommy scream, we take off. No talking, just evacuate. Everybody understand?"

We whispered, "Yeah."

Jamie Bordeaux said, "From now on, I speak, nobody else. The exception is if Tommy has to yell."

Bob slid up to the fence. Coleman pulled it out more from the pole so Bob had room to crawl.

Bob carried the aluminum part in his hand. He was an expert at the G.I. crawl from the movies we saw together and the times we played war. He disappeared into the darkness of the yard, but soon became visible in the light by the restaurant's back door. He made his way up the fire escape steps. Once he was on the landing at the top of the fire escape, you couldn't see him unless you knew he was there. He reappeared under the window of the kitchen to his apartment.

Chiamaka took her turn while Bob worked on the backdoor to his apartment. When she disappeared into the darkness at the top of the stairs, Jamie Bordeaux started his crawl. Coleman followed next. While Coleman crawled somewhere in the yard, Bob disappeared into his apartment. The open door cast more light onto the fire escape. Bob closed the door.

Coleman vanished into the darkness at the top of the steps so it became my turn to crawl. As I stepped past the wire fence, my foot snagged on a piece of the wire. That was when I realized I wasn't wearing my sneakers.

Both hands were clamped tight over my mouth while I danced in circles around Dickey Nelson's backyard. Muffled "ooooooo" sounds poured out into the night air like I was trying to imitate a train engine with a lisp. Who knew Dickey's yard had so many pebbles for a guy to step on? I muffled "ouch-ooch" noises. At the end of my jitterbug, I did knee bends to squish out the pain.

Creeping like a soldier was hard on the elbows and knees, but I kept the pain down with thoughts of Penny and the kiss I would plant on her lips in her bedroom in the dark. At the concrete area in front of the back kitchen door, I rose up and crawled the way a baby does. I dashed to the steps, but then remembered to slow down.

At the top of the fire escape, I found everyone except Bob parked on the little platform. Jamie Bordeaux pointed at Chiamaka and then at the backdoor. He whispered, "Leave the door open just enough to squeeze by. The light is bound to be noticed."

Chiamaka reached up and opened the door but not as wide as Bob did. Even in the dark, I could see everyone cringe when the door creaked.

A dull light streamed out of the open door. Bob did something to keep the light down. The cop in the garage must have been asleep.

Jamie Bordeaux pointed to Coleman who crawled into Bob's kitchen. When it was my turn, I saw Bob holding a blanket up to cover the door to keep the amount of light down. Jamie Bordeaux crawled in last.

The kids sat on the kitchen floor in a circle. I heard a quiet click of the door as Bob closed it. Jamie Bordeaux pointed at me and whispered, "Do your thing."

I checked my foot. The sock was torn and there were blood spots. I pulled off the sock and found a nasty scratch. It wasn't as bad as the one healing on my side, but it hurt just the same.

Time for me to crawl on the floor to stay out of sight from the windows. The bedroom door was closed so I reached up to turn the doorknob and pushed into the room. The hinges squeaked.

Penny and Mrs. Durkin didn't stir from the noise so I crawled to the bunk bed. The room was dark, but soon my eyes adjusted. Enough outside light slipped in through the window shade. Mrs. Durkin snored under a sheet on the double bed. Her head stuck out of the sheet and she faced me, but her eyes were closed. From the kitchen I heard whispers and giggles.

Penny slept in her shorty pajamas and top without a sheet. She faced me. In the darkness, I couldn't see the black and blue color of her skin. Instead, I saw pretty Penny with smooth white skin. I was scared to kiss her, but knew I had to.

This is where my heart belonged, now, to this place, this apartment, this bed. Here was my steel Penny.

I paused a moment, took a deep breath like I was about to dive underwater. I planted one on her lips for as long as I could hold my breath.

Penny's eyes fluttered and opened. She had a startled expression on her face. I put my finger to her lips to shush her. She smiled when she realized it was me. Then her face turned into a question mark.

I moved in close to her ear and whispered, "Get dressed and come into the kitchen, but crawl so the cops can't see you." While close to her ear I figured I might as well kiss it, too. After my quick little ear peck, she planted a huge, wet, tongue licker on me.

She pushed my head away and smiled. I could feel the proof plastered on my face as I crawled back to the kitchen. I had fun by keeping my face pointed to the floor until I had crawled well into the room. When I sat back, everyone grinned at my smile, except Bob and Chiamaka.

Chiamaka didn't say anything, but Bob whispered, "You were in my sister's bedroom a long time, buster."

Jamie Bordeaux whispered, "Tommy McConnell loves Penny Durkin. Bob Durkin, shut up and get used to it." Without waiting for a response, Jamie Bordeaux pointed to the backdoor. I held up my hand to stop him. He looked at me.

"Penny is dressing. Let's see if she can sneak out," I whispered.

Jamie Bordeaux shook his head up and down to indicate yes.

We waited about five minutes before Penny crawled into the kitchen. She had a big smile on her face, but in the kitchen light, her face appeared black, blue and green.

Jamie Bordeaux pointed to Chiamaka and she started out the backdoor. When my turn came, I tried to find Alan's bloodstain as I crept backwards down the fire escape, but didn't see it.

Once we were back in Dickey Nelson's yard, Jamie Bordeaux whispered, "Don't say nothing. Everybody go home."

We walked down the alley. Jamie Bordeaux headed north towards Market Street to go home while the rest of us crossed Walnut Street with me jumping every time I stepped on a pebble.

"What do we do with Penny?" Bob asked.

"Send her home?" Coleman asked.

Penny made a motion with her hands like she wanted to push us away. "What do you mean, what do you do with me? I'm out of here."

"It's the middle of the night?" Chiamaka asked. "Where can you go at this hour?"

Penny scrunched up her face like she wanted to spin her brain wheels. "I can't crawl back up to the apartment. It about killed me to sneak down."

"Have to keep her," Bob said.

"Keep her where?" Chiamaka's voice sounded suspicious.

"In Tommy's room, of course," Coleman said.

I put my hands up in protest. "Mom will kill us."

"My mom already killed me, Tommy," Penny said.

"She did?" I asked.

"I'll tell you about it later. Let's go to your house." Penny bumped my arm with her shoulder.

"What will we do in the morning?" Bob asked.

Penny pulled away from me. "Wait. Change of plans. I have a better idea. I'll walk home through the front door. See you later."

"Penny, wait." Bob snatched her wrist. "The cops will catch you."

"No, the cops are protecting me. Guy up in the firehouse ain't about to say nothing if I stroll into the apartment late at night."

"Why not?" Bob asked.

"So here's the cop," Penny began. "'Hello, dispatch. I caught Penny Durkin sneaking back into her apartment. No, I don't know how she snuck out or when she left. No, I wasn't asleep. Honest. I was awake the whole time. Yes, I watched nonstop. I didn't see her leave is all. How am I supposed to know how she left? No, I said I didn't fall asleep.'"

"You're brave," Bob said.

Penny pushed Bob on the shoulder. "What will they do, shoot me?"

"See you later," Bob said.

"See you." Penny walked over to me. "That was a pretty decent kiss, Tommy. Want to try another?"

"Well, I…"

Penny planted one right on my lips and tickled me with her tongue again. She pulled away and smiled. "See you later, handsome."

"Handsome?" Bob asked. "He looks like Howdy Doody, for Pete's sake."

Penny wandered off towards Market Street.

"What can we do now?" I asked.

Chiamaka said, "I bet the killer brags to his friends including those with little brothers and sisters. Some of the bragging be passed down to the young ones. I know the little colored brothers and sisters on the east side of town and a number on the west. Tommy, you know the little Catholic brothers and sisters in town. Bob knows the public steel penny brothers and sisters. Together we have the whole town covered."

"Too late to begin tonight," Bob said.

"We start tomorrow." Chiamaka held onto Coleman's arm and led him into the alley. She stopped by her house and waved at us before entering. Coleman put his hands in his pocket and whistled down the alley.

Bob and I walked back to my house.

"That was my idea, remember?" I patted Bob on the back.

"Yeah."

Back in my room, Bob bellyached about me and Penny. Some of it made me laugh, but I could tell he was ticked off.

CHAPTER 38

Bob raised a cloud of dust by pounding his foot into the dirt. "We've been here long enough."

"Don't know where he lives," I said, not for the first time.

Bob slammed a fist onto his seat on the kiddie merry-go-round at the Walnut Street playground. "You said Rig Town."

"Yeah, but I don't know the address." I kicked at the dirt to start the merry-go-round circling.

Walnut Street Park was on the south end of West Chester where Walnut Street dead ended into Rosedale Avenue. We were there to hunt up my school friend, Toby Gillis, but we didn't see him.

The merry-go-round spun us in a lazy circle while little kids played nearby. Six boys about our age strutted over.

"What are you kids doing in our park?" the tallest one asked.

"Your park? Thought it was a community playground." I was stalling for time because these were Rig Towners and they wanted a fight.

"You boys ain't from around here," another of the kids said.

Bob stood. He was like a brother so I didn't want to see him hurt.

I stood up and moved in front of him. "We live up the street on Walnut."

"And I live on Market." Bob pushed around me so we were side-by-side. I was his brother, too.

I thought it was a bad move to mention Market Street. I wanted these kids to think we were from two or three blocks away, not half way across town.

"You boys better head home," said the leader of this little gang.

I couldn't understand why Bob and I didn't know any of these kids. They were either Catholics or publics. One of us should know them.

"We're looking for my friend," I said.

"Yeah, who's that?" The leader stepped up to me, nose-to-nose.

"Toby Gillis." I made a fist and tapped Bob on the leg so he knew to be ready for action.

The tough expression on the leader's face melted into a smile. He patted me on the chest like I was a long lost relative. "So you're a friend of Toby's? Makes you all right by my book."

He turned to one of the other kids. "He's a friend of Toby's."

The other kids gawped at each other. "Oh."

The leader said, "Tony, run over to Toby's and tell him he has a friend waiting for him at the park. Tell him to come quick or we might think this guy is not such a good friend." He pounded a fist into the palm of his other hand to make sure I got his point.

The littlest one in the gang took off running.

The leader glared at me. He smiled. I smiled back. I stood my ground. If I stepped back, it would be to position myself to take a swing at him.

The leader patted me on the shoulder. "Sit down, boys. Your friend Toby should be here in a few minutes."

Bob and I parked back on the merry-go-round, but we didn't allow it to spin.

The leader turned to the gang. "This way, boys."

They wandered off towards a barn where there was a guy handing out checkers and other games to the kids. Several children took basketballs for the macadam court on the south edge of the park.

"Who are they?" Bob asked.

"Don't know. Don't want to know. Just want them to disappear."

Bob sighed. "We're leaving now and never coming back, aren't we?"

I poked Bob on the shoulder. "We have about five minutes for Toby to show up. Then they'll return. When they do, we high tail up Walnut."

"Deal." Bob stared ahead. We didn't speak for a few minutes. Instead, we heard the birds yacking at each other while the children sang below.

Out of this near silence, Bob dropped a bomb. "Chiamaka did it."

"What are you talking about?" I pushed my heals into the dirt to make the merry-go-round spin.

"Chiamaka. She's the killer." Bob kicked dirt to add to our speed.

"How do you figure?" I asked.

"Simple. She had easy access to her Uncle Walter's house. She snuck in and bop! Had nothing to do with Johnny Bruce."

I reached over and scooped up a couple of tiny pebbles on the fly. "Why did she kill her uncle?"

"Who knows? Maybe he was hitting on her when he was drunk."

"What about Alan?" I asked.

"She hid in the little alleyway that runs out to Market Street. When Alan escaped Menoitios out the backdoor of the Royal, bam!"

"Why?"

"Was Alan hitting on her?" Bob asked.

"Not that I know." I rubbed one of the pebbles between my thumb and forefinger. "What about Mickey? She would have had to sneak into your apartment."

"She snuck into your bedroom so slipping into my apartment's no problem."

I flipped the pebble towards a tree about ten feet in front of us. "She didn't sneak into my bedroom. We let her in. She couldn't figure out how to get past the screen, remember?" My pebble missed.

"She waltzed in through my backdoor. You saw how easy the lock is to get around with a flat piece of thin metal. Chiamaka even said she knew how to do it." Bob spun around to lay back on the merry-go-round seat with his feet pointed into the center. His head hung over the edge of the seat. He had to hold on to the metal framework with both hands.

"It sounds interesting, but I don't buy it."

"Why not?"

"Why would Chiamaka knock off Mickey?" I flipped another pebble at the tree as we spun by and hit it this time.

"She tossed him down the steps at the horsepistol, remember? And she knew that Mickey would want to kill her out of revenge so she nailed him first. She's a tough girl. Capable of murder." Bob let go of the framework with his left hand and rubbed the bruise on his forehead.

"It's a stretch from throwing your brother down the steps to killing him. Besides it was an accident. She was defending herself." I let another pebble fly and nailed the tree.

"Doesn't matter. If Mickey had landed on his head instead of his leg, she would have killed him at the horsepistol. She snuck into my apartment and finished the job. What's taking your friend so long, anyway? We're almost out of time." Bob stretched his arm out as far as possible. If a kid happened by, he'd probably whack her as we spun around.

"He'll be here. We forgot about Cynthia."

"So she bopped Cynthia for hating colored girls, Tommy Did it with the same axe or whatever she used on her Uncle Walter. Then she buried her in the woods."

This time around, the pebble missed. "How'd she get Cynthia into the woods? She was only eleven back then, like us at the time."

"Suckered her into going with her."

"Bob, you think she suckered Cynthia into the woods, while carrying an axe? Cynthia might have become a bit suspicious, especially since she never played with colored kids."

"Don't know. Did Cynthia go to the woods for another reason? Then along comes Chiamaka and whacks her a good one?" Bob let go of the framework with his right hand.

I waited to see if Bob would fly off, but he didn't. Then I scooped up pebbles as the merry-go-round continued its slow spin to nowhere. "Did Chiamaka carry a shovel with her?"

"Nah, she just buried Cynthia with the axe. All you have to do is stir up the dirt and cover her over so she's underneath. Then pile leaves and stuff. Bury her in the bushes and nobody finds her." Bob began to slide off the merry-go-round so he wrapped his feet in the metal support.

"How do you know so much about burying bodies?" I missed the tree again.

Bob had both hands hanging over the edge of the merry-go-round. "Commonsense, Tommy. Use the tool you have."

"Think so?"

"Sure, why not? Chiamaka did it. You can't prove me wrong." Bob grasped the handles and rose up to a sitting position. He faced into the center of the merry-go-round.

I still faced out. "How's Chiamaka a mad-dog killer?" I let about half a dozen pebbles fly. They made a staccato noise as they careened off the tree.

"You're blind to killer girls because you like them and think they're perfect."

249

"Nah, my sisters ain't perfect. Mom ain't perfect. And the nuns? We're not going there. But you are right about one thing. It adds up."

"Why do the girls like you anyway, Tommy? They should like me. I'm the good-looking one."

"Thought you didn't like them?"

"I like girls okay. I'm just not ready to hop into bed with them." Bob spun around to face out.

I wiped the dirt from the pebbles off my hands. "Neither am I."

"But you like to make out with them?"

"What them? I always had a crush on Penny. Ain't my fault she likes me. We like each other. We make out. Ain't no big deal, Bob."

"It's a big deal to me. She's my sister."

"You used to have a crush on Cynthia, you know."

"Yeah, I remember, but I was just a kid then."

"I was a kid to Penny until she decided that didn't matter." I gazed over at the Rig Town toughs. They rose from their checkers boards and headed our way.

CHAPTER 39

Toby showed up and waved his boys off before Bob and I had to run away. Toby was a friend, but we never saw each other away from school.

Toby frowned. "Tommy, why are you in my neighborhood?"

I stood to shake Toby's hand. "Need to talk for a minute."

"In Rig Town we become nervous when strange kids come around. We figured you wanted a fight. I don't recommend taking on the kids in Rig Town. Not unless you bring a small army."

"I hear you, Toby."

Toby took a gander at Bob.

"Toby, this is my friend, Bob. Bob, Toby."

They shook hands.

I caught Toby's eye. "We're trying to prevent a murder."

Toby's blue eyes lit up. He was a head shorter than me, about the same height as Bob. He was built solid with wide shoulders. Not tall like Coleman, but strong and tough. "Come over here," Toby said.

We followed him to an empty picnic table. We sat in a row with Toby in the middle on the tabletop with our feet on one of the benches.

"You want to tell me about this murder?" Toby asked.

"Somebody's out to kill my sister," Bob said.

Toby gazed at Bob for about a minute. "That's tough, man."

Toby turned to me. "So what do you want from me? I could send some boys up to your neighborhood for protection."

I waved a hand at Toby. "No, the cops have it covered."

"Cops?" Toby looked impressed. "This is the real thing then?"

"Yeah," I said.

Toby turned back to Bob. "What's your sister's name, Bob?"

"Penny."

Toby bowed in my direction. "Somebody's wants to kill your girlfriend."

"What makes you think she's my girlfriend?" I asked.

"Man, everybody in West Chester knows Tommy McConnell loves Penny Durkin." Toby faced straight ahead.

My eyes rolled. "We need your help."

"Yeah. Figures." Toby nodded.

I leaned back on my hands. "Whoever has it in for Penny may be in cahoots with somebody else. We don't know for sure because we don't know who they are."

Toby stared me in the eye. "And you think I might know?"

"Do you?" Bob asked.

Toby didn't move but he appeared ready to anoint Bob with the dunce of the year award. He let out a long, sarcastic, "Nooooo."

I gazed down at my hands to count with my fingers. "Some creep killed Johnny Bruce, Johnny's father, Bob's brother and my brother. And Cynthia Matting two years ago. And it's possible Salvatore's death was no accident."

"Salvatore? He fell down the steps at the hospital. Who'd kill a kid dying of cancer?"

"A cold-hearted killer who bashes in the heads of teenage girls and boys without mercy." I slammed my right fist into my leg above the knee. "Ouch, that hurt."

"Who's Cynthia what's her name? She the girl they found in the woods?" Toby asked.

"Yeah, Cynthia Matting. Bob and I found her."

"Creepy. You boys into digging up old bones?"

"Old man Utz's dog found her skull sticking out of the ground," Bob said. "We thought it was a rock, right Tommy?"

I nodded.

Toby said, "That's a lot of murders. Who's this Johnny Bruce?"

"Colored kid up our way. Was a senior in high school. A public."

"Never heard of him," Toby said.

"Doesn't matter." I shrugged. "We're checking around town with people we know to see if anyone heard about a kid or a man who brags they got away with murder."

Toby nodded. "You hear a lot of talk in Rig Town. Sometimes there's action to back it up, if you know what I mean."

"We're not the cops, Toby. We're not asking anybody to testify or turn in a buddy. We need to know who the killer is so we can protect Penny." I leaned forward to rest my forearms on my lap.

"No cops?" Toby asked.

"No need for any of your friends to talk to the cops. Bob and I will take the information to the police because it's their job to protect her. That has to be part of the deal."

"But you'll leave me and my friends out of it?" Toby asked.

I sat up straight and tried to crack my knuckles, but I couldn't make a noise. "We'll say we snooped around. Won't mention any names."

"Yeah, let me see what I can find out." Toby patted me on the back. "I see where you're headed with this. Older brother talks to little brother. One of my boys finds out and lets me know. I tell you. That about the size of it?"

"Yep." My knuckles went doink which was better than nothing.

"Here's the thing." Toby did a lot hand gesturing. "I don't call nobody. Never trust the government and never trust Ma Bell. Which Mass you go to?"

"Ten o'clock."

"If I learn anything, I'll see you in church. Don't look for me. You understand?"

I nodded. "Yeah, once you have the information, it'll be hot. You don't want anyone to know you told me."

"That's why I like you, Tommy. You're a wise guy, but you're a smart wise guy. You better leave my neighborhood, now. My boys don't like wise guys, you or Bob. Sorry but they're always on the lookout for a punching bag."

Bob stood up. "We're out of here."

Toby put a hand on my shoulder. "One more thing, Tommy. Sorry about Alan. I didn't know him well, but he seemed like an okay guy, and he played one mean game of basketball."

"Thanks, Toby." I shook his hand.

We repeated this conversation around town, with Bob and me covering the white kids while Chiamaka and Coleman checked in with the coloreds on the east and west sides of town.

CHAPTER 40

The more time Penny and I shared, the more I worried about how she may have been involved in the murders. The three weeks after Bob and I met with Toby made for a long stretch not to make any progress when the girl I loved may be the next victim. Or the killer of the next victim. I wasn't sure which. The good news was no dead bodies showed up during this time.

Penny and I wanted more time to be alone, but Bob hung around. I never said no to my best friend.

If no one tried to kill Penny, could it be because she was the killer? Was she playing with Bob and me? Except that was crazy. Why would she? It would have to have something to do with Johnny Bruce and Cynthia Matting. Mickey I can understand, but why would she kill Alan?

I loved her so much. She couldn't do anything wrong. Not anything really bad. She was a girl, for Pete's sake. She stole cars. Well, she borrowed them and put them back. I loved her so much my stomach hurt. You had to trust the one you loved, right? I loved her, but somebody killed my brother Alan. I couldn't let that pass.

Penny slept at night because she was pregnant and needed to heal from the beating she took. Her face became prettier every day, and our kisses hurt her less each time. If she was the killer, why wasn't she killing anyone now?

Chiamaka, Bob and I went on midnight adventures where we hid out around town and watched to see if the killer showed his face. We cut back to one midnight adventure per week in August because school started soon and we had to practice getting up early every morning.

Publics shopped with their parents to buy public school clothes and supplies. Catholics bought school uniforms, jumpers for the girls that came way down almost to their ankles so by spring they wouldn't be too far above their knees.

I attended the ten o'clock Mass every Sunday morning, but didn't see or hear from Toby Gillis until one Sunday in August when he shook his head no at me. I nodded back, but we didn't speak.

Breaking into Penny's apartment not only provided a way to know how a murderer could sneak in and kill Penny, but also gave Penny a way to sneak out at night. I made this discovery when I woke up in my bed to find Penny's lips pressed against mine and her tongue tickling my mouth.

I pulled back. "How did you get in here?"

"Walked in your front door. You don't think I'm about to start jumping around on your roof in my condition, do you?"

"What are you doing here?" I yawned and stretched.

"I want to sleep with you, silly." She stood, backed up and sat on Alan's bed.

My body and mind froze. My gut felt like somebody dropped a good size rock down there. My heart raced.

I must have looked more scared than I felt because Penny said, "We don't have to do anything yucky. I'm already pregnant. I want to hold you in my arms for a little while. You don't know how frightening it is when a girl is in a family way."

My heart did not slow down. The big rock in my gut waited. I considered whether my brother's killer was sitting on his bed staring at me. "I may not know much, but I don't think it's yucky from what the guys tell me."

Penny stood up. "Make room on your bed for me."

I moved over. Penny slid off her jeans and blouse to reveal her short nightie outfit. She slipped under the sheets. I wore shorts and a tee shirt, thanks to Chiamaka's midnight adventures.

I put my head on Penny's left shoulder and she cuddled me close with her left arm.

"Feel good?" she asked.

"Yes." My heart raced. Was she about to clobber bust me? Yet, I loved her. How could I feel so much love and loathing at the same time?

My mind floated around ideas of sex, which Alan once explained to me not as a yucky thing but more like yummy. He was eight and I was six at the time. He didn't exactly have his facts correct but the thought led me to want to play with Penny's head. "So tell me how your pregnancy thing happened when you're not married. Then tell me about the dots at the end of your sentences."

Penny crinkled her nose. "The dots at the end of my sentences?"

"Yeah, you know, about how you stopped having periods."

Penny laughed. "A girl can't have her period if she's pregnant. I thought you knew that."

"I get stupid sometimes." I still had no idea what a period was but didn't want to sound ignorant.

"Don't get stupid on me," Penny said.

"I'm already stupid in love with you."

"You are? You sound pretty smart to me." Penny hugged me tighter.

"At least I have my periods."

"Your periods?" Penny wrinkled her eyes.

"Yeah, at the end of my sentences."

I didn't realize how fast Penny could move until after she whipped the pillow out from under us and bopped me on the head.

She rolled on top and pinned me. "You're right, Tommy. You did get stupid on me. Didn't I tell you not to let girls sneak up on you?"

"You told me to not let colored girls cold cock me."

"Watch out for pregnant steel pennies, too."

"You promised to tell me how you became pregnant."

"Boy, you did get stupid. Can't you figure it out? Me and Johnny Bruce did the deed."

"The deed? I see." I didn't see.

Penny slid off me and released my arms. She snuggled her back against me as I wrapped her with my arms. I kissed her ear.

"Mmm, watch the ears, Tommy. They'll get you into trouble."

"You don't like when I kiss your ears?"

"I love when you kiss my ears. It makes me feel too good, if you know what I mean."

"You mean kissing like this is for serious making out when you want to do the deed?" I tickled her ear with my lips.

"Um-hmm."

I kissed her ear again and tried the little licky thing with the tongue.

"Tommy..."

"Hmmm." Her ear tasted good.

"See what I mean?"

"Yeah." I didn't stop.

"You're making me feel too good."

"I love you a lot, but..."

"Hold your 'but' this time and say the first part."

"Penny?"

"Yeah?"

"I love you."

Penny rolled over to face me. "Perfect. I love you, too." She planted one on me, and I felt like somebody turned the furnace on by mistake.

When she finished kissing me, she snuggled against me and planted little kisses on my throat. She rested her mouth against my neck.

"Penny, you were supposed to tell me about the deed."

Penny's voice came from far away. "Yeah, the deed. You mean with Johnny Bruce, right?"

"Yeah."

"Here's another rule for you. Never kiss and tell. Besides, we did it once, which was enough. I didn't think virgins could become pregnant the first time."

Since her forehead was in front of my lips, I kissed it "Thought you had to be married before you could do the deed."

"Sounds like something my teachers would say. You can do the deed anytime you want, but you're supposed to wait until you're married."

"If you can do it anytime, why do people wait until marriage?" Talk about feeling stupid as soon as you said something.

"So the girl doesn't end up like me, Tommy. You don't want to get your girlfriend pregnant before you marry her, do you?"

"My girlfriend's already pregnant." I kissed her on the forehead again.

She kissed my throat. When she spoke again, her voice was muffled by her lips tickling my skin. "No harm in doing it with her then?"

"You mean she can't get any more pregnant than she already is?"

"Right."

"It would still be a sin."

"You could always go to confession."

"The idea is to not sin in the first place. Confession doesn't count unless you're sorry."

"So, you'd be sorry."

"No, I wouldn't." I couldn't see her face, but I felt her smile against my skin.

Penny slid up and kissed me on the forehead. She lay back on her half of the pillow. My arms were around her neck, but she no longer pressed against me.

I hugged her close. "You said your mom already killed you. What did you mean?"

Penny turned her head to the side and then back in slow motion. "She used to love me, but the love is gone. It's like all she can give me is burnt ashes."

"Does she hate you?"

"No. If she hated me, she'd yell and punish me and be mean to me. It's not like that. It's more like I died and turned into a ghost. She ignores me which is the cruelest punishment of all. No more hugs. No more kisses. No more kind words. No more being in charge of Bob or other chores. Nothing."

We became quiet for a long time. She fell asleep. I leaned over and checked the clock. It was three-thirty.

I thought about Mom and how she never had time for me because of my younger brothers and sisters. Mom was too busy to squeeze me in unless she was complaining about me doing something wrong or forgetting to do something right. I guess that's a kind of loving where there's no time and the love is assumed.

Another thought crept into my brain and parked a big period at the end of my sentence. Mom would wake up soon and could walk in on us any second.

CHAPTER 41

Mom never walked into my room early in the morning. She was too busy with the little ones, but who knew? This could be the morning she would want to come in for some dumb reason. I started to wake Penny, but changed my mind.

More time passed, but I didn't fall asleep. Penny's body shuddered, and she sat up. She stretched and yawned. She planted a sweet, wet kiss on my lips with no tongue tickling stuff. Her breath smelled awful, but I didn't say anything.

"Let's go," she said. "It's late or early or whatever."

"Where?"

Penny pulled her pants on and buckled her belt while she watched me watching her. "I lost two more holes on my belt, Tommy. Soon everyone will be able to see my big belly."

I stripped off my walking shorts and tee shirt and put on dungarees and a new shirt as Penny watched me. "Where are we headed?"

Penny pointed to my closed bedroom door. "Out front. You don't expect me to walk down the steps arm-in-arm with you to breakfast, do you?"

"What? Oh yeah, guess not."

"We can talk outside and no one has to know about my midnight visit. If you're good, maybe we'll have more visits. Would you like that?"

"Yeah."

We tiptoed downstairs. Mrs. McGillicutty stomped on my feet, rubbed against me and meowed like she wanted to go out. But she pushed against me like she wanted me to stay in.

I petted the cat on top of her head. "She wants me to feed her."

"So feed her."

"No, it's too early. Mom will feed her later."

At the front door, Mrs. McGillicutty rested on her haunches. She dug her front claws into the back of my pants as I passed by. She meowed like crazy.

"You can wait a few minutes to eat, Mrs. McGillicutty." I opened the squeaky front door and started out. Mrs. McGillicutty stopped hassling me. She sat on her haunches to watch me leave. Her eyes were wet, something I'd never seen before. She gave me a melancholy meow and stared at me while leaning her head to one side. I turned and walked out the door with Penny.

We sat on the curb near the Brownell's big old Walnut tree next door. Penny picked up a rock with both hands and tossed it out of the way. We watched it bounce a few times before it stopped near my front steps.

"Penny..." I wasn't sure how to start, or even if I wanted to.

"What, my little, young love? By the way, you know I'll wait for you to grow big. Nobody else will want me once I have a nigger baby."

"It's your baby, Penny. Please call it a colored baby. They don't like when you use that awful word."

"Will that make you happy, dear?"

"Yes."

"Now I love you more because we had a disagreement and patched things up. We're like a real couple now except for one thing."

"You mean sex, don't you?"

"Yes, Tommy. I'll wait for you though. I play with your mouth when I kiss you, because I want to tease you with my love so you'll grow up faster. But we have to wait. I know that now like I didn't before. You're a child and I shouldn't love you so much. I don't know why I do. One reason is I've always been a bad girl. The other is you and Bob are the only people who ever loved me. Besides Mom, of course, but she doesn't love me anymore."

"Penny, this isn't what I wanted to talk about. We have to discuss your secret."

"It's no secret anymore. Everybody in West Chester knows I'm pregnant with Johnny Bruce's baby."

"That's not the secret. Your other secret."

"Everyone knows you and I are in love."

"That was never a secret."

"I have a big mouth sometimes, Tommy. I'm sorry."

I took Penny's hand and kissed it. "It was frustrating at first, but now I have these special feelings for you."

"It's okay to say you love me."

"I want to talk about the other secret." I dropped her hand so the back of my hand touched her lap.

"What other secret?" Penny did not move my hand.

"You know."

"You're a good boy, Tommy, but you fell in love with a bad girl. Is that the secret you're talking about? Dad always said I was evil. It's why he wanted to kill me. Now, you know, too. But don't tell Mom and Bob, okay?"

The wind blew cool morning air. I waited for Penny to say more, but she kept silent.

She squeezed my hand and slid it up her lap a bit. "I'm a bad girl, Tommy. How can I bring a colored baby into the world? You know Mom will kill me. Colored babies and steel pennies can't mix. Do you think God will forgive me, like you always say to Bob? I hope he forgives me for being so wicked. Dad never forgave me although I said I was sorry after each time he hit me. I must have said I was sorry a thousand, million times. Do you think God will be like Dad, Tommy? I will always love you so tell God to forgive me for getting pregnant with a ni... I mean a colored baby. I know, I'll ask him, too. In fact, I'll do it right now."

Penny bowed her head. She let go of my hand so it rested alone on her lap. My mind flashed with thoughts about how warm her body felt. In my excitement, I squeezed her leg and slid my hand into a hotter zone. She smiled like she wanted my hand planted that far into the secret territory of a woman.

Penny folded her hands in prayer. It looked faked, like in a cheap movie, but she was bawling now and I was convinced she was sincere. "Thank you, God, for sending Jesus to save the world. I accept him as my Lord and savior. Now, please save me."

"Confess your sins, Penny." I patted her upper thigh.

"I'm sorry I got pregnant with Johnny Bruce, Lord. Please forgive me, Amen."

"Don't forget to confess your other crimes." I kissed her on the cheek.

Penny's eyes turned crinkly and her lips pursed like she was a bunny rabbit. I wiped the tears from her cheeks, abandoning her high temperature lap.

The question marks dripped out of her eyes, and she gawped like she understood. She bowed her head again. "Forgive me, Lord, for falling in love with Tommy and making him fall in love with me when he was too young. Teach us to wait until we grow up. Forgive me for any other bad stuff I've done, too, like making out with boys in cars, which I stopped doing on account of that's how I became pregnant in the first place. Forgive me for borrowing cars without permission and everything else I ever did wrong, Lord, Amen."

Penny locked eyes with me. "There, Tommy, I confessed like they do in the Protestant church because you're not a priest and besides, I like this way better."

"I hoped you would admit your other guilt, and I wouldn't have to lay it out for you."

Penny glanced down with her hand rubbing her forehead. She shook her head a few times. She gazed at me with question marks in her eyes. "I don't know what else to admit to." She paused, taking a deep breath. "Why don't you start and I'll pick up when I know what you're talking about."

I fiddled with her fingers. "I didn't pay any attention when Bob came over to my house with his hatchet wet the last time we went out to the country. Remember the day Bob and I found Cynthia's skull and Johnny Bruce almost ran him over?"

Penny intertwined her fingers with mine. "Of course. Johnny didn't stop and Bob wasn't hurt. When you boys came back from your pretend funeral for Cynthia Matting the next day, Bob cried, but you held your tears. You shouldn't have. It's okay for a man to show emotion, but the look on your face not wanting to cry was what started me falling in love with you in the first place."

"Don't change the subject."

"You're the one who asked about the time Bob almost got run over."

I kissed her hand. "As time passed, the more Bob's wet hatchet bothered me. You would never wash Bob's mess kit, Penny, no matter what your mom said. You would make Bob do it. And nobody ever asks anybody to wash a hatchet. That was the first big give-away."

"What give away? I never washed Bob's hatchet. What are you talking about?" Penny squirmed so I figured she had lied and I must be on the right track.

I pressed her. "You chopped up Johnny Bruce's father on the same day Bob and I went into the woods to camp out, and we found poor Cynthia Matting. Bob used to have a crush on her but she rejected him so you killed her, right? No, maybe you didn't do that one. I don't know, Penny. Did you?"

Penny skewed her head at an angle. She glared at me without blinking. Her mouth opened wide but nothing came out.

I was in no mood to wait for answers. "Penny, you killed my friend Salvatore at the horsepistol by pushing him down the steps. You clobber-busted Alan for no reason unless he refused to make out with you because he knew I liked you. You killed your boyfriend Johnny Bruce because he made you pregnant or refused to marry you. You even kerpowed your own brother Mickey, who I admit deserved to be punished but murder is a bit harsh, don't you think? You are a cold-blooded killer, Penny Durkin, but I love you anyway. I can't stand it."

Penny stared at me with her jaw about down to her beautiful chest and tiny daggers appeared in her eyes. "Tommy, what has gotten into you?"

"I love you, but you have to turn yourself in." Tears rolled down my cheeks but I didn't care anymore. I was on a role. I was angry. I thought about Alan, and I was in love with Penny Durkin.

My brain twirled around as I tried to separate loyalty for my brother and love for Penny. While my head didn't blow up, I felt like I was twisting coils of nerves into a rope and the rope twisted into a bunch of knots.

"Penny, please turn yourself in. They'll put you in an insane asylum and make you better. You won't be put in prison like your Dad or reform school like Mickey. I'll be older when you come out, and we can be together then. Maybe I can visit you sometimes." My body shook as I cried out of control. I placed my arms around Penny's neck. My tears made the collar of her blouse wet.

She held me. "You poor goofball, I have to wait for you to grow up, don't I?"

Breathing became difficult. My head slid down the front of Penny's blouse, my face fell between the bumps on her chest and past her expanding belly. My head ended up on her lap. I hugged Penny around her legs. I whimpered, "Penny, Penny, Penny, I love you so much, Penny."

Through her tears, Penny said, "This is about my best day ever, Tommy McConnell. My boyfriend thinks I killed like a zillion people but he still loves me. Life doesn't get any better. And I confessed my sins to God, so I'm cool with him. The only thing missing is…"

CHAPTER 42

Chiamaka sat Indian style in a blur at the foot of the bed where she read a book. She must have sensed me watching her because she glanced my way. She wore one of those straight, studious but blurry expressions that melt under the pressure of a big grin. She crawled up and hugged me.

I made some sort of unghh noise because the pain hurt so much, and it was the only sound my mouth would make. She flashed a whimsical smile before kissing me smack on the lips. She held on for a while before breaking off.

My eyes began to focus.

She positioned her face about six inches above mine. "Thought I lost you, steel penny."

I felt her tears drip hot on my skin. She stroked my cheeks with her fingers to rub her tears in.

I squeezed out my own tears from the pain of her crushing hug. I wanted to speak, but all that came out of my mouth was "Uh, uh, uh."

"Lay back, steel penny. You slept three days. Takes a while for your brain to reconnect to your mouth. We can talk later. Let me smile at you." Chiamaka scooted back to the end of the bed where she flung me a quick, "I forgot" glance. She spun her head around to one side. I followed her gaze to where Mom slept in a chair by the side of the hospital bed.

Seeing Mom filled me with a new love for her like when I was small. Mom had responsibility for the five little ones at home, but she was not with them. She was here waiting for me to wake up. She must have left my older brothers in charge.

Tears poured down my cheeks.

Mom opened her eyes and smiled. Soon she was crying, too. She scampered out of her chair and hugged me as I discovered in this moment the undying love my mother bore for me and I for her, a love I hoped never to lose again.

"They said you might never wake up, Tommy." Mom wiped a tear from her cheeks.

I pushed Mom back so she had to stop kissing me.

"I swore to God I would not lose another boy. Not this summer, not never. Oh, Tommy." She set about kissing me again.

"Mom!" I tried to push her back again but was too weak.

"I've been praying for you, Tommy. Me in this chair three days with my rosary beads and God up in heaven on his royal throne. And see, he gave you back to me." More kissing followed, but I was too weak to care.

Days passed by. I don't remember most of them. They had a routine in the horsepistol of poking and pilling a guy until he had to get out or die.

Freeman the Cop stopped by and asked me about what happened. I didn't remember anything. If I ever did, he wanted me to call him. He told me what everyone else had been saying since I woke up – Bob's dad did something terrible over on Walnut Street that morning.

No one would answer me when I asked about Penny or wanted to know why Bob hadn't visited me. But the answers were in the choking silence and the tears that streamed from their eyes.

Will Barnes found his way into my room, tapping with his cane on the linoleum floor. His sister, Constance, who was in my grade at St. Agnes School, accompanied him.

Will told me about waking up and hearing Penny call him through the spirit world. She asked him to rescue me. "I asked her 'Are you a good thief or a bad thief?' Penny replied she was counted among the good thieves and Jesus had promised this day she would see him in paradise. I charged out into that rain as fast as a blind man can galumph along, Tommy McConnell, because I knew something happened horrible on Walnut Street. Loco, loco."

"Don't pay any attention to him, Tommy," Constance said. "He was out taking his morning stroll and about tripped over you."

"Oh, sweet Jesus," Will Barnes wept. "I found those dead white folks, and you were passed out in the gutter and bleeding to paint the road red. I held you in my arms and prayed sweet Jesus to rescue you and wrapped your head in my shirt and cried out, 'Loco, loco, Mrs. McConnell, come see what they done to your boy!' And then your people came running. Sweet Jesus, how they came running."

***

At home, I had to stay in bed and skip school for like a month. One night as I minded my own business, it hit me. If someone had punched me hard in the chest and in the stomach, I would have felt about the same. My head hurt. I became dizzy. Something awful happened in my stomach, like I was about to hurl.

I remembered Walnut Street.

I thought about Jesus on the cross. In the Bible Jesus called his Father "Abba." I asked one of my older brothers, Sean, to look it up for me in the college library on the way home from work and darned if he didn't. "Abba" didn't exactly mean "father." It meant "Dad" or "Papa."

On the cross the Father abandoned Jesus because the Father is holy, and Jesus had to take on the sins of the world. The Father doesn't hang around sin. Jesus said, "My God, my God, why have you forsaken me?" Jesus was so abandoned by his Father that he no longer recognized him as his

"Abba." Being abandoned by his Father was the last agony of the crucifixion.

My little anguish was nothing compared with what Jesus suffered for my sins while hanging between a good thief and a bad thief. And what he suffered for Penny's sins and even Bob's sins.

I'll see Penny Durkin again. The first pleasure of heaven for me, after apologizing to God for my sins, will be apologizing to her.

When you love someone as much as I loved Penny Durkin, and if it's your first love, you should honor her memory and not hurt her family. Besides, I found out the police had already killed Bob's dad for resisting arrest when they caught him. So why change the official story? Everyone seemed satisfied blaming Penny's dad.

***

I remembered waking up that morning as I lay in the gutter with something sticky around me. The dim light of the sun marked its rising in the distance. I heard no cars on the street so it was still early. Gray, churning clouds released the first rain of a dry summer that August morning. I smelled a mixture of blood, raw meat and street tar.

I glared up at a monster born of the asphalt, a black blob rising out of Walnut Street itself. The tar bubbled and oozed in the rain as it took on the shape of Bob Durkin. He wrapped a rope around the branch that jutted out of Mrs. Brownell's tree next door and hung over towards my house. Long, deep scratches covered his face and continued down his neck. His bare arms displayed the same deep abrasions. He ignored the blood oozing out of his cuts.

Bob spoke to me. I'm not sure he realized I could hear him. He may have thought I was dead, and he was talking to my body or to my soul in purgatory.

"I spent my whole life following you around. Then you wanted my sister. You can't have her. You thought you were so smart trying to figure out who was killing everybody. First with me and Chiamaka. Then later with Penny. Yeah, I heard you accuse my sister of killing people. You're so stupid for a kid who gets good grades. How could you think she would ever hurt somebody? But you were too close to the truth.

"You know I liked Cynthia Matting just like you cared about Penny. Penny didn't pay any attention to you two years ago either. Cynthia Matting told me to get lost even though we played together for years. She became a teenager before we did, so I wasn't good enough for her anymore. She didn't need me, and so I didn't need her anymore. Then I found her in the woods making out with – guess who – Johnny Bruce, just like Chiamaka told us. Yep, the same Johnny that did my sister. Boy, did he deserve to die, but he ran away when he heard me charging up the hill. He wasn't afraid of a little kid like me, but he didn't want anyone to see him with a white girl.

"Cynthia wasn't smart enough to run away. She just said hello and turned away from me. I was so angry I threw my hatchet at her. I did it without thinking. Never meant to hurt her. Almost took the top of her head off. Blood flew everywhere. Buried her for Utz's dog Logan to find two years later. I should have chased that dog home when he followed us into the woods that day.

"For a long time, I felt real bad about killing Cynthia, but it was my secret. Then one day it stopped bothering me. Got to where I wanted to try it again. Didn't act on the urge until I found out about Penny and that rotten Johnny Bruce. Yeah, I knew already when you told me, but it made me mad enough to kill her, knowing you knew. I get mad sometimes, you know. Real mad. Like now.

"Then we went camping, and you asked me about my wet hatchet. I chopped up Johnny Bruce's father that morning. I had to wash away the blood. Why Johnny's dad? How'd I know the old man was in the bed and not Johnny until after I swung away in the darkness? Johnny wasn't even home when I chopped his old man. Johnny found him later and that's when he ran away in his dad's Caddy. You know how the cops will grab any colored guy when there's a crime committed and not care which one. That's why he didn't stop when he almost ran me over.

"Then like an idiot you tried to pin your friend Salvatore's death on Penny. She ran an errand to the horsepistol for Mom the same day. Did you ever stop to find out what time your friend tumbled down those steps at the hospital? Penny wasn't there when it happened. Gave the time in the paper. If you had read it, you'd know his death was just a stupid accident.

"You thought Alan was smacked at the bottom of the fire escape and then climbed up. Wrong again, clever detective. Alan came up the steps. I walked out the apartment backdoor. He nodded at me but didn't see my hatchet because I kept it behind my back. Alan decided to launch a lunger into the kitchen fan of the Royal, to get even with Menoitios. While he faced down at the fan and worked up a spitball, I conked him on the back of the head. He spun around and wham went down like a rock. He smacked the back of his wounded noggin on one of the steps. It was the sixth one, Tommy. Remember the one with the blood stain? When he hit it, his feet kept flipping over so he did a somersault until he landed at the bottom.

"Why did I kill Alan? No reason, except Will Barnes had said, 'Woe be unto Alan,' so I figured I'd bring a little woe unto him. I knew it would screw up your head, and I knew Menoitios would get blamed. I hate the sucker. The one mistake I made was you were too dumb to take the hint and try to prove Menoitios committed the murders.

"Penny never saw me bop Alan. You know why? She was taking a nap like she said. Girls need extra sleep when they're pregnant. If you ever paid attention to your mom who had, what, a dozen babies, then you would know. I knew and I'm not even in your family."

Penny moaned but was still knocked cold.

Bob kept talking to me. "I enjoyed watching Johnny Bruce burn. You didn't notice I had disappeared long enough from you and Jamie Bordeaux at the golf course to sneak over to the housing development. I wasn't planning to kill anybody, but I spied Johnny Bruce's car. Penny was climbing out of it. She never saw me. I waited for her to disappear. I snuck up behind the car and shoved it. The stupid idiot had left it in neutral.

"Of course Penny lied about being out with her friends that night. Remember when Jenny said she and Michelle had been driving to the shore on weekends?

"Mickey was easy. All I had to do was slip out of your house while you slept and sneak into my apartment. Smack! Old Mickey became history. Cleaned up my trusty Boy Scout hatchet and put it back. I even dried the hatchet this time so you wouldn't find it wet. Mickey will never beat on me again.

"You were so sure we could solve these crimes together except you missed another little detail. Your pal Bob was as evil as his dad and brother."

Bob yanked on the rope and hoisted Penny up by the neck. Her hands were stained red. Blood dripped from her sharp nails. In my paralysis, I wanted to stop Bob, but all I could do was scream inside my head while I watched in silence and listened.

Bob said, "Goodbye, Penny, who sneaks around to sleep with boys." He gazed my way. "Yeah, I know where Penny spent last night."

He fell silent for the rest of his task. Penny was still alive when Bob hauled her unconscious, bleeding body up to hang from that limb. She came to, and I gazed upon her panicked, shocked eyes. She noticed me as she squirmed about before her body relaxed. She drifted around and around while Bob stood back to admire his handiwork in the sunrise.

Then another black blob arose from the tarmac of Walnut Street and reshaped itself into Bob's dad. Even then I tried to shout a warning to Bob who wasn't looking, but I wasn't able to move or make a sound. His dad smacked Bob over the head with a rock, maybe the same one Bob used on Penny and me before tossing it aside.

Cynthia Matting strolled by then, like it was the middle of the day and she had nothing else to do but ramble down Walnut Street. She wore the maroon and green striped blouse she had on the day Bob killed her. Her outfit appeared new and pretty. She had on a grey skirt and black penny loafers with white bobby socks. The pennies in her loafers were steel. She carried her purse, the one the police found with her body and used to help identify her. She glanced down at Bob and then over at me. She shrugged, smiled, and waved to say goodbye before ambling on. Whatever message she had tried to deliver was past receiving, except for one word mouthed in the balcony of the Warner Theater. Was she miming boo or Bob? I had guessed wrong and paid the price with my steel Penny.

Mr. Durkin gawked at me. Did he wonder if I was still alive? His eyes were black with red flames in the center. He faded out of my field of vision as the tarmac itself lifted up in anger and swallowed me.

I floated above the streets, houses, businesses, schools, churches, and the great college of West Chester. Directly below, almost dead center in the town, stood Mrs. Brownel's walnut tree with the long branch extending over towards the sidewalk in front of our house. I couldn't see through the foliage of the tree so I zoomed down to street level and gazed upon Bob Durkin with his head split open and blood splattered on the sidewalk where it mixed with rain below Penny's dangling feet.

My beloved twisted in the wind, her shoes and pants wet and soiled, but her blouse dry under the protection of the walnut tree. I couldn't look more than a second at her face with its cold bulging eyes, but her blonde ponytail still dangled sweetly to her shoulders, held with a pink ribbon tied in a bow.

I gaped at my body on the street. My eyes were closed. Rain mixed with the blood leaking from my face and skull. I heard the tap-tap-tap of a cane upon the wet brick sidewalk.

My last memory of the Walnut Street Horror was Will Barnes' face green in the world of the spirits and four times its normal size. He glared at me in the blackness of the asphalt void and laughed like he knew something I didn't.

***

Sometimes late at night, I found myself waking in a sweat despite the West Chester weather turning cold and the trees shedding their leaves in preparation for a bitter season. At these moments I whispered, "I'm sorry." But no one answered.

With length of years came understanding, or so said Will Barnes, blind in body but with eyes that saw in the darkness. He said we were all either good thieves or bad thieves. And he was right, I suppose. Whether steel pennies or copper, we carried the same value in the marketplace of Heaven. And in all things, it was faith that ultimately saw us through the day.

I wanted to run away to where they never heard of me or Bob or Penny or the Walnut Street Horror, somewhere out west where in my dreams I saw a wilderness of trees, mountains and childish pleasures awaiting me. I envisioned an Indian tribe adopting me, and a young squaw helping me to forget West Chester, Pennsylvania.

Penny took my accusations when I was wrong. She was a tough girl. Chiamaka said I had to be strong, too.

"Childhood," Chiamaka said, "is like the Garden of Eden, full of innocence and sweetness. Then comes the devil, and when you gaze about, you ain't in Eden no more. You're an adult. Look around us, Tommy McConnell. We don't see no gardens, but you won't stumble on none wherever you wander either. What you do have here that you can't have no place else in the world, is me.

"Where you headed off to anyway, my steel penny? All you'll find is Pittsburgh or Chicago. You're too old for cowboys and indians and running away from home. Stay here and let Chiamaka hold you. Then we be having our own midnight adventures right here in West Chester, Pennsylvania, and take our pleasure in waiting upon the morning star."

THE END

Thanks for choosing **Steel Pennies**.

Purchase more of my books, including **Snpgrdxz and the Time Monsters,** Book 1 of the Snpgrdxz Series by searching Snpgrdxz on www.amazon.com.

Or keep reading the Snpgrdxz series now…

SNPGRDXZ AND THE TIME MONSTERS

BOOK 1 OF THE SNPGRDXZ SERIES

BY PAUL R. LLOYD

CHAPTER 1

CRAZY IS AS CRAZY DOES

From where she stood at the foot of my bed, fifteen-year-old Jennifer Hawkins couldn't miss, but would this sweet girl shoot me?

Yes, I meant that Jennifer Hawkins, the prettiest sophomore at Lincoln High in Wheaton, Illinois, with her skinny-but-tall body, the daughter of Principal Hawkins and old Mrs. Hawkins, the choir director at our church.

"Bryan, I'm sorry you won't understand what I'm about to tell you, but that's all I'm sorry for, you little –" Here Jennifer referred to the male anatomy in a derogatory way. I'm certain she didn't mean my personal anatomy. How would she know? Mine's not like that. Honest.

" – I'm about to blow your head off so you won't survive to shoot me again later. Now you know why I will kill you. I guess that explains everything, doesn't it? There's nothing sweeter than avenging your own murder."

I ducked and covered my head while admiring Jennifer's tight blue jeans and white blouse.

Okay, maybe I wasn't her type. Or she'd prefer a date with Lionel Nipgrinder, the senior quarterback who was unaware of her existence. But these were not reasons for her to shoot me on the Monday night before my junior year. At age sixteen, I was a year older. She should have shown respect for her elders. Instead, she wore an evil grin I hadn't thought she was capable of.

"Why?" I sat up and pointed my hands to the ceiling. Tears welled up in my eyes. I knew nothing about weapons so I had no idea what type of pistol was about to end my brief life but my soon-to-be murderess gave off a perfume that hinted of soaking wet toy poodle or sweet animal perspiration rather than flowers.

The gun Jennifer held had an extra-long fat attachment on the barrel which I assumed meant a silencer. That's what it would be in a James Bond or Jason Bourne movie. Noticing the little add-on made my stomach push up into my heart.

At a moment like this, you're supposed to have a brilliant insight into the meaning of life, but all I noticed was Jennifer's cup size under her white blouse. She must have grown over the summer.

I also couldn't help notice as the sweat poured down the side of my face that James Bond and Jason Bourne had the same initials. Why was that?

What else could I do? Someone, I assumed Jennifer, had switched my bedside lamp on while I slept. But how had she made her way into my house without waking me or my parents or my little sister, Katie? We Ganarskis are light sleepers.

How was she avenging her own murder? Did she mean I had killed her or was about to? Why would I harm the girl I had a crush on? Besides, I couldn't kill a cat or a mouse. I'm just not made that way. I'd slap a mosquito no problem, but Jennifer Hawkins? I don't think so.

I was about to plead my pacifist nature to Jennifer when an Asian girl I didn't know slammed through my bedroom door with my best high school buddy Gilbert Armstrong right behind her. My door banged against the plaster wallboard and flapped back against Gilbert. As he ricocheted off my bureau, my body began to shake.

The force of the rebounding door almost knocked the Army rifle out of Gilbert's hands. I mean the weapon with the bayonet attached. The Asian carried one also with a long banana clip loaded and a bayonet mounted that had a shine on the edge of the blade like she had just sharpened it. Where Jennifer's aroma was sweet but animal like, their aroma was a mixture of the musk of hard sweat and dirt.

"Turpelator will be pissed." Actually, Jennifer dropped the f-bomb before "pissed." In her fifteen years, Jennifer Hawkins had never uttered rough language harder than "crap" in my presence so you can imagine my shock at her little f-ing speech on top of her derogatory comments about my private anatomy which she knew nothing about.

From the dark depths of my parent's bedroom, I heard my dad call out, "Quick making all that noise, Bryan."

Jennifer backed away from the foot of my bed until her back banged into my open bedroom window hard enough for her butt to almost pass through the open window space. She caught herself and bounced off my window before firing without aiming because she was busy focusing her pretty eyes on Gilbert and his Asian cohort. Some people worry about distracted driving. I had to worry about distracted shooting.

Before I could react to any of this, Dad hollered again from his bedroom, "Bryan, cut out the racket already. Your TV is way too loud."

The Asian skewered Jennifer through the chest with a bayonet thrust packing enough force to knock both of them out my open window. The blow shocked my mind off Jennifer's cup size and onto Dad's direct order earlier today to replace the broken window screen in my room or I would have to pay hell or hell would pay me, I forgot which. Either way, you don't ignore one of Dad's mighty commands, but there was the window hole without the screen.

With the aluminum structure of the window destroyed when Jennifer and that Asian terrorist flew through it, I wasn't sure I needed to replace the screen anymore, but I had to keep Dad happy or else.

While I took in the fresh aroma of burnt sulfur and hot lead, Gilbert bellowed through the window hole, "Nice going, Snpgrdxz."

He turned his black, baldy cut head in my direction and smiled a shit eater at me. "This didn't happen, Bryan."

Before I could ask what a Snpgrdxz was, Gilbert left my bedroom the old-fashioned way as he charged out the door.

"For the last time, turn down that TV," Dad hollered.

I had no problem thinking this had been a wild late night TV flick. I wanted it to be a nightmare movie. Wouldn't you?

Maybe I had replaced the window screen, and Jennifer Hawkins' increased cup size was a figment of my imagination. How else do you explain Mr. Turpelator, our high school physics teacher, who flew in through my open window uninvited? I wasn't hyperventilating, but I wasn't playing catch with my breath either.

And why had Jennifer mentioned his name before shooting at me?

Mr. Turpelator hovered above the place where Jennifer had stood with her pistol before the Asian girl gored her. He didn't have a gun, but he opened his mouth about a foot and a half to reveal the longest fangs I had ever seen. He floated closer to me on the bed like he wanted to suck my brains out. His breath made me think of dead rats in the rain. To be precise, the aroma was more like dead rats in the gutter two days after they had drowned in a flood and now the sun beat down on them.

Either my breath was worse than I thought (it was after midnight) or Mr. Turpelator had spotted the big crucifix

Grandma Ganarski had hung above my bed the year I received Communion for the first time, no matter that we were Protestants. Either way, he threw his hands up to block his face and flew backwards out the window at a speed that suggested a balloon struck by a pin or a puppet whose strings had been hard yanked.

As I checked the crucifix, I couldn't help but notice that Jennifer had missed Jesus by a quarter inch.

Dad would kill me if I didn't replace the shattered window and clean up the broken glass, but would he be pissed about not replacing the screen? A new window, paid for by my summer job, would include the screen.

I tried to sleep, but what if it hadn't been a dream? Was the girl I was crazy about in high school at this moment bleeding to death right under my second floor bedroom window? If these midnight events were real, then Jennifer's bloodstains would cover the floor and the wall. I'd also find bloodstains around the window, right?

I climbed out of bed and checked my floor. I didn't see any blood, so it must have been a dream except how do you explain the evidence of broken glass, bits of aluminum, and the bullet hole in the crucifix? Besides, the aroma of animal sweat still wafted in the air. But what if Jennifer had been so close to the window when the Asian girl had stabbed her that her lifeblood flowed out the window with her?

CHAPTER 2

ESTABLISH A FEW FACTS

Scuffling noises from the backyard tore my attention away from the broken window. I padded barefoot down the hall to Katie's room. From her window, I glimpsed two shapes next to the storage shed by the back fence. As my eyes adjusted to the dim light, I identified Gilbert and the Asian. They patted down a dirt pile in the shape of a grave where Mom's mums grew in the fall.

"Bryan?" Katie asked.

"Go back to sleep." I rushed downstairs to the garage to grab Dad's flashlight. I tripped over the one-hundred-foot long electric cord Dad used with our plug-in lawnmower. Okay, I mowed the lawn, and yes, I was supposed to wrap up the wire and drape it over the mower handle out of the way when I finished. I knocked over the recycle bin which started the empty cans and bottles clanging around the garage floor. The plastic gallon milk jugs clattered in their muffled plastic wuss noise until they ended up under Mom's Malibu and Dad's Explorer. Dad was going to slaughter me.

From my position with my butt on the garage floor, I heard Mom shriek loud enough to wake the possibly late Jennifer Hawkins. I discovered one of Dad's crushed aluminum beer cans under my left big toe as I danced and hooted out of the garage through the family room and back into the kitchen.

283

"It's okay, Mom." I checked my right foot for blood. There wasn't much. The empty was a twelve-ounce can so how much damage could it do? And I didn't think this was the best time to tell Mom that Gilbert and some Asian terrorist murdered sweet little Jennifer Hawkins up in my bedroom.

Besides I was still alive so someone watched out for me. I mean other than Gilbert and his Asian girlfriend. She was attractive despite her warrior ways.

"What's happening down there?" My sister Katie this time. Could Dad be far behind?

On cue, Dad wandered out of the powder room off the kitchen dressed in his t-shirt and boxers trailed by the aroma of long dead pork. "Why are you bothering me with so much racket in the middle of the night?"

"Sorry, Dad. I was checking on a noise in the backyard when I tripped."

"Be quiet and go back to bed so I can sleep undisturbed by the likes of you."

"Yes, sir."

Dad appreciated an occasional expression of respect, which worked wonders when there was more to a story I didn't want to tell. Dad headed for the stairs as I searched the kitchen for a flashlight. I found one in the drawer next to the refrigerator.

I checked the flashlight to see if it lit. You know how it is with flashlights. They sit in a kitchen drawer for years. When you need them, you discover acid leaking out of the batteries. Mom must have been at this flashlight recently because it worked, but the bottom of the drawer had acid stains from the previous set of batteries.

In the yard under my bedroom window, I discovered blood stains and shoe impressions on the lawn. I followed the footprints and blood smears until they vanished at the storage shed by our back fence. Someone had dragged Jennifer's impaled body across the lawn to the dug up spot.

I noticed two shovels and thrust one into the dirt. It hit something below the surface that was too soft for a rock. The sugary animal aroma from my bedroom escaped into the air.

My butt hit the ground. I backed up until I came into contact with the shed. I couldn't breathe. I had liked Jennifer Hawkins since preschool, and had a crush on her since puberty, but never realized how deep my feelings for her went until my chest collapsed around my heart and the tears flowed.

I heard a rustling noise by the back fence. I took a gander in time to spot shadow upon shadow as something dark and mysterious vanished into the night.

***

Where blood had darkened the lawn during the night, black muddy spots appeared like the remains of a well-scrubbed cleanup campaign gone awry. I woke up on the dirt spot next to the storage shed, but was stiff and chilled by an August morning in the Chicago burbs. I searched around the yard again under my window. The lawn had a dish detergent aroma. Bubbles floated over the grass, but there were no blood stains.

I had survived a wicked dream about blood on the lawn, or one of the local coyotes must have caught a bloody rabbit. But who served on the cleanup committee and why didn't they wake me?

I went inside for breakfast. I should have gazed up at my window. So sue me. I'm not a detective. I'm a teenager.

The first day of my junior year of high school was a few days away. And a guy had to eat. This was no time to panic about a nightmare that turned my bedroom lamp on while leaving perfumed soap bubbles on the lawn and a grave by the storage shed.

It didn't take long for the reality of my looming craziness to hit home. The words spoken by my evening visitors were right out of a nightmare where the girl you like tries to kill you so you won't kill her later. What insane logic was that? But upstairs in my bedroom, I had to replace the shattered window and face the reality of a bullet hole in Grandma's crucifix.

***

"You didn't happen to invade my bedroom last night with an Asian beauty queen who rammed a bayonet between Jennifer Hawkins' boobs, did you?" I passed a towel to Gilbert on the bench of our basketball game in the summer league. The season ended with this game, and our school's football players were already gone to their practice so Gilbert and I became the beneficiaries of their basketball game minutes.

"I think I would remember that." Gilbert peeled off his left sneaker and rubbed his foot.

I spun my head to face the other way to avoid the aroma of old gym, but it followed wherever Gilbert's feet went. I turned back to him. "Then my dad drove me crazy."

"Did what?" Gilbert asked.

"Drove me nuts. I'm having hallucinations." I yanked a soda out of the ice chest, but before I could pop the tab, Coach Corbin, aka our youth director at church, roared for us to get ready to return to action.

We made our way down to Mr. Romano, the art teacher at Lincoln High, who served as timekeeper for the summer basketball league as well as the regular interscholastic winter league. He stopped the game long enough for us to jump back into the game.

Later when we returned to the bench for a rest, Gilbert asked, "So this Asian babe? Was she a hottie?"

"Yeah, kinda. I paid more attention to the gun with the silencer Jennifer fired in my direction."

"If she was a hottie, then I went out with her."

It was my turn to scrunch up my face while I sipped the soda I had eyed since the previous break.

Gilbert slapped my back. "Kidding, Bryan, okay?"

"So you're not dating any new girls?"

"I'm not dating an old girl either. Who has money for dates?"

"Then it must have been a wild dream."

Gilbert leaned forward with his elbows on his knees. "Trust me, Bryan, you can relax. Oh, wait. Did your mom dump chemicals into your corn flakes? She's the drug-crazed hippie type, right?"

I pictured my church deacon mom dumping weed into my breakfast bowl. The picture didn't work, but my experience last night didn't fit anywhere near a sane place. "Gilbert, there's a brand new bullet hole in the big crucifix above my bed, and somebody smashed my bedroom window. And I found blood stains on the grass in my yard under my window, but somebody cleaned it up while I slept."

"So how did you get Jennifer Hawkins up in your bedroom past your parents, especially your dad?" Gilbert put his sneakers back on.

"I didn't. I woke up and there she was with her gun aimed my way."

"And what are you doing with a crucifix?" Gilbert tied his sneakers.

I took in the aroma of fresh sweat coming off the basketball court, a sweeter smell than Gilbert's feet. "You've seen it. Grandma got it for my first communion."

"Did you ask Jennifer Hawkins about any of this?"

"Are you crazy? I'm not in her league."

Gilbert gave me a cold stare. "What are you talking about? We're in youth group with her, and we've known her since preschool."

"I can't call her about this."

"Text her."

"What if she's dead? When you wake up insane is no time to text your friends."

CHAPTER 3

MY IRRATIONALITY CONTINUES

In the darkness before dawn on Wednesday, Jennifer Hawkins kissed me awake. She snuggled close on the bed with the aroma of sweet flowers around her. "Darling, I'm so happy we're together again at last."

I turned on the lamp by my bed and sat up certain of my new irrationality. Jennifer wore the same blue jeans and a white blouse she modeled for my Monday night reality dream. "How? Why?"

She kissed with a mouth open, tongue-probing passion that shocked me. Sure, I've known Jennifer Hawkins all her life, and I cried for her when I thought she was stabbed to death by my best friend Gilbert's Asian terrorist girlfriend, although Gilbert didn't have a girlfriend, Asian or otherwise. But where did this sweet Christian teenager learn to kiss like that? No girl had ever pushed her tongue my way before so you can imagine my surprise. She pulled away like she needed air before the next French dive with me.

"Jennifer, I'm so glad you like me, but isn't this a bit fast?"

"Darling, I missed you so much." She brought her open lips almost to mine but stopped. "Did you say 'a bit fast'?"

Not waiting for an answer, she pulled away while the passion on her face morphed into a scrunched up question mark that transformed into an "I screwed up" expression. "Snpgrdxz?"

Jennifer studied my face for something that wasn't there. I have to admit I was happy her lovely, kissable mouth had returned to saying words like "crap" instead of real curses and swears.

It was my turn to speak, but what can a guy say at a tender moment like this? I should have asked who or what was a "Snpgrdxz," but all I could muster was a weak "Huh?" I would have to wait until another time to ask Jennifer to explain Snpgrdxz to me.

Jennifer stomped across the room hands on hips. "I missed. Sorry I frightened you. This didn't happen, okay? And if you see Turpelator, run like hell."

She crept out through my open bedroom door as I considered that it was too late to worn me about Mr. Turpelator.

I went over to the hole where my window used to be and pushed aside the cloth I hung for a covering. The evening breeze wafted in cool, damp, clean suburban air as I gazed at Jennifer running down the driveway.

The Asian girl appeared by the side of the house. She headed towards the shed with two shovels as her short skirt billowed in the night breeze.

Gilbert joined the Asian girl. He spoke barely above a whisper. "Jennifer."

"What?" Jennifer asked in a normal volume.

"We have to get rid of your body before the sun comes up. Can you help us?" Gilbert asked.

"What will you do with it?" Jennifer asked.

Gilbert pointed to the shed. "We can't leave it here. Let's take it out to the woods where we burned those cars that time and cremate her."

"Good idea. But please respect my body," Jennifer said.

"Why don't you come with us to make sure we do it right," said the Asian.

"Okay, but I wish my Bryan were here. He always knows how to do these things right." Jennifer took off around the front of the house. I ran downstairs to open the front door for her before she rang the bell and woke my family.

I had no idea what Jennifer meant about me knowing how to do something right. I'm not the do-it-right sort. I'm more the goof-it-up-the-first-time-and-fix-it-later kind of guy. But if Jennifer Hawkins wanted my help to dig herself up and burn her other body, then I was ready. Insane but ready.

I remembered she snuck into my house earlier with no problem. I ran back upstairs to put my jeans on. For a teenage girl to kiss a guy clad in his skivvies in his bed was one thing. But to answer the front door dressed that way was another. Crazy or not, I had to respect the proprieties.

When I arrived at the front door with my pants zipped and belt buckled, no one was there. I whispered, "Jennifer."

No one answered.

I went outside and checked around, but saw no sign of her.

The squeal of tires caught my attention in time to observe a dark sedan peel out of my driveway and take off up the street. It went too fast to tell the make in the dark.

Jennifer must have changed her mind about inviting me to help burn her extra dead body. I stopped as another hallucination or wild dream invaded my mind. In a dream, would Jennifer Hawkins burn her own dead body? She needed two bodies to pull it off, and she mustn't need the extra one anymore.

I wandered back by the shed to discover an open, empty grave. I shoveled dirt in. As I patted down the last of the muck, my dad arrived.

"What are you up to?" he screamed.

Never was a clever answer so needed and never had one not bothered to show up on time. What could I say? "Nothing."

"Don't you nothing me. You buried drugs or booze. Dig them up and remove them from my property or you move out. Am I making myself clear to you, young man?"

"Yes sir, but this is not about drugs or booze."

My dad turned his back and wandered off in the direction of the house. He mumbled, "Burying dope? Burying booze? It's what they used to do during Prohibition. What's with that kid?"

I returned to bed as the red glow of the morning sun broke over Chicago in the distance. I was more convinced than ever that I needed psych counseling, but who goes to the guidance counselor before the school year begins?

***

When I awoke several hours later, Jennifer's visit seemed like another insane dream or vision, but as I dressed, I realized my bedside lamp was still lit and my jeans bore the telltale signs of mud on the cuffs and knee area. What nightmare invades reality?

You can have hallucinations without dropping off your nut. Two nights of insane visions that disturb the real world don't prove anything, do they?

I spent half the day arguing with myself over whether to speak with Jennifer Hawkins about what happened. I was shy, and she was hot which didn't make for the best combination. On the other hand, I was a junior and she was a sophomore which had to count for something along the lines of a "more mature man" or "big man on campus," right? Although I wasn't sure art club qualified you for BMOC status. Girls dug the BMOC stuff, but in the end I didn't call or text her. Turned out I didn't have to.

The other half of the day, I eavesdropped on the window installer in my bedroom. Mom insisted I clear a path through my dirty laundry and junk for him. I figured as long as I had to pick up clothes, I might as well take the pile down to the washing machine for Mom. The window guy didn't seem to mind the gym locker-room odor I stirred up while picking up my long dead laundry. He appeared old enough to have teenagers of his own so he may have been used to it.

It's a special day when you can make your mom happy while preparing for a midnight visit from the girl you have a crush on at school.

While I had no reason to think Jennifer would stop by my room tonight, I also had no reason to believe I wouldn't see her. After all, I was the one having insane hallucinations that left an imprint on the real world.

Gilbert texted after dinner so we chatted for a while. No surprise here, but he denied digging up dead bodies in my backyard last night. The Asian girl didn't text which made me happy. I would have dropped down dead if she had.

CHAPTER 4

BONKERS

What could make me so bonkers as I climbed into the sack on the night before my first day of junior year? Think what you want. I wasn't crazy, was I?

Without waiting for me to fall asleep on Wednesday evening, Jennifer Hawkins crept through my brand new window, turned on my bedside lamp, and plopped down on the bed next to me. My eyes laser-locked onto the clear, clean skin of her smooth thighs sticking out of her white lacy jammie shorts. Her fat ruby lips curled into a kiss-me smile that brought out her high cheek bones. She didn't wear perfume but should have because she smelled like one of the guys after gym class.

She grabbed my face in her hands to drag my attention up to her sultry green bedroom eyes. "Hi, Bryan. I guess you want to know why I'm in your room the night before school starts, huh?"

"Kinda." I morphed into a puddle of teenaged crazy goo and angst. I didn't know what Jennifer Hawkins had in mind this time, but the crucifix on the wall above my bed still had a bullet hole in it the last time I had checked.

"Yeah, I guess I like you."

"Wow. That's cool, Jennifer, because I sort of like you, too." I ran my hand through her brunette hair and noticed blond highlights that weren't there the last time I had seen her in that other dimension I sometimes visit, the one where she takes pot shots at me and digs herself up for the funeral pyre.

She planted a kiss on my lips that would have blown my socks off if I wasn't already stripped to my undies. We broke apart at the sound of the big crash.

***

If you sneak down to the kitchen for a snack in the middle of the night, why mess up by dropping the plate or the fork? But that's my dad. Or my little sister, Katie. Or Mom. One of them made the big noise in the kitchen. We Ganarski's are a night-snacking family.

"I have to skedaddle." Jennifer placed her index finger over my mouth.

"But Jennifer…" I muffled through her finger. I wanted to ask her about last night and "skedaddle." Where did skedaddle come from? What fifteen-year-old girl says "skedaddle" these days? Isn't it Bronze Age speak? I can hear two Romans guarding Jesus's tomb and when the rock rolls back by itself, one Roman guard says to the other, "Time to skedaddle."

The word is like Latin or the name of some city in Washington State. But it's not uttered by anyone under age fifty. Not today. Not since the nineties, anyway. The eighteen nineties. The word was last used on the Titanic by a crew member right before he jumped onto a lifeboat.

But the next thing Jennifer said got my attention because her voice became husky and hoarse. She smiled, her finger still warmed my lips. "Next time you see me in school, Bryan, mosey on up to me and plant a big kiss smack on my lips so everybody will know we are a couple."

"What about your old… I mean father?"

"Especially the old man. He is so antiquarian. Our little PDA will give him a wakeup call."

As Jennifer Hawkins disappeared out my window, I thought about how I've known her forever and how she has always been attractive but on the quiet side despite her good looks.

Kids change over the summer, don't they? Her bra size sure improved. New school year, new Jennifer Hawkins. And a much happier me if I could get past the insanity of these past few nights.

I definitely had to clean my room enough to entertain midnight guests.

The good news is Jennifer Hawkins visited me in my bedroom three nights in a row. We both may still be virgins, but we were moving in the right direction, weren't we?

I spent the rest of the night with a grin that slung off my face and stretched out across the remaining dirty laundry scattered about the floor.

In the morning, I remembered my bedroom was on the second floor and no way did Jennifer Hawkins makes that jump out my window.

To continue reading, please search **Snpgrdxz and the Time Monsters** on www.amazon.com.

ABOUT THE AUTHOR

Paul R. Lloyd is an accomplished writer of suspense and thriller fiction. He leads the Write Time Writer's Group in Geneva, Illinois. His career spans more than 30 years of marketing and business writing experience, including projects involving print, video, film and online media. Paul is married and lives in the Chicago area.

Visit him online at: http://paulrlloyd.blogspot.com

To read more paperback books or ebooks by Paul R. Lloyd, please search Paul R. Lloyd on www.amazon.com.

Paul R. Lloyd

FICTION BY PAUL R. LLOYD

NOVELS

Fulfillment

Hags

Steel Pennies

Snpgrdxz and the Time Monsters
Book 1 of the Snpgrdxz Series

Snpgrdxz and the Time Warriors
Book 2 of the Snpgrdxz Series

Snpgrdxz and the Time Hunters
Book 3 of the Snpgrdxz Series

SHORT STORIES

Angel Thorns

Little Miss Forgotten

Egbert

To Dwell Among Us
Prequel to Fulfillment

Paperback and E-Book versions available by searching the
title or Paul R. Lloyd on www.amazon.com.

www.ingramcontent.com/pod-product-compliance
Lightning Source LLC
Chambersburg PA
CBHW070307260626
47160CB00003B/756